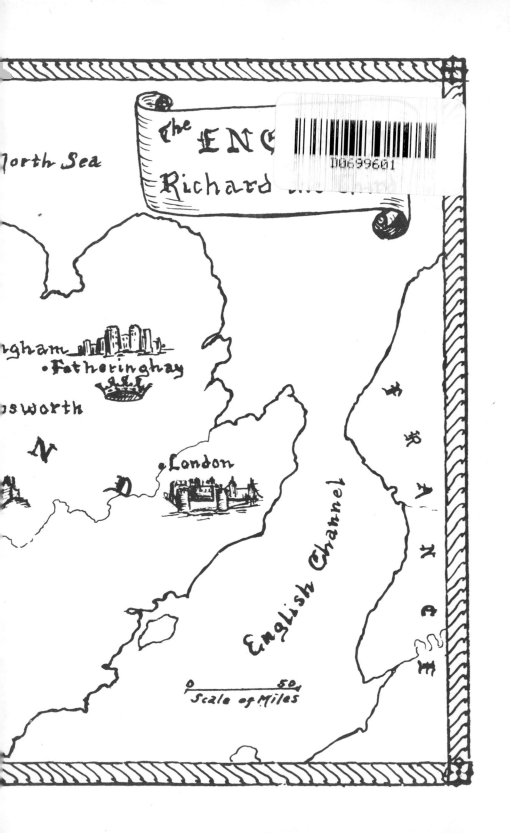

The ENG[...]
Richard [...]

North Sea

[...]ngham
• Fotheringhay
[...]sworth

N

[...]

• London

English Channel

FRANCE

0   50
Scale of Miles

Under The White Boar

Books by Mary Dodgen Few

CAROLINA JEWEL
UNDER THE WHITE BOAR

Under The White Boar

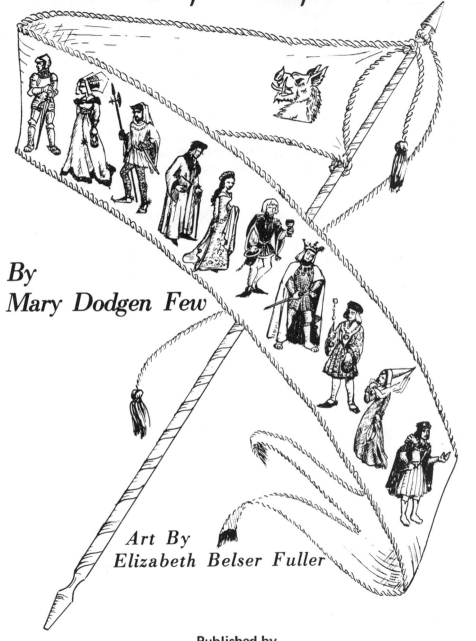

By
Mary Dodgen Few

Art By
Elizabeth Belser Fuller

Published by
DROKE HOUSE/HALLUX
Publishers of Books
Atlanta, Georgia

Standard Book Number: ISBN 0-87667-069-9
Library of Congress Catalog Number: 70-161090

Manufactured in The United States of America

Published By
DROKE HOUSE/HALLUX
116 West Orr Street
Anderson, S. C. 29621

Cover Portrait of King Richard III reproduced by permission of The National Portrait Gallery.

For
My Menfolk

Joe

Robert   *Kendall*   *Jo Jo*   *Nace*

Bobby
John
Allan
Wes
and
Marshall

TEN little Englishmen
Standing in a line
One got too biggety
And then there were but nine.

NINE little Englishmen
At the Palace Gate
One wed the Duke of Burgundy
And then there were but eight.

EIGHT little Englishmen
Thought the throne was heaven
But one got in the King's way
And then there were but seven.

SEVEN little Englishmen
Thought two kings didn't mix
The Dukes went to the tower
And then there were but six.

SIX little Englishmen
Were all who stayed alive
The Duchess went to heaven
And then there were but five.

FIVE little Englishmen
The King could brook no more
The Duke sent in a cask of wine
And then there were but four.

FOUR little Englishmen
One wanted to be free
Of all the cares of kingship
And then there were but three.

THREE little Englishmen
One proved to be untrue
They laid his head upon the block
And then there were but two,

TWO little Englishmen
Both sitting on the throne
For one the crown too heavy proved
And then there was but one.

ONE little Englishman
Ruling all alone
The Tudor landed on the shore
AND THEN THERE WERE NONE.

BOOK I

THE WOULD BE KING'S SON

I

TEN LITTLE ENGLISHMEN

Richard came suddenly awake. Sweat bathed his neck, his feet were like blocks of ice. His mouth felt dry. It hurt to swallow. He wanted to turn to relieve the awful pain in his shoulder, but a terror to which he could put no name held him motionless. His stomach and bowels began to churn in the old familiar way when something was wrong. His clammy hands seemed to belong to someone else.

Where was he?

Fotheringhay?

The boy sniffed tentatively. No, it couldn't be. The seeping cold had not the marshy stink of the fens around his birth place.

Ludlow, then? Neither had the air the crisp vigor, sign of the heights from which his brother Edward's castle guarded the Welsh country side.

Coventry? Home of dread Marguerite, wife of feebleminded King Henry VI and bogey of all the children! Richard retched at the thought. His body servant's stern face and wagging long finger swam before his tortured mind's eye. His bodily eyes were screwed tight closed in fear.

"Dame Marguerite will get you if you don't watch out!" Scogan was wont to threaten when Richard's misdemeanors were more than trifling. More effective than a thousand thongs was this dire threat. Virtue followed immediately on its heels.

"No!"

Had he cried aloud? He clapped a hand over his mouth.

A thousand times no. Had he gone to sleep under the awful Queen Marguerite's roof, surely he would have had nightmares of witches with boiling cauldrons of pitch in which to souse him at the slightest wrong doing. Instead he had slept dreamlessly, if briefly.

Kent?

Scarcely better. This memory was still a throbbing scar. There he had watched his proud mother with head unbowed — pretending she was not a hostage — while her husband the Duke of York tussled with the wife of addle pated Henry VI for the regency of England.

The low rumble of a cart caught Richard's ear. His eyes flew open.

London!

Baynard Castle! Relief caused his knotted muscles to relax. The pain in his shoulder made his head reel. He bit his tongue to contain the agonized cry that rose in his throat. The pain did not pass. His teeth chattered. The cold was more than his eight year old determination could stand. Hunching his left shoulder to where the pain seemed a mite less searing, he slipped from his bed in the boys' dormitory and crept on icy feet to his brother George's bed.

"George!" His miserable croak reached no one's ears but his own.

"George!" Richard cleared his throat and tugged his brother's coverlet urgently. "George, I'm cold. Let me in with you!"

"Umph, go away."

"George, please! I'm freezing." His voice was almost a wail. Richard's dizziness increased with the pain in his shoulder. He hunched it closer and tugged frantically at George's foot which was the only available part of his anatomy under the mountain of velvet coverings.

Richard was not prepared for the blow. George's foot caught him squarely in the stomach and sent him flying against the heavy tapestries that covered the clammy stones of Baynard Castle's thick walls. His fear and chill bound stomach revolted violently. When he could control his vomiting, he crept to the closet where the flux, even more awful than the pain in his shoulder, took over.

There in the pale watery dawn of a London December day Edward found him. Pleasantly drunk from an even more pleasant night of revel, Edward Plantagenet looked down from his great height on the sorry spectacle of his puny, scrawny little brother, certainly no whit a Plantagenet in looks. Sallow, dark, ugly and obviously on the brink of freezing, Richard looked up in pleading adoration at the golden giant who was his oldest brother. Even in the flush of wine, virile vigor, and nineteen years of lusty manhood, Edward felt a stirring of pity for this changeling whose lips were almost as blue as his intense deep set eyes. There at least he is Plantagenet, thought Edward as he swept the shivering boy into his

12

arms and carried him to his own great bed. When his brother cuddled him against his own animal warmth, Richard could not suppress a cry of pain.

"What is it, Dickon?"

"My shoulder, Edward, it hurts so."

"What ails it, lad?"

"I fell out of the tree that George and I were climbing to see a bird's nest."

"You? Why you climb like an ape. What made you fall?" Edward paused in thought. "Why was brother George in the tree? 'Tis not like that lazy rascal to exert himself so."

Richard lay silent, drawing on his brother's warmth and vitality against the pain and cold.

"Dickon?"

"Yes, Edward."

"Why was George in the tree?"

"He-he wanted the bird's nest."

"Your pipit's nest?"

Richard nodded against his brother's chest. Even that slight movement made him moan with pain.

"Here, let me feel it." Edward probed gently. "We must let the doctor see it." For a moment they lay still. "The dirty rat."

"Nay, Edward, he didn't mean to," Richard said drowsily. "Please don't tell, they'll tease me. Please, Edward."

For a while the great blond giant cupped his undersized brother against himself exuding warmth and comfort. Richard sighed.

"Edward, tell me a story," he said sleepily.

In the bleak dawn, Edward, Earl of March, filled his young brother's ears and mind with tales of his own exploits on the battlefield; of their father, the great Duke of York who was in reality a ruler if not a king; and of their cousin of Warwick, himself not a king, but powerful enough to make or break one.

Comforted and enthralled, Richard slept.

Memory of his brother's warmth was yet a comfort when the shoulder pain stabbed Richard viciously awake to the cold reality of broad daylight and the clank of harness beneath his window. For a moment the spell was still upon him. But where was Edward?

Richard sprang from the cavernous depths of his brother's bed and unmindful of his shoulder ran to the casement. Below him in the narrow street, a weak December sun was not so fair as its reflection on the unhelmeted heads of his brothers Edward and Edmund. Their golden beauty was in sharp contrast to the stocky and slightly dour

13

solidity of their father the Duke of York who, as yet unhorsed, was bidding their mother a formal farewell that told nothing of the great love they shared in the rare privacy of magic moments stolen from the increasing stress of campaigning.

"Edward!" Richard's cry was lost in the stamping of impatient horses and creak of harness.

"Richard!" But it was only the restless reminding voice of his uncle of Salisbury to his father. "'Tis past time."

Richard whirled at the sound of a firm but motherly voice at his back.

"Dickon?"

"Meg!" The pain staggered him against the splendid tapestry, a copy of a luscious nude by the budding Italian painter Sandro Botticelli, that horrified his mother's somewhat pious soul while it hid the clammy stones of Edward's room.

"Isn't she gorgeous, Mother?" Edward was wont to tease, omitting the title of respect her other children felt was due Cecily of York from whom they took their beauty. "Someday, somewhere, I'll find one just like her."

"Are you certain that you are looking in the right places, my Son?" Cecily replied dryly. "Your father thinks the Mowbray girl . . ."

"Bridget?" Edward had exploded. "Cease, Mother. That flat breasted virgin shall remain so as far as I am concerned. I'll wager her knees are knocked, though who could find her charms sufficient to investigate, I wot not."

"Have done, Edward." Cecily's famous calm was as ever unruffled as she smiled upon her eldest. "Be not so lewdly free before the children — besides she's a great heiress."

"Not great enough for such a sacrifice," Edward had taunted winking at the Botticelli.

Now standing beneath Edward's coyly lovely nude whose luscious color made her seem warm in spite of the room's biting chill, his sister Margaret was all concern.

"Dickon, are you ill?"

"Nay, but help me dress, please, Meg. I must see Edward."

"Edward? You'd best not tarry longer then. Our Uncle Salisbury is in a fever to be off to challenge Dame Marguerite."

Even in the witch-scattering daylight the dread name made Richard shudder to the hurt of his plaguing shoulder.

"Will they best her, Meg?"

"Of course, silly. Did our father ever fail?"

"Then who will be King?"

"Henry, as always, goose. Why do you ask?"

"Scogan says he's daft."

"A king is a king for all that," said Margaret sternly. "Scogan talks too much."

"Scogan says our father who already rules King Henry would be a better king."

Margaret clapped one hand over Richard's long, thin mouth while she helped him tie the latches of his hose with the other.

"Scogan, Scogan! I wonder what his loose tongue would prattle with a noose around his neck," Margaret snapped tartly. "I'd better have a word with him."

"Nay, Meg, don't," pled Richard. "His tales are almost as good as Edward's."

"Edward! There, and you'd better hurry or he'll be gone, lad."

Richard smiled up at Margaret. Even at fourteen she was the nearest thing to a mother he knew. Through France, England, and Ireland during the uncertain years of Henry's doddering reign and the certain menace of his French wife's domineering rule, Cecily Neville, Duchess of York campaigned with her lord pausing only briefly at regular intervals in one of his bleak castles for the birthing of his heirs. Twelve times she was brought to bed to serve this dynastic purpose but through it all, Cecily Neville remained more wife than mother.

"To horse!" The Duke of York's voice carried plainly up from the roil of preparation in the street. Margaret noticed with a start how like their father's pleasant but authoritative voice was that of his youngest son Richard who was now calling impatiently over his shoulder as he dashed from the dormitory down the winding stone stairs.

"Make haste, Meg, or we'll miss Edward!"

Margaret clucked and shook a head as fair as this brother Edward's. She grabbed up Richard's forgotten marten lined cloak, made a mental note to inquire of her baby brother about a shoulder he seemed to have favored during his dressing, and — forgetting as hastily all such motherly concerns — raced after Richard in fourteen year old impatience to wave big brother Edward off to the wars with that witch, Dame Marguerite.

Richard shot out into the December sun to trip over his brother George's practiced foot and sprawl in an undignified heap. In the excitement of leave-taking no one noticed save big brother George who smiled with sadistic glee and bigger brother Edward whose usually genial countenance darkened in a scowl.

15

"I'll be back, brother George." Edward's lips merely formed the words. But George got the message as the two fair brothers of York faced each other over the changeling who was their younger brother.

"Edward!" The premptory voice of his cousin of Warwick, all bluster and martial vigor, recalled Edward to the business of the day. A wave of annoyance pricked the eldest son of York as he donned his helmet and with a last glance at his brother's crumpled figure clattered off northward over the stones.

It was Scogan who picked Richard up and carried him gently into the castle. Even Margaret had forgotten.

"Who are you?"

Richard looked down into a pair of direct and grave brown eyes. The left side of his long thin mouth shot up in a crooked but not unhumorous smile.

"And who are you?" he retorted.

"I asked you first." The solemnity of the small pointed face under its ridiculously mature headdress did not change.

"And so you did. I'm Richard."

"I thought so. Help me up."

Richard extended his right arm.

"Both," demanded his small visitor lifting her own arms trustingly.

"Pull up," the boy in the embrasure ordered back. "The other one hurts."

"Why?" the little girl obeyed and plopped down beside the boy amidst a billowing of velvet skirts.

"I fell," Richard answered shortly. "Who are you?"

"I'm Anne," his visitor's grave eyes regarded him in surprise. "Didn't you know?"

"Why should I?"

"I'm your cousin, silly."

"My only cousin?" Richard's eyes began to twinkle.

"Well, my sister Isabel is, too," Anne conceded smoothing her gown and moving her head tentatively. "Help me take this thing off."

"What thing?"

For answer Anne bowed the heavy hennin directly into his face.

Richard laughed and drew the cumbersome frame off the small head to reveal a length of soft, straight, chestnut hair that fell to Anne's narrow shoulders and framed her now smiling face.

"You aren't so bad," she appraised him matter of factly.

16

"Am I supposed to be?"

"My lord father says you're a throw back. What's a throw back, Richard?"

Richard squirmed, but there was no escaping that direct gaze. Anne waited.

"Well, I'm not exactly like my brothers and sisters," Richard began uncomfortably.

"You're nicer than George." Anne peeked around the heavy velvet hangings of the embrasure to where George at eleven was lounging against the mantle in apt imitation of his brother Edward's insouisance. Anne looked back at Richard. "He *is* better looking," she granted.

"But I like *you*," the child crossed small white hands on her lap and regarded her cousin Richard, as if she had just given him a fair gift.

Richard was not sure but what she had.

Silently now the snow that had begun to fall the day after the departure of Richard's father and brothers held London in its unrelenting grip.

"We shall be back by Twelfth night," the Duke of York had assured his Duchess.

Confident as always in the word of her lord, Cecily turned to her remaining children in sudden and unusual loneliness. For the first time in twenty years of conjugal unity with a husband whose passion for his beautiful wife was second only to his love of England, Cecily experienced the belated joys of motherhood in the diverting preparation for Christmas. Diverting from the white snow monster that was beginning to assume frightening proportions, diverting from an unwonted uneasiness that plagued her as much as the clammy, biting cold that huddled them all to the great maws of the gigantic fireplaces of Baynard Castle.

It was Christmas.

Cecily's warm cheek touched her kinswoman's cold one. Anne Beauchamp's wealth had made her husband the Earl of Warwick's household a byword in splendor. But all the countess of Warwick's wealth could not warm the greal pile of their London mansion which this December of 1460 earned its name of Cold Harbor. Her small daughters, as unused to their mother's companionship as she was to theirs, came into the York household as joyfully as a pair of greyhound pups let out to the chase. Isabel, her face sparkling with cold and the sheer delight of being alive, bobbed dutifully to *my Aunt of York* and rushed over to Margaret. Her heavy fur cape slid in

17

an unheeded soft fur pile to the floor.

"The girls were lonely," The Countess of Warwick explained.

"Of course, my dear, I understand." Cecily smiled at Isabel chattering gaily with her cousins Meg and George. "And where is Anne?"

"That is a good question oft repeated in our household," the countess sighed drawing near the great fire and chafing her cold hands. "Anne is a law unto herself, always present at awkward moments with her incessant questions, never when required. She is probably presently inquiring of your head cook the mysteries of stuffing the Christmas boar's head. Her curiosity is insatiable — to her father's right complete vexation."

Cecily could well imagine, knowing her nephew of Warwick's habitual annoyance at anything that went not exactly as he laid out. Now her eyes fell on Anne and Richard kneeling together in the window embrasure — Richard's sharp gaze on the road from the North in anticipation of his brother Edward's return, Anne's inquisitive face turned confidently up to Richard's. Cecily smiled fondly wondering what the question of the moment might be. She completely shared Anne's confidence that her son could supply the answer. She noticed of late that Richard was a canny child himself, enquiring with his ever alert ears and eyes rather than his questioning tongue.

"You ask too many questions," Richard was saying impatiently.

"Well, nobody ever tells a girl anything," Anne replied without rancor. "How else will I learn?"

"You know too much already," Richard had to smile down on her precocity. "You talk like a woman grown."

"How else should I talk?" Anne reasoned. "I never see anyone other than *women grown*," she giggled at her own mimicry, "or *men grown*." She was suddenly thoughtful. "Will you be like my lord father when you are a man?" she demanded.

"How should I know?" Richard's voice was tart. He wanted to go back to his vigil . . . Edward! His mind's eye beheld his great golden brother, so handsome and strong, so gay and yet so kind to a miserable, hurting younger brother. He touched his still aching shoulder that he had managed to hide from all but kindly Scogan. Why was he so unlike his brothers? Even Edmund the scholar and George the . . . . He wondered exactly what George was. Both were over six feet tall though neither so large as Edward. Their hair was fair and golden, glistening in the sun like their mother's. His older sisters Anne and Elizabeth, now great ladies both with husbands and titles of their own, and Margaret . . . he watched Meg now laughingly forgetful of her dignity in a frivolous game of cards with George and Isabel. Firm, motherly Margaret, though inclined to plumpness, was almost as tall as their stately mother who was discussing with Anne's mother the meager news of their husbands far off to the North battling the hated French Marguerite. He had forgotten Anne and her question.

"I believe you will be," Anne broke in reproachfully on her new friend's reverie. His now brooding and forbidding look reminded her of her father's habitual scowl.

With unseeing eyes Richard watched her as she slid unaided off the high seat and wandered disconsolately toward the fire and the card game. His blue eyes came to rest on his mother whose own lovely gold hair glinted in the firelight. Cecily refused to wear the fashionable though cumbersome hennin because it made her appear taller than her lord.

Why, thought Richard gladly, *I'm like my father!*

Short and stocky, dark of hair, too, but powerful and mightily strong withal, the Duke of York was of a height no more than that of his duchess. Richard flexed his fingers and tried his muscles. He winced at the pain in his left shoulder. He would be as strong for his father — and for Edward!

Singularly comforted and regretting his ill temper with his little cousin, he made his way toward the fire in whose glow Anne stood vainly seeking admittance to the game.

"Come, I'll teach you to play chess."

Anne looked up, at once grateful and confident.

"I already know how."

"Very well," he smiled the crooked smile, "You must not beat me badly. It is neither mete or proper for a lady to beat a gentleman."

"I know that, too."

"What don't you know, my Pigeon?" Richard laughed aloud.

Cecily turned a surprised face on her youngest son in whom laughter was rare.

Why he's like his father, she thought.

"Your move, my lady," Richard spoke with mock gravity.

"How can I be a pigeon and a lady at the same time?" his cousin Anne matched his tone.

They smiled across the board at one another. He was twice her age.

But he was only eight.

During the twelve days of Christmas, the numerous inhabitants of the House of York stuffed themselves with fine foods while the Lord of Misrule led his riotous band of mummers through well rehearsed disguisings. The ladies of Warwick joined their voices to the Yorks in carols as the traditional boar's head — into the preparation of whose succulent goodness the little Lady Anne had truly inquired — was brought in pomp to the high table. Cecily had even permitted George to turn his greyhounds in to chase a cat and then a fox around the festive board. However, she put her firm foot down when George would have his beasts tear their prey to bits before the eyes of her guests. When George turned sulky, Cecily's soft shod toe sent her son, who was kneeling to better enjoy the bloody fray, sprawling in the rushes from whence he was recalled to his manners by her indignant face. George was quick to apologize but not so quick to forget his resentment of his chastisement at the hands of a woman albeit his mother. Later in the smokey rush lit halls he tried to vent his spite by cornering his cousin Isabel and kissing her in a manner that he had no cause to have learned at his age. His lively cousin slapped his face soundly and kicked his shin to boot with a not so softly shod toe.

Altogether Christmas was not a good day for George. He sneaked off nursing his bodily and spiritual injuries.

The great snow held and called for more which came softly but relentlessly to complicate the festive life of the great, bustling household. Even the enormous demands of the season and her numerous dependents could not keep Cecily's mind from her lord and their two eldest sons engaged in what — she admitted only to herself — was a death struggle for control of their poor worthless King Henry. Between her lord and Henry's termagent French wife, there could be no quarter. One must go. Cecily shuddered, ordered the great fires built even higher, and tried not to reveal her mounting apprehension.

On the eighth day of Christmas the scurrier she had come to dread rode out of the snow.

Cecily, Duchess of York, gasped and almost tottered under the blow. Almost, but not quite. She summoned her children to her. Tall and pale of face she leaned on nothing for support as she told them in a voice which would have been flat with sorrow had it not been tinged with the fire of hatred for the French woman.

"My children, my lord your father is no more. Nor is my brother your uncle . . . ." she paused to swallow hard. Her voice steeled with pain almost faltered — but not quite. "...nor is your brother Edmund."

The iron band of fear that had begun to tighten on Richard's heart relaxed a mite.

"And Edward?" he heard his own voice ask.

"There is still Edward."

There is still Edward! Richard's heart sang with joy. His father and his brother Edmund, one a slave to his campaigning, the other to his books, he had scarcely known. Thus he could feel scant loss at their going.

"You may leave me now."

Richard was striken with remorse as he looked at his mother's face struggling for control until she could be alone with the aching bitterness of her own loss. He had thought only of himself. He shook off Margaret's guiding hand and remained behind as his sister led an unprotesting George from the hall.

"Mother!" For the first time he addressed her without the habitual courtesy title. His voice spoke his sudden sympathy in a new found maturity.

Cecily turned on her youngest son. For a moment they stood apart. She opened her arms and he was crushed against her fragrant warmth. It was the first time she had ever caressed him.

"Even your voice is like his," she cried out at last. "At least I have that."

"And Edward," he reminded her in a voice muffled by the pain in his shoulder.

"Yes, and Edward," she conceded.

He felt her tears raining down on his dark head.

From Scogan Richard learned of Dame Marguerite's atrocities. He learned that in ghoulish derision — like the witch all children of York thought her — she ordered the Duke of York's head striken from his dead body, encircled with a paper crown, and spiked on the Micklegate barbican of the Duke's own city of York. Her scurrilous mercenaries commandeered and guzzled tuns of good York ale, and bowed in shrieking mockery before the sightless and crow picked eyes of the once mighty duke. Finally urged out timorously but firmly by the city fathers of York, the undisciplined tatterdemalion army struck south toward London in an unrestrained orgy of sacking, raping, and burning.

Richard shuddered and sought the closet frequently with the flux.

21

Dame Marguerite — ran Scogan's lurid tales to his shaking charge — shrouded in witches' weeds, her black velvet hood relieved only by a single white ostrich plume, rode in their midst biting her pale lips and muttering curses.

But the French witch had only replaced one deadly enemy with another.

In London's Baynard Castle the party of York gathered around the indomitable Cecily in rush lit nightly conferences.

"And Edward?" Richard demanded of Scogan. "What of Edward?"

Scogan's hard-bitten face lightened at the thought as he rubbed Richard's left shoulder gently and inserted a pad in the right shoulder of his tunic.

"You should have let me call the physicker, Master Richard," Scogan clucked. "See how you've hunched one shoulder until it's higher than tother?"

"Never mind, Scogan," Richard prodded him impatiently. "What about Edward?"

"Does that pain you?" Scogan began exercising his left arm clasping elbow and wrist.

"Of course it doesn't!" snapped Richard. Scogan worked harder. "Ouch!" yelled Richard. "Of course it does. Stop it!"

"It may have to bear a shield one day," Richard still avoided Scogan's ministering hands, " — for Edward."

For Edward! Richard submitted meekly to his body servant's healing, but hurting hands. Scogan, smiling wisely, relented.

"Never fear, young master. Your brother Edward will ride out of the West like St. George and witch Marguerite will rue the day she ever set foot on English soil!"

He was right. But before Richard's god could ride out of the West and join with his cousin of Warwick in the bloody snows before Towton, Dame Marguerite was fast closing the gap between her forces and London.

Cecily summoned her children to her again. This time it was the Duchess of York who spoke and not the mother of whom Richard had had so fleeting a glimpse.

"Dame Marguerite is at the gates with a detachment of cavalry." Cecily spoke as a general discussing a matter of tactic. Richard glared fearfully at Scogan. Was the witch going to get them after all? He shuddered, but not with cold.

"Should anything happen to your brother Edward, the future of the House of York," Cecily paused a moment looking from George

22

to Richard, "nay, even the future of England may depend on you boys. I am sending you to Burgundy and safety with Duke Phillip."

George threw back his broad shoulders proudly, a gesture that did not escape his mother's sharp eye. She bore down on him.

"Should it fall your lot, you will be England's, George, not England yours!" George tossed his fair head but his shoulders sagged a little.

"And you, my Lady Mother?" Richard ventured.

"I shall stay here."

"Then I shall stay with you," Richard tried to shut his young mind to the terrors of Dame Marguerite and speak bravely. "England has no need of me."

Cecily studied her two sons in the flickering, eerie rush light that smoked mightily in the great hall. One so tall and fair, so seemingly grand and strong, one so puny and dark, yet trying so hard to be a man. Did the one have a flaw in his great Plantagenet frame? Could the other bear the weight of York and England on his slight shoulders if called to such a destiny? She resolved to know them better.

"You will go with George," Cecily commanded.

"But I wish to stay with you," dared Richard stepping forward from his place one step behind his brother George. "A lady needs . . . . "

"You will do as you're told," Cecily cut him off coldly. "You must always do what England requires of you, not what meets your inclination. Never forget that, Richard."

"Yes, my Lady Mother," Richard stepped meekly back to his usual position one step behind George. He was dumbly grateful for Scogan's comforting hand on his shoulder.

The channel is a fearful thing in February and Richard was miserably seasick. The pitching and tossing of the little barque had no apparent effect on George except to make him feel a flash of unwonted pity for his retching little brother. Richard's blue eyes were big with gratitude. A love for his brother George almost as great as that he held for Edward — and his mother — grew in his heart. Ah, these new devotions were filling his pinched and lonely spirit. His heart felt as if it would burst with the fullness of love for his beautiful, golden family. And they loved him, too! Hadn't his brother Edward fondled him and warmed his freezing body with his own animal vitality? Hadn't his mother held him and wept — a thing unheard of in the proud Duchess — into his dark hair? Even Meg, though she loved George more — and who wouldn't — was always doing him small kindnesses and protecting him from George's pranks. In his new born love, Richard saw George's meaneness as boyish jokes, an outletting of his spirits that hurt only because he, Richard, was so small. And now George was mopping Richard's sweating brow and telling him stories, much too bawdy for a lad of eleven to know, much less to tell a lad of eight to distract him from his misery. Yes, Richard's heart was full to bursting with love given and received from his wonderful family. Would they could all be together soon to share their love for each other — and England!

Through thin blue lips Richard smiled up at his brother George and slept.

Scogan's face was a study as he covered his young charge and listened to the creaking of the tortured vessel. George had swung himself confidently aloft into the shrieking February wind.

After the rigors of a London winter and the hazards of a February storm on the channel that churned like a treacherous moat separating England from her traditional enemy France, spring at the court of his Uncle of Burgundy was a fragrant paradise to little Richard. Not understanding his sudden importance but relishing the flattering attention it brought him, Richard conquered his jinx. The flux left him. His thin body began to fill out and a new color crept into his sallow cheeks. One day after the daily exercising of his left arm and fingers, Scogan announced that he had grown an inch! He pronounced his patient cured although Richard would always carry his left shoulder higher because the broken collar bone had mended thus. Richard felt the knot on the bone that ached even now when it rained. But it rained seldom in Burgundy and life was one long holiday.

Uncle Burgundy replaced George as jokester. Richard, used to being the goat, laughed good naturedly when one of his uncle's jewel encrusted books blew dust into his eyes. George, on the other hand, did not laugh when a cleverly contrived little bridge collapsed and pitched him unceremoniously into a garden pool.

"It's only a joke, George," Richard soothed as he tugged his brother out, a bedraggled and undignified looking mess in his soaking velvet tunic and splotched gaudy hose. But the look of angry resentment on George's face did not pass although he did refrain from kicking — as Richard was afraid he might — his highly amused uncle's shins. His uncle roared off down a path of his fabulous gardens to an even more fabulous mid-day meal that had caused him to suffer pangs of gout years before his time. But Uncle Burgundy had had his fun. The tunic that he sent George that evening to replace his ruined one was so heavily embroidered with gems that even George's luxury accustomed eyes popped in unbelief.

George was mollified.

On Richard, nurtured in the rigors of the north, this determined leisure and grandeur were not long in palling. An April sun was outdoing itself when he wandered idly into the beautiful library hung with Jason tapestries where his ingenious host, the wealthiest lord in all Europe, had contrived to simulate thunder and lightning, snow and rain. This amazing feat caused his guests, even the clever Italians with their bent for startling inventions, to gasp in awe. Richard had long since ceased to be surprised at his uncle's splendor and ingenuity. He began to feel a real affection for Duke Phillip which grateful and happy subjects had long felt, an affection which was not shared by Phillip's cousin Charles VII of France who glared down from his fortresses to the North in envy and distrust. Duke Phillip even had more and handsomer mistresses than his cousin of France. Duke Phillip even had Charles' son, Louis. Charles stormed about and swore to get even while this hated son the Dauphin languished at ease along with Richard and George writing dutiful letters to his aging father that never failed to keep his furious parent, who was continually beleaguered by his recalcitrant barons, informed of the splendor, the ease, the comfort, and above all, the peace of the Burgundian court.

Richard had taken an instinctive dislike to Louis whom he now found in the library in deep discussion with a strange man. The boy turned to leave.

"Tarry, my Lord," called Louis in the pleasant voice that did not match his unpleasant soiled appearance.

"My Lord?" Richard tried not to show his distaste for the only person he knew that he considered uglier than himself. He looked around to find whom Louis was addressing.

"Master Caxton and I," Louis' unctious voice continued while his darting eyes pierced the young boy standing uncertainly before him, "were discussing the right glorious news that has just reached these parts."

Richard waited while Louis' sharp tongue moistened his lips in a darting catlike motion and the stranger's kind eyes examined him slowly.

"Your brother Edward has just been proclaimed King of England! Is this not wonderful news, my Lord?

Edward King! Why, then the Dauphin was addressing him, Richard. He was a king's brother! For a moment he was stunned speechless. Then a smile lightened his narrow child's face and touched its solemnity with momentary beauty. He turned and ran from the room forgetful of the manners that Scogan and the times demanded.

"Scogan! George!" he cried. "Now we can go home!"

William Caxton smiled and turned back to the shelves groaning under their priceless loads of illuminated manuscripts.

Louis, Dauphin of France, did not smile. Neither did he fail to record in the rat's nest of his intelligence that Richard Plantagenet now second in line to the throne of that hated land of England, called for his body servant before he called for his brother George. These insignificant threads, who could tell how they might fit into the pattern of the tapestry that someday he, Louis, would weave? His bandy legs carried him into the April sun that hurt his eyes as he turned them northward toward France.

Home? Louis wondered when he might go home, too.

BOOK II

THE KING'S BROTHER

II

AND THEN THERE WERE NINE

Louis went home, too, in the blistering summer of 1461. But not, however, before Edward Plantagenet, that biggest and handsomest man in all Britain had been crowned King of England in such glittering pomp and circumstance that reporters to the different courts of Europe present for the occasion wrote home enthusiastically.

The King is a person of most elegant appearance and remarkable beyond all others for the attraction of his person.

Charles VII's ambassador had the misfortune to have his master die before his account reached Paris. It fell into Louis XI's hands.

The new King is the handsomest prince in England — nay! in all Europe! He prattled on carried beyond tact by the beauty of Edward and his splendid coronation, *His visage is lovely, his body mighty, strong, and clean . . .*

The ambassador was replaced.

Richard trembled with joy as he was prepared for his initiation with George as Knight of the Bath. Three knights of the Order drew his sumptuous bath. Richard flushed with embarrassment as Scogan pushed him forward.

"Must I, Scogan?" he pled holding back.

"You must, my Lord."

The title on Scogan's lips startled Richard.

"Before all these people?" he whispered as a company of squires entered the chamber singing and dancing.

"Do like George." Scogan demanded.

Richard glanced at his brother whose ivory perfection was gleaming as he luxuriated in the warmth of the water and in the deference duly paid him as the King's brother and heir to the throne.

"But I am not like George," moaned Richard.

"Praise be to God," hissed Scogan devoutly crossing himself. Suddenly reasserting himself as master, Scogan pushed his young charge forward into the ridiculing eyes of the assembly.

"Hurry and get it over with," he commanded for Richard's ears alone.

Richard made it and was grateful for the water that slid over his naked body giving it back its dignity that he had carefully preserved by a hard fought for modesty in the complete lack of privacy of a great mediaeval household.

Scogan deftly continued to rub the anointing water into his shoulders while the knights instructed him in the rites and ideals of the Order. He even managed to dry and clothe his charge. But his body servant could not follow Richard as he was conducted to the chapel.

Suddenly alone Richard tried to take George's hand, but his brother shoved him off impatiently.

"Don't act like a child," whispered George.

But I am a child, thought Richard trying to walk tall and not look like one.

There was Edward, golden smiling Edward, sharing his greatness with his brothers. Richard started to break into a run but was rudely jerked back by his brother George. Gulping his shame, Richard fell back into the solemnity of the procession stretching his short legs in a vain effort to match George's stride.

What had his mother said?

Do what England requires of you, not what meets your inclination.

With eyes straight ahead, Richard strode into the Cathedral.

He was sleepy and the Cathedral, thronged with the governors of the Order, was too hot. His eyes drooped and his body sagged. George kicked out at him although he was sleepy, too. Richard's eyes sprang open to meet the cold disapproval of the priest. He tried to ease his knees that ached from the all night vigil. The pain nearly made him cry out. He made his body rigid and began to count to keep himself awake.

Would dawn ever come!

. . . five, six, seven . . . four, three . . . .

By Holy Paul! He unconsciously borrowed the only oath his mother permitted herself. *Have I slept?*

A watery, uncertain mote of dawn light sparked in the great ruby of the Bishop's mitre and cast a bloody red glow on George's face. Richard was fascinated. His eyes began to cross.

He was suddenly swept up by a pair of powerful arms.

"But your Grace, the confession," whined the priest as Edward turned to stride down the Cathedral aisle.

Edward looked down at the crumpled pile in his arms. No weight at all. Just like a sparrow.

A sleepy smile again beautified Richard's face as two pair of Plantagenet blue eyes met.

"Has anyone so young and so little anything to confess?" Edward tossed over his shoulder to the nervous prelate. "Take my Lord George, there. He should have enough for two!"

George's sulky gaze followed his two brothers down the aisle. As the King of England carried his small burden out into the summer dawn and handed him over to the waiting Scogan, he whispered:

"Be thou a good knight, Dickon."

Richard's eyelids stirred, the crooked smile started and was gone. "Edward!" he murmured sleepily.

The lord of Middleham castle examined his young charges critically as they tore up and down the tennis green under a brilliant October sun laughing and shouting gay taunts at each other. Today was young York's birthday and thus a holiday — at the instigation of the Countess of Warwick and her daughters — from the vigorous regimen of training in the knightly arts that the stern Earl demanded of his wards. The habitual forbidding look of the Earl of Warwick's face did not relax even for the occasion. Warwick was troubled.

Richard smashed a ball with brilliant accuracy far out of his cousin Harry Stafford's reach. Harry retrieved it with poor grace. Rob Percy laughed frankly at Harry's discomfort but Francis Lovell, impatient of his partner's lack of sportsmanship, cried out:

"Come on, Harry! It's just a game."

Harry's obviously surly reply was lost in the bustle of arrivals.

Warwick had watched the play in amazement. He wondered how sheer will could drive such a spindly body to feats of superiority over obviously better endowed opponents. Warwick had to admit that young Richard of York, who had looked hopeless as a knight at the outset, had something vital in his frail frame which lacked all physical beauty. Richard's determination and stamina were astounding, Warwick's chamberlain had reported to his master. Laced into his cumbersome harness, Richard excelled on foot with sword, dagger, and even battle axe. His thin legs hugged his mount the more securely as he galloped over the moors. His natural knack with all animals made him a master of the hawk. His arrow or spear seemed to seek out stag and boar.

Rob Percy and Francis Lovell took their friend's excellence in good humour and unjealous admiration, but Harry Stafford . . . .

Warwick's frown deepened.

There was a strange one. He wondered again if he had done well to take an orphaned Lancastrian bird into his Yorkist nest. But God's blood! He had to consolidate this position, had he not? He would have to tame many a bird of Lancaster if he meant to keep Edward of York on the throne. And *that* he most certainly meant to do.

Unease touched his mind again as he thought of Edward — young, handsome, popular with his new subjects beyond Warwick's wildest dreams — but beginning to like the feel of his crown withal. Warwick looked back at Richard and made a mental note. He might be useful if Edward tried to get out of hand. Harry Stafford, even with his near-royal blood and possibilities of fine title and fair fortune, he promptly forgot as of little consequence.

The Earl of Warwick made a determined effort to throw off his broodings and perform the duties of host to his stern best.

"My Lord Nephew," Cecily of York bowed gracefully. Her head but not her spirit paid him homage, Warwick's calculating mind jotted down. Looking at his royal aunt, he wondered if she would not be a more formidable enemy than Dame Marguerite — if aroused. He decided not to arouse her.

"My Lady Aunt," Warwick's craggy warrior's face tried to smile. "Each year you grow more handsome. It is obvious from where the King and his sisters and brothers obtain their great beauty."

And their determination, he added mentally thinking again of unbeautiful Richard.

"You are most gracious, my Lord," replied Cecily with a knowing smile that Warwick did not miss. They bowed again formally, having long since taken one another's measure.

Cecily swept into the crowd. Warwick did not. He stood apart accepting the accolade to the splendor of his court as his just due. The Earl of Warwick was not a joiner. His magnificence and beneficence were calculated.

"His household is more splendid than the king's," some whispered as they gorged on the sumptuous feast of roast oxen, swan, jellied quail, stuffed boar's head, spun sugar confections, and heavy pastries.

But where was the guest of honor?

Finally exhausted, even his iron will consumed by activity, excitement, and the heavings of his over stuffed stomach, Richard lay supine under a hawthorne bush. He was grateful for a moment of privacy after the sickness from the unwanted food. Forced to abstinence by his uncertain bowels, Richard usually chose his food with care from among the thousands of rich dishes that daily crossed the great Earl of Warwick's board.

"Will you play chess with me?"

"Hello, Pigeon." Richard neither moved nor opened his eyes.

"Will you?" the voice persisted.

"I'm too tired," Richard was surprised to hear himself admit.

"You're sick to your stomach, too, aren't you?" Anne squatted complacently at his head.

Richard managed a weak smile as he opened his eyes and met a wide, brown-eyed stare.

"How do you know?" He demanded. She always knew everything.

"That's easy. Your face is greener than spring grass."

He rolled over on the offending stomach. Already he felt better.

"Will it make you fell better if I play for you?"

Richard's eyebrows rose but he smiled in amused surprise.

"Do you play the lute, also?"

"I'm learning."

"Then, my Lady. Please play for me. I am certain the sound of your lute will be better medicine than any Dr. Oliver has to offer."

Anne giggled as always when he addressed her so formally.

"I like *Pigeon,* best," she remarked as her tiny fingers strummed an instrument almost her size.

"All right, Pigeon. Coo!"

Anne giggled again, and Richard hid his face in his arms to keep from laughing. The strings twanged unmusically.

> *Itt was a blind beggar, had long lost his sight,*
> *He had a faire daughter of bewty most bright;*
> *And many a gallant brave suiter had shee,*
> *For none was soe comelye as pretty Bessee.*
>
> *And though shee was of favor most faire,*
> *Yett seing shee was but a poor beggars heyre,*
> *Of ancyent housekeepers despised was shee,*
> *Whose sonnes came as suitors to prettye Bessee.*

33

"Shall I teach you?"

"Please do sometime," Richard struggled for a straight face and added hastily. "Now, we'd better go back for the fireworks." He surveyed the October sky. The sun was sinking in a great red disk. This fine weather would not last much longer, he thought as they raced hand in hand across the grass, the lute and upset stomach both forgotten.

As the years passed in the routine of living at Middleham, Anne's lute playing improved, Richard's prowess in knightly conduct and his love for the North developed — as did Anne's sister Isabel. This charming fact did not escape the lustful eye of young King Edward as he made one progress after another around his realm stopping frequently to visit with his brothers at Middleham Castle. Edward was hugely enjoying his position. His subjects loved their georgeous King who brought glamour and royal dignity to a throne whose prestige had begun to totter under addle pated, pious, lackluster Henry VI. Edward also loved the sumptuous living that the Earl of Warwick affected on all his manor lands but especially at Middleham the favorite abode of his countess and daughters. It was cheaper, too, thought Edward whose coffers were continually over taxed.

Edward smiled inwardly at Warwick's pretensions. The Earl with all his might had been able to beget on his countess only two daughters. Edward couldn't say much for that least one that followed his brother Richard around like a faithful puppy. But that older one! Edward smacked his full, sensuous lips.

Isabel Neville at thirteen, just a bare six months short of marriageable age, was much more the woman than Edward's sister Meg, at seventeen with all her motherly pretensions.

"Holy Mother of God." Edward swore aloud. If lasses developed at thirteen in the manner of Isabel Neville he'd better find a husband for Meg quick. Now, who would bolster his throne in Europe, and yet give Meg a good time in bed? Did Meg want a good time in bed? He wondered. Meg was so wonderfully complacent. Could anything shatter that serenity?

Serenity was not a subject to hold the interest of the lusty King of England over long. The image of his own sister's calm beauty was suddenly replaced by a life and blood Isabel Neville with curling chesnut hair, high ripe bosoms, and sparkling eyes above a very red mouth.

The new Duke of Clarence had also noticed the charms of gaily heedless Isabel. For some months after receiving his glittering title from his brother the King, whose bland nature could nurse a grudge against no man, George had ricocheted around the countryside with his proud new standard blazing before him in his own progresses that aped the King's. But Edward, hard put to support his own extravagancies, frowned on them in others. George's activities were abruptly curtailed. Forced to amuse himself at Middleham which was home during his knightly schooling, George's appreciative eyes also fell on Isabel. George had been physically precocious at eleven, as Isabel had already reason to know. At fourteen he fancied himself a man.

Now Isabel was cornered again. However, laughing Isabel was on the alert this time. Isabel loved fun, but the wet, sucking kisses of the Duke of Clarence were not her idea of fun. They parried like a pair of wrestlers taking each other's measure.

"Isabel!" George's changing voice betrayed him with a croak. Suddenly the desire for vengeance was submerged in just plain desire. For all his cockiness George did not understand his bodily urges. Isabel was so pretty. He felt as if he would burst. He sprang suddenly forward. A cry like that of a maddened animal escaped him as Isabel dodged under his outstretched arms and flew down the corridor. Her mocking laughter floated back over her shoulder as lightly as the gossamer stuff of her hennin.

Escaping, headlong down a flight of narrow stone stairs, from one brother Isabel ran helter skelter into the willing arms of another. Edward's solid frame withstood the impact of her plummetting descent. Bear like arms closed around her slight but tall body, a sensuous mouth covered her laughing lips. Taken by surprise, and something else she did not understand, Isabel gave herself up completely to his embrace. Not until she felt the frenzied groping of his hands at her bodice did she recollect her reeling senses. She struggled against him uselessly. Nor could she free her mouth to cry out. In terror she bit his mouth viciously and tasted the salt of his blood on her tongue. Taken by surprise, Edward relaxed his hold a moment and felt the tearing of her nails across his cheek. Stung to frustrated fury he reached for her again and felt the crack of her well aimed toe on his shin.

Dancing on one foot in tingling agony, Edward did not see the stricken look in Isabel's grey eyes beneath a pile of tousled chestnut curls. She was gone on flying feet, but this time no laughter floated over her fleeing shoulder. Only her torn hennin lay crumpled at his feet.

The Duchess Cecily's eyebrows rose when Isabel pleaded a

splitting headache as an excuse for her absence at the evening meal where Edward sat glumly silent.

"Cousin Edward," demanded Anne, "what's the matter with your face?"

"Nothing, Child, nothing," snapped Edward before he shouted angrily for more sweet, heady malmsey wine to soften the blow to his masculine pride.

"It looks like a cat scratched you," the child persisted.

"Perhaps it did," growled Edward not meeting his mother's eyes. "Ungrateful bitch!" he grumbled, not quite under his breath.

Anne surveyed the handsome young King gravely.

"What's a . . . ?"

"Let's play chess, Pigeon," Richard interrupted hastily.

Anne Neville's face was wreathed in smiles as she looked up into her other cousin's darkly kind face.

"Let's," she replied happily, placing her tiny hand confidently in Richard's. Bad tempered Edward was already forgotten.

"Isabel, why don't you like Cousin Edward?" asked Anne as she drove her needle into the fabric on her needlework frame. "Ouch!" she cried wringing her hand then sticking a finger in her mouth to suck the blood from the wound. "I don't like to sew. I'd rather play the lute. Isabel, will finish this for me so our lady mother won't be cross? I'll play for you."

"All right, Pigeon," adopting Richard's pet name, Isabel smiled at her younger sister.

For a moment Anne strummed the strings aimlessly as she examined her sister's face, bent intently over the needlework. Isabel wasn't nearly as much fun lately as she usually was. She was peevish and cross for no apparent reason, refusing to play tennis with the boys and moping around in her room. Anne even thought she had been crying one evening when she came upon her unexpectedly. Anne wanted to ask her sister why, but budding maturity held even Anne's persistent tongue silent. She shrugged mildly piqued. If it weren't for Richard, Middleham would become a dull and sombre place as the bitter winter softened into the spring of 1464. Even Rob and Francis noticed Isabel's fits of moroseness and missed her gay laughter. They finally ceased to ask her to play tennis and contented themselves with Harry's or George's bickerings until in desperation they even let Anne join in their game. With this Anne's cup of happiness was like to overflow. Now she smiled as she sang,

Fair lady Isabel sits in her bower sewing,
Aye, as the gowans grow gay
There she heard the elf-knight blowing his horn
The first morning in May

If I had your horn that I hear blowing
And yon elf-knight to sleep in my bosom
This maiden had scarcely these words spoken
Till in at her window the elf-knight was luppen.

"Why, Isabel?" Anne interrupted to ask.

"Why, what?" Isabel did not raise her eyes from her work.

"Why don't you like Edward?"

Isabel's busy fingers slowed and dropped listlessly into her lap.

"I declare, Anne, your threads are so snarled, how shall I ever untangel them," she fussed pettishly, "why shouldn't I like our cousin?" she snapped as Anne waited for an answer. "Everyone should love the King, shouldn't he — or she?"

Anne eyed her sister speculatively as she resumed her song softly.

"It's a very strange matter, fair maiden" said he
"I canna blow my horn but ye call on me
But will ye go to yon Greenwood side
If you canna gang I will cause ye to ride . . .

"Then why don't you?" Anne persisted idly strumming the lute.

"Don't I what?"

"Love Edward."

"You ask too many questions."

"That's what Richard says," Anne observed, "but how can I . . . ?"

"Richard's perfectly right," Isabel cried out springing to her feet throwing brightly colored yarn everywhere. "Leave me alone, will you? Leave me alone!"

Anne's troubled eyes followed her sister from the room. For a moment she continued her song listlessly.

If I had your horn that I hear blowing
And you elf-knight to sleep in my bosom
This maiden had scarcely these words spoken
Till in at her window the elf-knight has luppen.

37

Anne laid aside her lute and with a sigh began to gather up the scattered yarn. Richard found her seated, a small figure among her wide skirts, running strands of yarn idly through her fingers.

"What's the trouble, Pigeon?"

Eight year old Anne Neville, second daughter of the great Kingmaker Warwick grinned up at her twelve year old cousin, brother of the King.

"Cousin Richard," she declared, "I don't understand *women grown!*"

"Who does?" Richard grinned back.

But it was not Isabel that Richard had in mind.

In the busy, happy-go-lucky childhood years at Middleham, Richard and George had begun by sharing equally in the great honors the King chose to bestow on them. But Edward, whose body was inclined to indolence although his mind and eye were not, was quick to notice important differences between his two younger brothers. George he had made a duke months before he had granted a similar honor to Richard. Edward remarked that his least brother accepted the Dukedom of Gloucester with dignity and pride while George used his Lordship of Clarence as a peacock uses his tail. In the land grants of 1462 George felt that Richard was favored although his honors preceeded his younger brother's. George raised such a fuss that Edward who loved his ease retracted some of Richard's revenue and reissued it to George. But at the same time he made Richard Admiral of England, Ireland, and Acquitaine.

Edward, often rode north to Middleham in those formative years. He inquired into the progress his brothers were making in their schooling and took young Richard on many of his tours to quell intermittant outbursts of Lancastrian sentiment which Marguerite managed to keep stirred up, first to the North on the Scottish border, then to the South in the Welsh Marches.

"That French bitch is like a nettle under my saddle, Dickon," Edward complained in exasperation. The young King had much rather have spent his time in the ease and adulation of his London court — or in the austere grandeur of Middleham Castle where the warm beauty of the Lady Isabel tantalized him to the point of madness in its inaccessibility.

As a result of these constant trips with the King, Richard became an apt student of his brother's temperament. Even at twelve years Richard recognized full well that a storm was brewing. Edward's temper was frayed to the breaking point. Failing as a man, he called upon his powers as a king.

"Dickon," he commanded, "fetch the Lady Isabel to my chambers. I desire to speak with her."

Richard was well aware that Edward desired no such thing. Although he loved his brother to the point of adoration, that adoration was not blind. Edward's propensities and failings were common knowledge to an indulgent populace who, like his young brother, recognized their King's budding abilities as a leader and, unlike his younger brother, willingly condoned his sins.

Now Richard thought first of Isabel whom he liked enormously for her friendly gaity and happy laughter. She was like the birds of gay plumage and soft eyes that depended on him for their sustenance, but flushed away skittishly if he approached too closely.

And then there was her father Warwick whom Richard acknowledged frankly as the mainstay of his brother's throne. Richard had no illusions about Edward's intentions toward Warwick's elder daughter, nor had he any doubts about Warwick's reaction if harm should befall a member of his house, king or no king. Warwick would not defend his daughter for fatherly love, but as a pawn in the struggle for power, she was a priceless jewel.

So Richard hesitated.

"But, Edward," he demurred.

"Dickon!" Edward's voice had an edge to it.

"Edward," Richard drove on not recognizing the look in his brother's eye, "you have no right . . . . "

"My Lord of Gloucester . . . . " the King warned in a cold voice restrained with fury and frustrated desire. "Do you deign to tell the King what is his right?"

"Isabel is no tavern wench to be taken to bed at a man's pleasure," Richard retorted indignantly.

"I am not just a man. I am the King!"

"You may be the King but you are first of all a man. Would you have Isabel love the King or the man?"

"Have done, Boy!" Edward shouted pounding the table. "Even from you there is a limit."

Equally but coldly angry Richard faced up to his brother.

"From you there should also be a limit! You lack restraint in all things. It will be your undoing if you don't check your greed!"

For a moment Edward was aghast at such effrontery. When he spoke at last his voice was soft but full of menace.

"Do you dare to criticise the King?"

"I dare to criticise my brother. I would be derelict in my duty to my King if I did not warn the man."

Edward's chest swelled with rage. "You sorry little popingjay!" he yelled. "Do you propose to dictate a code of morality to the King?"

Shock hit Richard like a physical blow. Edward wasn't joking! His eyes widened in surprise as he surveyed the magnificent bulk of his brother's frame, now towering above him in righteous, kingly anger with legs like tree trunks wide spread, ham-like, jewel encrusted hands on his broad hips.

"No, your Grace," Richard replied quietly. The title was as yet unfamiliar on his tongue.

"Then be gone and fetch the wench!" roared the King.

Unconsciously Richard imitated his brother's stance. The cock glared down on the bantam rooster. The bantam rooster stared back bested but not intimidated. Rather a new dignity and assurance vested him.

"Very well, your Grace." Turning on his heel without permission Richard headed for the door. "But there are some rights that even a king does not have."

"I'll wait outside," Richard promised a shaking, white-faced Isabel. "That is the best I can do, for what it's worth."

Isabel nodded gratefully and disappeared into the King's presence. Her trembling increased, her grey eyes widened in anguish as they rose to the magnificent — and beloved — figure that awaited her.

Edward's bombast and bluster faded as he examined the slight but uncringing figure with its bowed chestnut curls.

Damn it all! I love the chit.

He approached her cautiously and touched her hair gently.

"Isabel?"

He felt the shiver pass through her body at his touch. With a finger under her chin, he forced her eyes to meet his. A shock passed through his own body into his very vitals. Why this child loved him, too! So this was the reason for her avoiding him, not just feminine coquetry.

The great arms encircled her again as he whispered into her fragrant hair.

"Isabel?"

This time the sensuous mouth covered her trembling lips gently drawing on their sweetness for a long moment in time that stood suspended for them both. But the demands of Edward's virile body were not to be denied. Fired by her unexpected quiescence, his kisses became more frenzied. He swept her up and carried her almost fainting into his bed chamber. In his great bed hidden from the world by curtains of cloth of gold trimmed with ermine and powdered liberally with the suns and roses that were his emblem, Edward tore at her gown until his hands could cup the white softness of her breasts.

Isabel recalled her reeling senses with a monumental effort. She stayed his caressing hands.

"Please don't do this to me, Edward."

"Why not?" he demanded startled, "You love me, too, I can see it in your eyes."

"That's why, Edward," she whispered shakily, "I do love you. Please don't take what I cannot give — not like this."

"That's ridiculous!" he snorted in a haste to satisfy the wild clamorings of his body. "You love me, what more is there to it?"

"There's marriage."

"Marriage!" Edward exploded at this new idea. In the moment of surprise he relaxed his hold, and Isabel was gone on flying feet that took her past Richard who paused in his anxious pacing to watch with troubled eyes her headlong flight and the disheveled condition of her hair and clothing.

"Richard!" The bellow nearly startled Richard off his feet.

"Yes, Edward?"

The quickness of his response took Edward by surprise.

"Were you spying at my door? No, I know you weren't, but your God-damned righteousness is the cause of it all!"

"All what?" Richard asked quietly.

"Nothing!" Edward snapped. "Get my horse. We ride tonight. And call Hastings."

"Where do we ride, Edward?"

"We just ride! And you don't go! Bring me some wine!" shouted the King finding his silver gilt decanter dry. He hurled it at the door that closed on Richard's retreat. A page scurried in with a replacement. Edward started to kick him, but decided against it. Edward IV, King of England, was sometimes ruthless in his punishments but he was always just. Now he even managed to thank the surprised page who remained, nevertheless, out of reach but within easy ear shot.

Edward was already drunk by the time his company clattered out of the courtyard at Middleham, and turned southward on the road that led to London — and Grafton Regis. Richard had not failed to

41

notice that although Hastings matched his master cup for cup, as usual, he was as coldly sober as the forbidding walls of Middleham Castle.

In their ridings together over the northern countryside of England, the King and his little brother Richard had come upon a maiden so fair that even Richard was impressed.

But Richard had been quicker to see than his aroused brother Edward that the Lady Elizabeth Woodeville of Grafton Regis was after something more than just an amorous adventure. Informed of the frequent passing of the King and his company to and from Middleham through their estates at Grafton Regis, and prodded by her voluptuous and ambitious mother, the gilt haired Elizabeth, mother of two small sons and early widow to Lancastrian pretensions, found herself and her two sons frequently on the King's path. Her patience was soon rewarded. Edward had come upon the lovely widow seated under a great oak tree, her fair head bowed in studied innocence to some childish question.

"Your Grace," Elizabeth Woodeville rose to a graceful curtsey dumping her two boys unceremoniously on the ground.

"Madam?" Edward inclined his head, his eyes sparkling with interest.

"Elizabeth Woodeville, Lady Grey, your Grace," Elizabeth replied prettily, curtseying again. Drawing her protesting sons into her arms and pinching them to pouting acquiescence, she sighed. "And my two poor fatherless lads Thomas and Richard Grey." Pinched again, they bent a reluctant knee.

"Grey?" questioned King Edward frowning in the effort of memory.

"Lord John Grey, your Grace," William Hastings, Edward's closest friend and the Lord Chamberlain was quick to supply. "Lancastrian, killed at St. Albans."

Edward frowned.

"Lancastrian?"

"Through no fault of my own," Elizabeth Woodeville's eyes fell modestly. "A lady has no choice but to follow her Lord — and master. Has she, your Grace?"

"What? No, of course not!" Edward recalled himself from his examination of two bulging breasts bare almost to the nipples. Lancastrian or no, he had seen none so tempting.

"My Lord," Elizabeth Woodeville who was well aware of the direction of Edward's eyes dropped a gossamer scarf over the tantalizing prospect. "Would you and your company care to refresh

42

yourselves at my mother's manor? It is close by and she would be well pleased if you cared to honour her humble home."

"I do have a great thirst." Edward smacked his lips to prove it, "And you, my Lord?"

William Hastings smiled in indulgent understanding into the hungry eyes of his King and friend in revels.

"Indeed, I have, your Grace." He leaned forward on his horse to whisper into the King's ear. "Mayhap the lady has a sister?"

"Sister, I know not," hissed Edward in delighted reply. "Would a mother do? I have heard the charms of the lovely Jacquetta noised abroad."

"A mother should be the better for experience, eh, Edward?" Hastings slapped his King's leg familiarly.

They roared with laughter as they turned their mounts to the east and Grafton Regis.

The whispered by play had not been private enough to escape young Richard's ears, nor that of the lovely widow, who smiled with satisfaction as she jerked her sons homeward.

Richard, who neither laughed nor smiled, had followed slowly in the rear.

Now, after the unsatisfying interlude with Isabel, Edward was in a towering rage of frustrated desire and the confusing new sensation of love. However, the young King had no intention of complicating his existence with sentiment. The lust of the body for women, war, and wine he could handle. Sentiment was foreign to his nature. He wanted nothing to do with it.

From the towering battlements of Middleham Richard watched his brother ride out across the moors of Wensleydale. He turned disconsolately away from the star-studded April night and went slowly below — in search of Anne.

The summer of 1464 was hot and dry. The plague struck early in London and worked its way relentlessly toward the city of York, hard by Middleham Castle. Although the Earl of Warwick came often to enquire after health of his Countess and her household, Edward came not at all.

Richard understood that the great Warwick was busy with affairs of State which fell heavily on his shoulders while Edward caroused around his country winning hearts and subduing abortive Lancastrian uprisings. Chief among these momentous affairs that made the King's right hand man frown — something always made the Earl of Warwick frown, thought his daughters — was a brilliant marriage for his

Sovereign. Fascinated by the ugly scheming spider that sat on the throne of France manipulating all Europe to his own advantage, Warwick listened to an attractive offer held out tentatively by Louis XI. Warwick, usually clear eyed and himself a practiced schemer, failed to see that Louis of France's offer was but a reaching tentacle to enclose the hated England in his well knit web. In any case, Bona of Savoy would be a nice political plumb to pluck. Besides being Louis' sister-in-law, by prudent managing Warwick might secure the Duchy of Savoy as her dowry.

The tennis games continued. Isabel rejoined them, although her laughter rang less frequently and her gaiety was of a quieter sort. Francis Lovell often gave up his racquet and came to lie at Meg's feet while she sewed or sang to Anne's lute, or fashioned a light poem to please him. Meg was quietly pleased at his attentions, her serene beauty took on a new grace, and she spent less time mothering George and Richard.

Richard noticed and was pleased for he loved them both and thought how well suited his friend and sister were. In these thoughts at least he found a certain peace although his worry about Edward plagued him sorely.

Meanwhile with the help of Warwick's brother Montagu, whom he gratefully rewarded with the Earldom of Northumberland, Edward, by September had crushed Dame Marguerite's Lancastrian forces and confirmed himself as King of all England. Lancastrian heads to the number of two dozen rolled, among them the heads of some of England's greatest barons, it is true. But English gentry in general considered this a fair price to pay for peace and were well pleased with their young King. The fact that in his campaignings around the countryside, the King was a frequent visitor at Grafton Regis did not escape notice, which fact Scogan duly reported to his young master.

"They are saying that Lord Rivers, the Lady Elizabeth's father and her brother Sir Anthony Woodeville have been pardoned." Scogan's usually genial face was glum.

"Just a political move," Richard tried to shake off his worry.

"My Lords of Hungerford, Roos, and Somerset fared not so well," Scogan reminded him. "Some say 'tis because they had no lovely daughter or sister to petition the King with personal favors as a bribe."

"Hush thou, Scogan," Richard flew quickly to his brother's defence. "Repeat not such scurrilous gossip. You know full well the King does not sell a man's life at the price of a kiss. Edward is just."

Scogan shrugged.

"Edward is also a man." Scogan's dour face relaxed a bit in thought. "And the Lady Grey is every bit a woman." He wagged his head, "And *what* a woman!"

Richard could think of nothing to reply. His body servant rounded up his wandering thoughts and went to fetch his master's evening livery of candles and firewood. The nights grew chill early at Middleham.

On September fifteenth the Earl of Warwick arose in Council to present his plans for the King's marriage. Edward sat glumly with bowed head while Warwick extolled the physical and financial charms of the French King's sister-in-law. The lords, usually quick to resent any rapprochement to its traditional enemy France, could find no objection to the match. It committed them to nothing and might get the spidery Louis off their backs while they prepared for a new attack on France, now that King Edward had brought peace to the realm. The duchy of Savoy was not to be lightly refused.

Hastings watched Edward covertly during the lengthy harangues.

"Have you nothing to say, my Lord?"

"I bow to his Grace's opinion, my Lords," Hastings replied blandly.

All eyes turned on the King. Edward for a moment did not raise his head. When he did his vivid blue eyes searched each one of his advisors, daring them. He arose to all his majestic height in an atmosphere charged with expectancy.

"My Lords," Edward began deliberately. "I thank you for your efforts in behalf of my good will and domestic happiness." A faintly mocking smile flitted about his full lips but failed to touch his defiant eyes. "I regret that I cannot taste the charms of this lovely Bona, sister to our beloved Cousin Louis of France, whom my Lord of Warwick our dearest friend and councilor has so thoughtfully secured," the usually genial voice took on an edge of steel, "without our knowledge."

The silence was deafening.

"However," Edward took a deep breath, "I am already wed."

The gasp that arose from the assembled lords shattered the silence into a thousand shimmering pieces.

"Your Grace!" Lord Howard, the first to find his tongue, dared in angry protest. His temerity was quickly imitated by other lords who sprang to their feet.

"My Lords!" Edward's thundering voice quelled the riotous clamors which subsided under his icy glare.

"On Michaelmas Day in Reading Abbey, you will honor the Lady Elizabeth Woodeville Grey as your Queen!"

Although the lords in council crooked their knees in obeisance many a heart beat in unbending anger over this new whim of their young King. William Hastings, the King's chamberlain and boon companion, noticed with grim satisfaction that the Earl of Warwick, his face livid with fury, strode from the council chamber without the King's permission.

Over tortuous roads wet with September rains the news flew north to Middleham. George, Duke of Clarence, Richard, Duke of Gloucester, and Harry Stafford, Duke of Buckingham, the three premier peers of the land were summoned to give immediate attendance upon the King to do homage to the new Queen of England.

George had correctly assessed the affair between his brother and Isabel with the canniness of guile rather than intelligence. Now he sought her out in sadistic glee hastening to be the first to impart the tremendous news. If George's shallow nature had been capable of love, he would have loved Isabel. As it was, she was the object of all his passions — lust, hatred, jealousy. He was well rewarded by the stricken look on her face.

"Married? Edward? He can't be!" She shook her head vigorously as if to prove it to herself. "Why our lord father . . . . " Isabel's voice died out piteously as Richard entered the room. The look on his dark, narrow face confirmed her fears.

It was true! She wished now, too late, that she had done his bidding. Anything even eternal shame would be better than this terrible searing pain that swept through leaving her alone in the awful loneliness of lost love. But in someways Isabel was a true daughter of her stern, unbending father. Her face was white with the palor of death, but her head was high as she sailed from the room pulling aside her skirts so as not to touch George as she swept by.

Not many days later the Duchess of York stormed into the King's antichamber at Westminster with her youngest son in tow.

"Where's Edward?" She demanded.

"Madam, the King . . . . " someone ventured before he was swept unceremoniously in the wake of the Duchess of York.

Cecily charged into the King's private suite and there found her son undignifiedly clad in his small clothes. His esquires of the body, listening gleefully to one of Edward's lurid jokes, found the smiles frozen on their lips.

"Get out!" commanded Cecily.

They got, never looking to the King for confirmation of the order.

"You bastard!" Cecily turned her furious face on her son. Richard blanched.

"Madam." Edward bowed with as much dignity as he could muster. He groped for his dressing gown.

"Never mind," snapped his mother. "Every strumpet in England has seen you less clothed than you are at this moment. Why shouldn't your mother?"

"Madam, you forget yourself. You are addressing the King!" Edward blustered angrily.

"And you forget that you are the King only because you carry my blood in your viens, not from any ability of your own," Cecily stormed at him.

"Mayhap your blood has put me there, but my ability that you deny me has kept me there," Edward stormed back now thoroughly aroused.

"That ability you claim failed you when you took that gilt haired strumpet to wife!"

"Madam, you go too far," Richard endeavored to soothe his furious mother while he kept one eye on the choleric color of Edward's face.

"You're always on his side," Cecily shook off Richard's restraining hands. "To think that you, Edward, would cast aside the weal of England just to mount a woman!"

Richard closed his eyes against the shame of his mother's coarseness.

"Nay, Mother, calm yourself. You don't realize what you are saying."

"I realize full well what I am saying," Cecily nevertheless submitted to the calm voice of her youngest son and allowed herself to be seated. "'Tis your brother who has failed to realize the greatness of his destiny."

"There's naught you can do about it." Edward's ruffled dignity returned as he wrapped his nakedness in his robe. "She is my wife."

"I can declare you a bastard," snapped the Duchess.

"You wouldn't dare!" Edward and Richard cried in unison.

"You would be surprised at what I'd dare for the good of England," Cecily declared.

"Would it be for the weal of this England whose love you so fondly profess to make George her King?" Inquired Edward with a

47

mocking smile.

Cecily, Duchess of York, looked long at her son.

"Nay," she replied slowly, her anger changed to dismay. "What a mess you've made, Edward. You shall certainly suffer for it. I hope England will not."

Before the majesty of his mother's disapproval, the King of England tried not to quail.

"Come, Richard," Cecily was suddenly tired, "take me home."

"Will you not stay the night, my Lady Mother?" Edward's anger died as quickly as it had flamed. He loved his mother as he did all mankind.

"Nay, not under the roof with that . . . . "

"Mother!" Richard chided gently.

The Duchess of York swept from the room with never a backward glance at her recalcitrant son.

The Duke of Gloucester bent his knee to the King.

In spite of her grand words, the Duchess of York was on hand that Michaelmas Day, to watch in stoney silence while the Earl of Warwick and the Duke of Clarence escorted Elizabeth Woodeville, a graceful hand on an arm of each, to be crowned Queen of England.

But the Queen's mother and the King's boon companion had reckoned without the fair Elizabeth. Hastings found himself suddenly *persona non grata* at court and the lovely Jacquetta was expected to dance in attendance on her regal daughter as if she were the lowliest serving maid. For an ambitious mother with twelve children to be provided for in a ruthless world, such a position might not be so galling as long as the Queen doled out favors to the rapacious satisfaction of her six sisters and five brothers with a lavish hand.

Elizabeth Woodeville, the erstwhile poverty stricken Widow Grey, now Queen of England, was a woman of great passion, and little love. What love she was capable of she gave to her family. Her passion was slaked in a highly satisfactory manner by her virile husband. She also realized that her voluptuous body more than answered Edward's urges. Hastily she set about placing her family in high places, her sisters by glittering marriages, her brothers by flashy positions at court close to the King.

With Hastings, who was looking out only for himself, it was another matter. He found he had helped to remove the Earl of Warwick from between himself and the King, only to have him replaced by a beautiful and haughty woman, who frowned upon the

48

escapades the King was wont to share with his chamberlain. For the moment, Edward found his wife's bed sufficient to his needs while Hastings found life at court extremely dull. In the chamberlain's little soul, the fire of ambition was replaced by the brush fire of hatred that if not quickly brought under control might consume a whole forest.

But Edward would have an enemy in no man. He sought out Richard.

"I'm sorry, Dickon," he was truly contrite. "I didn't mean it."

Richard said nothing. He knew without saying that Edward was referring to his words of last April when he had stormed from the loving arms of Isabel into the greedy arms of Elizabeth Woodeville. What was there to say? He had known all along that Edward hadn't meant those words. He had struck out at his brother whom he loved because he could not strike out at Isabel — whom he also loved. Edward tried to squelch this traitorous thought.

"How is she?" Edward asked tentatively.

"Well, when last I saw her," Richard replied shortly.

"What did she say?" Edward turned his back to hide the sudden pain in his face.

"Naught. What was there to say?"

A constrained silence lay between them.

Edward put on his genial smile and turned to face his brother.

"Come, Dickon, say you forgive me. I'll make you Admiral of England."

"You don't have to buy me off, Edward."

"Come, Richard, don't be stuffy. I need your help." A faint shadow clouded Edward's handsome face. "Warwick . . . . " his voice faded.

Richard understood. Through the all knowing Scogan he knew that Edward and his right hand man had quarreled furiously.

Warwick had berated Edward soundly until Edward was stung to reply.

"My Lord," Scogan reported Edward as saying. "What is thy name?"

"Richard, your Grace," Warwick had replied coldly, astounded. "Is this some joke?"

"Me thought for a moment, my lord, that it might be Edward so kingly was thy voice . . . "

Warwick said nothing.

" . . . and that mine might be that of Warwick, a mere *servant* of the crown."

49

Edward drove on noticing Warwick's discomfort.

"And who is King of England, my lord?" Edward's mouth but not his eyes smiled. For a long moment after the softly caressing voice ceased one could hear a pin drop.

"Surely thou art jesting, your Grace. Who but thou, the mighty Edward," Warwick managed a mocking bow, "art England's King?"

"And who but thou, the mighty Warwick, art England's ruler, is that it, my Lord?"

"Sire, I pray thee desist this unseemly joking at my expense . . . . "

"Take heed," Edward interrupted, "that it become not a test of mights, my lord of Warwick. In which case it will surely be at thy expense."

Warwick said nothing.

The genial expression returned to Edward's face as the sun slips from behind a cloud to warm an earth chilled by its withdrawal. His ire now fully spent he turned his great charm full heat upon his general.

Warwick's face showed nothing of his soul's inner raging as he bowed a graceful knee to the blond giant who, it appeared, had already forgotten him.

But Edward had not forgotten.

All this crossed Richard's mind as he felt his own frozen soul melting under the warming charm that only Warwick seemed able to resist.

"I hope I can always help you in your need, Edward," Richard replied stoutly.

The court that Edward was permitting his luxury loving consort to create was the most magnificent in all Europe. Wherever the King and Queen lay, the walls were hung with the newest and most costly tapestries. Rich velvets and satins for her ladies' gowns drained the royal coffers while Elizabeth's demands increased daily. The customary filthy floor rushes disappeared — replaced by extravagant Turkey carpets that created more warmth while creating a dog hazard. The King was forced to establish the position of Dog Butler to the Royal household else relegate his hunting dogs to the outside.

If the people of England could complain of the extravagance of their royal family they could point with pride to a new learning. Along with the deep piled carpets that John Tiptoff, Edward's constable, brought back from Jerusalem, came a valuable cargo of books, Sallust, Tacitus, Lucretious. True, few could read them beside the constable and men like George Neville, Warwick's brother and

50

Edward's chancellor who found time from his duties of State to employ a scribe to translate the works of Plato and others which he presented to growing university libraries. Music was heard on every occasion. Minstrels, bands and choruses of many voices enlivened every ceremony and entertainment.

Dress became so worldly that the Pope frowned. Ladies costumed themselves in heavy satins that amply concealed their feet but frankly revealed much bosom. Gentlemen wore such long pikes on their shoes that brass chains were required to latch them below the knee to keep a lord from tripping on his own toe. The Pope's frown passed unnoticed.

Some men say they shall wear long pikes whether the Pope will or nil, a garrulous Italian ambassador wrote home, but *not* to the Pope. *For they say the Pope's curse will not kill a fly.*

God amend this, he added as a pious afterthought.

All this cost money.

Queen Elizabeth had just consulted her comptroller and found there were no more funds available in her treasury to finance a great jousting tournament she wished to engage with her favorite brother Anthony as its star contestant. Her calculating eyes fell upon young Harry Stafford.

Biting her full under lip thoughtfully, she dismissed her comptroller who found difficulty getting to his feet after a two hour session upon his knees before the haughty Queen. Elizabeth made her way magestically to the King's private quarters where she entered unannounced to find the King in a heavy drinking conference with his personable young guest the Earl of Desmond and the inevitable William Hastings. Desmond was Deputy Lieutenant of Ireland acting for George during his minority, a man both active, educated, and convivial — a man after Edward's own heart. The day had been a satisfactory day, a man's day of good hunting to be topped off by good heady wine. Women would come later. As yet it was not the time.

So Edward's eyebrows rose when his wife invaded his masculine privacy.

"Madam," his geniality had a slight edge," was there none in the ante room to announce your visit?"

"Edward, I wish to speak with you alone. Dismiss these men!"

"Later, Madam," Edward was stung to retort. "Gentlemen, the Queen." Edward swept a gracious bow. The young Earl taking his cue from Hastings fell upon his knees.

Edward saw the bare white breasts of the beautiful woman

51

waiting before them swell with anger and push their voluptuousness against her gown until they were like to split it. He felt a tingling in his massive hands to be at them. He even liked her spirit. It was a good thing to have in bed . . . but not here.

"My Lord Desmond," Edward was unwary enough to crack a heavy compliment as he rubbed his hands to still their tingling. "Think you any man in his right mind would be willing to trade such beauty for noble blood and a foreign alliance?"

"Certainly not, your Grace," Desmond mumbled as he ducked his flaming face lower.

"Then you retract your statement of this afternoon?" Edward persisted, hugely enjoying his joke.

"I was but jesting, your Grace," the young Earl's dry throat made his voice crack. "Surely her Majesty . . . " he croaked.

But her Majesty was gone in high dungeon followed by the King's boisterous laughter.

Hastings, who understood the Queen's nature better than did the King, scrambled to his feet wondering how any man could be so naive as the King where his wife was concerned.

Young Desmond arose more slowly his face deeply troubled.

"Your Grace, I fear the Lady Elizabeth is offended. Could you . . . . "

"Forget it, man," Edward clapped him heartily on the back. "Forget it. The Lady Elizabeth already has."

But the Lady Elizabeth had not forgotten. The Queen never forgot a slight.

After Edward had sent his uneasy guest away loaded with gifts, and was himself pleasantly loaded with heady hypocras, he thought again of the bursting roundness of the Lady Elizabeth's white and satiny breasts and made his way to her apartments whistling softly between his teeth. His hands began to tingle again. A good end to a perfect day, he thought in anticipation as he rapped on her door.

Having a matter of her own advantage to discuss with the King, Elizabeth forbore to quarrel with him on the subject of the afternoon's affair.

"My Lord," she began demurely, "I have a petition to make to the King's Grace."

"Madam, I did not come here to discuss business," Edward replied testily, already removing his garments.

But Elizabeth held him off.

"Had you thought of young Harry Stafford's wardship?"

"Harry Stafford? No, why?"

52

"'Tis quite a plumb. The Buckingham estates bring in fabulous rents."

"I know all these things." Edward snapped impatiently. "Why need you discuss them now?"

"I want you to grant them to me as his guardian."

"Holy Mother of God, Elizabeth, what will you want next?" He knew full well what he wanted at the moment. "Take him and be done with it. Now come here."

Still Elizabeth delayed although the sight of the King's now naked body sent chills up and down her spine.

"He has not been confirmed as Duke of Buckingham."

"Will tomorrow do," Edward bellowed sarcastically, "or must I get my sword and run out now as I am?"

"No, my Lord," Elizabeth smiled enigmatically, dropping her own gossamer night robe to the floor. "I have need of thee now."

"For that at least, thank God. Woman, get into bed!"

A storm was brewing. Edward sighed heavily as he recognized its portents. Some storm was always brewing since he took the beauteous widow — and all her rapacious family — into his bed and board. Now from a hidden spot on the balcony he watched the revelling below. He was prohibited by court etiquette to be present in person.

The occasion was the churching of the Queen who had just given birth to her first child. A girl, thought Edward in disgust. Oh, well, they still had time and he could think of no better place to spend it than in bed begetting other heirs.

Now, he saw his Queen below, arrogant and beautiful still in spite of, perhaps more beautiful because of, child bearing. Her animal spirit was supplied with animal health to sustain it. In her golden chair before her fabulous tapestries, the Queen dined in solitary splendor, clothed in costly cloth of gold — paid for from the Buckingham coffers — and served by her mother and the King's sister Margaret.

The storm was brewing on Meg's face.

Margaret for all her serenity and motherly ways was a Plantagenet with the fiery spirit and pride that name engendered in its heirs. Like her mother the Duchess Cecily, who had the temerity to be absent on this occasion, Meg hated the Queen. Of this the Queen was well aware and had specifically commanded her sister-in-law's attendance. Forced to kneel in the Queen's presence, to interrupt her dancing with Frank Lovell, to bow and curtsey each time she passed the Queen's board, Meg was in a slow burning rage that did not escape the notice of the King, the Queen, nor her brother Richard, wandering disconsolately on the edge of all this splendor. Nor did the way Margaret looked at Frank Lovell escape the Queen's keen eye.

How old is Margaret? Edward thought.

In the confusion of the years since Middleham, he had completely forgotten his resolve to marry Margaret off to his own advantage. Charles of Burgundy? He felt his mind ease. A widower would be just the thing for a girl so long past the marriageable age. Why Meg was every bit of twenty years old! A veritable old maid. Charles was just the man. Rich, newly become Duke of Burgundy, a much needed ally to bolster England's wool trade in which England's King had just begun to dabble like any common burgher — and to his advantage. Holy Mother of God! He needed some advantage to maintain the sumptuousness below.

Margaret swung into view on Frank Lovell's arm. As his sister turned and bowed in the stately dance, the King correctly read the look on her glowing face as had the Queen.

"By God's mercy! Am I too late?"

"Too late for what, your Grace," Warwick spoke from his elbow where he had arrived on silent feet with George in tow.

"You walk like a cat, my Lord," snapped Edward, annoyed at being taken unawares. *His face is as unrevealing as a cat's, also,* Edward added to himself. Aloud, he spoke his mind.

"Charles of Burgundy is seeking a bride. I shall send him the Lady Margaret."

Warwick's eyebrows rose.

"And what will King Louis think?" he enquired tentatively.

"What the devil do I care what Louis thinks," Edward snapped.

"Louis has offered the hand of his son to the Lady Margaret."

Edward spat.

"He's just an infant, and uglier than Louis, it is said. I wouldn't do that to Meg. Besides, we need Charles' friendship and Meg is a book worm. She'll like that library Richard describes so glowingly."

"But will she like Charles?" George asked superciliously.

"Is that necessary, Brother?"

"You seemed to think so, Brother!" George was driven to retort.

The veins in Edward's temple began to pound as they had occasion to do often of late.

"You forget yourself, my Lord Duke," Edward's voice was ominous.

"Pardon, your Grace," the look on George's face was bitter. "I was under the impression that it was *you* who had forgotten *me,* your brother."

So that's it. Edward eyed his handsome brother closely, noting the puffiness under his eyes and the dissolute looseness of his mouth. He'd heard George had been drinking more of the strong malmsey than was good for him. *He's jealous. That's the reason he's dogging Warwick's heels of late. Two discontented birds in the nest. I'll have to look into this.*

Richard, nurtured in the rigorous life of the North, was lost in the sea of luxury and idleness that surrounded him at the Palace of Westminster. He missed Middleham. *He missed Anne,* he thought with surprise. The hour was late, long past midnight, as he ventured to quit the hall without the King's — or the Queen's — leave. He wandered through the winding halls chill with the lateness of the spring that year, hoping he'd find Scogan still awake. His shoulder throbbed. He hastened his step and almost fell over Harry Stafford vomiting up his heels on the cold floor.

"Harry!" Richard cried in alarm. "What is the matter? Are you ill?"

From his knees Harry looked up at Richard with unseeing eyes. There was a certain wildness in them.

"What's the matter?" Richard demanded again, trying to help him to his feet.

Harry was shaking like a leaf, his teeth chattered audibly in the empty hall. He could only stare dumbly at Richard. Taking him by the arm, Richard led the new Duke of Buckingham to his own chambers where, by Blessed Saint Paul, Scogan was still awake before a merrily crackling fire.

Scogan's eyes questioned Richard.

Richard shook his head.

Scogan, took over, handling Harry like a child. Bit by bit the shaking ceased, reason returned to the blank eyes and the ugly story poured out between sobs.

The next day Richard sought an audience with the King.

"Your Grace, I wish to leave London," Richard began with cold formality when he was admitted to the Presence.

Edward's eyebrows rose. It had been a bad night, all in all. He had eaten and drunk too much and had had little sleep. To top it off, Elizabeth had been difficult. Her mind, as fertile as her body, was full of scheming rather than love making. The King's eyes were as

55

puffy as his brother George's. His temper was short.

He's getting fat, thought Richard idly.

"Why the formality, Dickon?" Edward made a pass at joviality. His head ached, and he didn't want to solve any problems at the moment. He belched loudly to relieve the burning in his chest.

"There's nothing for me to do here," Richard replied in a flat voice.

"So?" Edward watched his brother's dark face. Richard's eyes had a new hooded look that kept a secret. "That's not it, is it Dickon?" He clapped his brother fondly across the shoulders. *How slight he is to be so strong!* "Out with it, Boy. You can tell your brother. Is it a woman?"

"Yes, it is," Richard let it slip out reluctantly.

"Oh, ho," shouted Edward boisterously. "At your age! So you are a man after all. Forget it, Boy. You've more conscience than the rest of us, but it's only natural. Who is it?"

Richard flushed darkly.

"It's the Queen's sister," Richard began in embarrassed confusion.

"Holy Mother of God, for a beginner you start in high places! I gave you credit for more discretion."

"Wait, Edward, please." By now Richard's face was flaming.

"Wait?" shouted Edward. "It's you who should have waited — at least until I could give you some advice."

"It isn't me at all!" Richard shouted back.

"Oh," Edward was deflated. "Then what's all the fuss about?" His head ached worse after his outburst. He reached for his wine cup, although he usually forbore it until noon.

"It's the Lady Catherine — and Harry."

"They're married, aren't they?"

"Yes, Edward, but he's too young to bed with her."

"Did he try? The little whelp. The marriage was not to be consummated until he's of age."

"Not he, Edward," Richard stammered in miserable embarrassment. "She took him into hers — as — as — a playtoy."

"Why that aging slut!" he exploded. "She had not my permission."

"She had the Queen's," Richard replied.

Edward regarded his brother a long moment while the terrifying color receded, leaving the King's face livid.

"So!" was all he said.

56

Richard rode out of London with Harry Buckingham in his charge. They wound slowly toward Brecon the Buckingham estates in Wales. The two seldom spoke. Harry, though not sullen, was withdrawn. Richard wondered what was passing in his mind behind those blank eyes. He shuddered with disgust when he thought of Catherine the aging sister of a Queen who aroused not disgust but cold fury in his heart.

And she was Edward's, his beloved brother's wife.

Although Richard knew that Warwick had been furiously angry at Edward's marriage to a commoner, so had the Lords who resented not being consulted. Even the Commons had made a sour face. Now, as Richard turned his face northward after leaving his charge in the hands of a capable steward and household appointed by the King, he cheerfully set about putting the disappointments of his life at court behind him. He had no reason to realize how deep the rift between Edward and his mentor Warwick was, nor how it widened daily as Edward became more the King and Warwick less the ruler. With all his greatness, Warwick was a man of limited scope, a man prone to resent any who dared shatter the image of himself he had built up in his own mind. In this he was akin to Richard's brother Clarence.

Of all this Richard knew nothing. He had liked the stern man who was his tutor in knightly training during the three happiest years of an otherwise bleak life. Warwick's sterness was like the austerity of his castle at Middleham and the rugged beauty of the moors of Wensleydale that surrounded it. Richard, inclined to solemnity himself, loved them all. The ease and luxury of the life at court held nothing for him.

> *Wherefore in great sorrow faire Bessee did say*
> *"Good father and Mother, let me goe away*
> *To seek out my fortune wherever itt bee."*
> *This suite then they granted to prettye Bessee.*
>
> *Then Bessee that was of bewtye so bright,*
> *All cladd in gay russett, and late in the night*
> *From Father and Mother alone parted shee,*
> *Who sighed and sobbed for prettye Bessee.*

Richard caught himself singing Anne's song as he quickened his horse's gait. His crooked smile broke out as he thought of home. Scogan also glad to be away from the pitfalls of an increasingly Woodeville court, joined his voice to Richard's.

Shee went till shee came to Stratford-le-Bow
Then knew shee not whither nor which way to goe;
With tears she lamented her hard destinie.
Soe sudd and soe heavy was prettye Bessee.

The first person to greet him at Carwood Castle, one of Warwick's lesser estates, was William Hastings. Richard expressed his surprise.

"Enforced vacation by orders of the Queen," Hastings confided intimately into Richard's ear. "The King must not be contaminated."

Richard felt a pinch of resentment in Hastings' tone. Disloyalty to the Queen, in spite of his dislike for her, was disloyalty to the King. He excused himself hastily and went in search of Anne.

He started to question a young girl he saw approaching him when she cried out joyfully.

"Richard!"

Before he could reply she had flung her arms around his neck in a bear hug and laid her soft cheek against his. For a moment he held her close, the ice in his heart melting yet a little more in the warmth of her sweet affection.

He held her off from him and looked at her hungrily. At ten she was as tall as he at fourteen. She was still very slight, her cheeks pale. Her eyes enormous. Lacking Isabel's vividness, her beauty was quietly serene.

"Anne!" His voice was hoarse with emotion. Here was something he could love without fear of complication, something he could cherish to his heart's content. Something that he could understand and that might understand him, although he could not himself. He drew her warmth back against him and closed his eyes.

This time it was Anne who wiggled free.

"Come and see the gorgeous preparations for the banquet," she took his hand and pulled him forward. "You've never seen so many dishes," she chattered on gaily. "Swans, and oxen, and egrets, and spun sugar sub-tle-ties," she stumbled over the new word. "What are subtleties, there I got it out," she giggled. "What are they, Richard?"

Richard laughed joyfully and clasped her hand tighter. It was really Anne. The questioning had begun.

"Little Pigeon," he mumured happily.

Much later after the long tour on which Anne conducted him they came out on a high battlement overlooking the peaceful spring greening countryside. As they gazed at the cold clearness of a trout stream, her questioning took a more serious turn.

58

"Why did he marry her, Richard?"

"Because he loved her." He knew full well of whom she spoke.

"My Lord Father says Kings don't marry for love. That's for common people. Is that true, Richard?"

Across the twilit softening vale, Richard seemed to hear his Mother's voice.

Do what England demands of you, not what meets your inclination. Never forget that, Richard.

A shadow of pain and doubt crossed his face. His eyes took on that hooded look that helped him hide his true feelings.

"Is it, Richard?" Anne tugged on his sleeve drawing him back to reality.

"I don't know, Pigeon. Perhaps your father is right. Who knows?"

"You don't like her either, do you, Richard?" It was a statement rather than a question. As usual, she was seeing straight through him with her clear brown eyes.

"Hush, Pigeon. Say not so." He touched his fingers to her lips. "She is very beautiful and regal, every inch a queen. And," he added, as he must for had he not chosen as his slogan *Loyalty Binds Me,* "she is Edward's choice."

For him that was, must be enough. Edward was his brother whom he loved. Edward was the King!

He might convince himself, but he saw by her eyes that he had not convinced Anne.

"But Isabel is not a queen."

Richard's puzzlement showed in his face.

"My Lord Father has decreed that she shall marry George."

Richard's heart constricted.

"Are you certain?" he demanded sharply.

"Of course, I'm certain, silly. I heard him."

Even in the state of near shock her news had invoked, Richard could not forebear to smile. A vivid picture of Anne hovering behind one of the exotic potted plants the Earl affected to beautify his bleak northern manors crossed his mind's eye.

"You were spying," he accused playfully, tugging a straight chestnut lock.

"I was not!" she pouted. "Anyway how else . . . ?"

" . . . can a girl learn? Nobody ever tells a girl anything," they chorused and ended in gales of young laughter.

But even young laughter must end.

"This is not Edward's will," Richard commented.

"It is not Isabel's will, either." Anne's great eyes snapped with excitement as she recalled the events of a recent evening for Richard. "Isabel stamped her foot and said she wouldn't be caught dead in George's bed. My Lord father didn't stamp his foot, he didn't need to. His voice was awful when he warned Isabel she'd be caught dead somewhere if she didn't do as she was told! He wouldn't kill her, would he, Richard?" If possible, Anne's eyes grew even wider with fear.

"Of course not, Pigeon," Richard soothed, wondering just how far the great Warwick might go if crossed.

"I don't know," Anne shook her head gravely. "He was terribly angry."

They were both silent a while.

"I don't like George." Anne stated flatly.

Richard squirmed uneasily.

"I don't think I like my father, either."

Now Richard turned on her, his own eyes wide with horror.

"Hush! That's treason!"

"It is not," she retorted warmly. "Isabel may have to do what he says, but she doesn't have to like it."

And Edward certainly won't, Richard mused as he followed her straight back down the outside stone stairway that led round the donjon and into the beehive activity of the great banquet given by the Earl of Warwick in honor of his own brother George Neville's enthronement as Archbishop of York.

It had taken more than half a hundred cooks weeks to prepare the sixty course feast that outdid the King's recent fifty course banquet in honor of the Queen.

Let him outdo that, thought Warwick, preening before the image of his own greatness. That the King was ungrateful enough to think himself capable of handling the realm without the man who had made him King, rankled in the Earl's bosom. Now that he felt he had George safely under his thumb, he turned to Richard. He noted with satisfaction that Richard's scrawny body was filling out. He no longer looked so crow picked, although he was still short of statue. His palor was a healthy paleness. The Earl noticed that the gleam of will burned the brighter in his dark blue eyes which were his only physical Plantagenet feature. There was something honest and likeable about Richard, and Warwick could count the people he liked on one hand. There were many to be used, but few he had found to like. Now he watched his daughter Anne chatting gaily with her cousin who smiled indulgently into her eyes.

60

This will be easy, thought Warwick. *Not like Isabel. . . .* His face darkened and he shook his head as if to clear it of unpleasant thoughts. Putting on his best face, he approached the table of state to refill Richard's cup with his own hand. But Richard had not touched his wine.

"Is the wine not to your liking, my Lord?"

"I like it, but it doesn't like me," Richard smiled. "If I could but have a cup of water?"

Water? God's blood! Warwick shared the opinion of most Englishmen that a man drank water only as a penance! For all his likeableness, the King's youngest brother was a queer one. He'd hardly touched his food either.

"By all means, my Lord," Warwick said unctiously, giving the order to a shocked butler.

He noticed his younger daughter's eyes upon him, but could not read the meaning behind them.

Beneath the enjoyment of the occasion and his pleasure at being in Anne's company, Richard felt an unease. The Earl of Warwick was too cordial, the feast was far more sumptuous than the occasion called for, and why were his two oldest sisters, the Duchesses of Exeter and Suffolk, whom he had not seen since Edward's coronation five years ago, here without his foreknowledge? It smacked of a family party. He wondered if Edward were aware . . . He decided to discuss it with his sister Elizabeth as soon as he could get her in private. His sister Anne? He didn't know the Duchess of Exeter well enough. Although having long since departed the bed and board of her Lancastrian husband, he wasn't sure of her. Elizabeth, Duchess of Suffolk, he knew to be staunchly loyal to Edward.

He looked about him at the brilliant assembly. There were certainly some queer ducks on this pond, rarely seen at Westminster. It somehow smacked of intrigue. He *must* talk to his sister.

But before he could corner the Duchess of Suffolk, Richard was himself cornered by no less than the Earl of Warwick. Taking the young Duke of Gloucester's arm companionably in his own he propelled him to his privy chamber where he fussed over him, plied him with water to his body servant's complete astonishment, and settled down to chat. Again the family gathering feeling.

Richard felt his uneasiness return. What was up?

Warwick who fancied himself a student of human nature recognized that Richard's forthright nature demanded a direct approach.

"Have you thought of marriage, my boy?"

Richard was startled completely out of countenance. Besides such a thing had not entered his mind.

"Nay, my Lord," he struggled to keep his voice level. "In its time, that will be a matter for the Crown to consider."

"And you, Richard, how do you feel about it?"

"I am certain that my brother the King, has my future, as it will best to serve England, in mind, my Lord." Richard replied stiffly. "There are yet my sister Margaret and my brother George to be provided for as your Lordship very well knows."

"Ah, yes, George. And if I tell you that George is already provided for?"

"There is still Margaret," Richard parried gingerly. "The King has not confided his plans for George to me."

"The King does not know."

Richard stiffened.

"The Duke of Clarence may not marry without the crown's permission. He knows this full well."

"Many are dissatisfied with the Woodeville influence on the present holder of the crown," Warwick began carefully.

A touch of anger flickered across Richard's mind.

"Meaning yourself, my Lord?" he enquired coldly.

Warwick saw that he had gone too far. Richard was not yet ready. His stiff back was not so easily bent as George's. He tried another tact.

"How old are you, Richard?"

"Fourteen, my Lord," replied Richard puzzled.

"Many men are already married at that age."

Richard said nothing.

"Does the Lady Anne please you?"

Richard smiled warmly.

"The Lady Anne pleases me very much. Why do you ask, my Lord?"

"You also please the Lady Anne. Methinks she would count herself lucky to call you husband."

Richard sprang to his feet.

"The Lady Anne is but a child, my lord. How can you thus speak of your own daughter?"

"These things are done every day, Richard," the Earl spoke with calm distain. "I offer you my daughter and you act like a churlish boor."

"My Lord," Richard spoke stiffly, his eyes aflame. "I respect you greatly, nay, one might say I love you for the affection you have heretofore shown me. But this conversation is not to my liking. I beg to be excused."

Again Warwick retreated. He had underestimated this boy.

"Nay, Richard. We'll forget it. I'll say no more about it. Come, let's join my friends."

Not mollified but used to the authority of the Earl of Warwick, Richard acquiesced. They entered an inner chamber where more wine and sweet biscuits were being served to a select few.

"Water for my Lord the Duke of Gloucester," Warwick called out thoughtfully but with evident distaste.

Richard conveyed his congratulations to the new Archbishop and taking his jeweled cup of water to the nearest corner tried to make himself as inconspicuous as possible. At his entrance the talk of the Queen had subsided quickly.

"Continue, my Lords," Warwick boomed aimiably. "The Duke is one of us." The company accepted the great Warwick's word, animated conversation crashed over and around Richard's ears. Richard listened with amazement. To rid the country of the hated Woodevilles was the topic of the evening. Some were patently weathercocks who turned with the political wind, some spoke vaguely of George of Clarence if Edward refused to come to heel and cast out the gilt haired strumpet who ruled England through her lascivious husband.

Aghast Richard sought out Warwick.

"My Lord," he spoke in a choking voice, "I beg to be excused. I can no longer reside in this house. What these men say is little short of treason." He bowed stiffly. "With your permission, I ride tonight."

The permission was granted for the Earl of Warwick knew his cousin of York would ride with or without it.

Warwick had gambled and lost. What a pity! This lad with the great Warwick's help might have some claim to greatness. George? Faugh! If he was the best he could get he must use him. Anne would have been happy with this boy. Somewhere in his austere soul was a grain of love for the wide-eyed child, who was his last claim to dynasty. What a pity that she could not have been a boy. A woman had no chance in this ruthless world. Richard, Earl of Warwick, watched reluctantly as his young cousin Richard, Duke of Gloucester, departed his household and his dynastic plans.

Richard sought out Anne. When he found her, words failed him.

"My father?" she inquired her eyes solemn.

"Yes." He squeezed her hands tightly, searching for the right thing to say.

"He has offered me your hand."

Anne looked down at her hand.

"What in the world for?"

"Marriage," he blurted.

They looked at each other with new eyes. Gone were the lovely carefree days, the gaiety, the fun, the sharing, the precious moments of childhood, all destroyed by one word.

"That's silly," Anne declared flatly.

"Of course," said Richard.

They were silent. What was there to say?

"Even if you were a *woman grown,*" Richard tried for brightness and failed. "I couldn't accept. You know that, don't you?"

"Of course, I do. I don't want you for a husband. I want you for a friend."

But both of them knew it would never be the same between them.

"Good-bye, Anne."

"Good-bye, Richard."

A slight girlish figure with straight chesnut hair and sad brown eyes watched a slight boyish figure of no beauty but great charm ride out of her father's house and her own bleak life. Her cousin Richard was the only touch of love she'd ever known besides her sister Isabel.

Anne didn't wave and Richard didn't look back.

Richard wound his way over the tortuous, rain soaked roads toward Corfe Castle in Wales granted him years ago by the King, but which he had never seen. For the first time, he was truly alone, if one excepted the faithful Scogan who plodded along on a mule more suited to his own stubborn temperament than the spirited steeds Richard urged on his body servant. Richard needed time to think. Scogan's lusty and tuneless singing hardly pierced the fringes of his mind.

> *How happy is he born and taught*
> *That serveth not anothers will;*
> *Whose armour is his honest thought,*
> *And simple truth his highest skill?*
>
> *Whose passions not his masters are;*
> *Whose soul is still prepar'd for death,*

Not ty'd unto the world with care
Of princes ear, or vulgar breath;

Who hath his life from rumours freed;
Whose conscience is his strong retreat;
Whose state can neither flatterers feed,
Nor ruine make oppressors great?

What was Warwick up to?
And more alarming, what was George up to?
Here in the bleak North Richard was brought face to face with
the politics and intrigue he had left the court to escape. He thought
of Edward, great golden, beloved Edward caught in the luxurious
wcb the Woodevilles were cleverly weaving about him. Edward
needed him! Suddenly Richard felt himself a man. *England has no
need of me* he had told his mother sadly but without bitterness.
Now, he felt a wholeness, the gentle tap of destiny. Someone needed
him! And that someone was Edward whom he loved. His heart lifted.
For a moment he joined in Scogan's unmusical singing.

Who envies none whom chance doth raise,
Or vice? who never understood
How deepest wounds are given with praise,
Nor rules of state, but rules of good.

Who God doth late and early pray
More of his grace than gifts to lend,
And entertaines the harmless day
With a well-chosen book or friend!

This man is freed from servile bands
Of hope to rise or feare to fall;
Lord of himselfe, though not of lands,
And having nothing, yet hath all.

But George? He ceased his singing and examined the image of his
brother George, whom he loved also. Wasn't he so like Edward? At
least he looked like Edward although he was weak and foolish at
times. George needed him, too. Richard's great heart swelled in its
small frame. He no longer felt alone. He must see George first and
show him the error of his way. Then he would see Edward and report
the events at Carwood Castle.

He frowned at two facts Scogan had gleaned below stairs. In the emotional confusion caused by the interview concerning Anne he had completely forgotten them. As his mind swung from himself to his brothers, these facts took on a new and sinister significance.

First, the newly enthroned Archbishop of York was already using his high ecclesiastical office to negotiate secretly with the Pope for a Papal dispensation for the marriage of George and Isabel who were first cousins.

Scogan had also reported that Edward meant to marry Margaret off post haste to Charles of Burgundy in order to cement the alliance with Burgundy that the people of England desired above all things in order to bolster their wool trade. Two facts had not escaped the King's attention. Such an alliance would be aimed against France, whom his people hated with a purple passion. Best of all, it would annoy Warwick who was seeking Louis' friendship to bolster his own failing influence over Edward.

Richard thought of Margaret. Perhaps she needed him, too. Edward certainly would not consider his sister's feelings in the matter. Richard, who fully concurred in the Kings's right to negotiate such an advantageous marriage — had he not pointed out this right in his own case to Warwick — nevertheless felt a pity for Meg. Charles of Burgundy had the reputation of being stubborn, violent, and arrogant. Richard could remember him but dimly, for he had come seldom to the court of his father Good Duke Phillip who had played pranks on boys but had been as quick to make amends. He had hated his father and this was not a point in his favor in Richard's eyes. Earnest and reserved, Charles was known to be well educated and a fine musician. These last were good points and would please Meg. He would tell them to her and, although they could do little to counterbalance in his sister's mind the qualities of the handsome and gentle Frank Lovell, they would be of some comfort.

Feeling some better, he urged Scogan on to new musical effort until they rounded a hillock and came in sight of Corfe Castle frowning down on them. The rusty chain screamed in protest as the bridge banged down across the moat admitting Richard and his company into an evil smelling, filthy courtyard, surrounded by bat and rat invested rooms. Down their clammy stone walls, bare of the luxurious hangings to which he was accustomed, ran rivers of condensed moisture that puddled up muddily on the floor. Richard shuddered and looked helplessly about. Not so Scogan. He blossomed in efficiency. Used to being overlooked as the mere body servant of an unimportant third son, he revelled in his promotion — as yet unconfirmed by his Master — to Steward in the household of the great (Scogan had no doubt he would be great some day) Duke of Gloucester. Right and left his bellowed orders sent the slim and slovenly staff scurrying, and by night fall Richard was warm, freshly bathed, his belly full of the simple but ample fare he preferred, and realizing fully that he was also in as great need of comfort as were his brothers and sister.

Madame he wrote in the firelight with what tools Scogan could scare up. *I recommend me to you right heartily; beseeching you in my most humble wise to come to me here to my singular comfort in my need. I pray you give credence to my servant Scogan the bearer of this missive in what we are sadly lacking at this my castle.*
Written at Corfe, the tenth day of May, 1467 with the hand of
Your most humble son,
Richard

Cecily, Duchess of York, read her son's plea and with the speed and stamina acquired in years of campaigning with her lord Richard's father, rode out of London astride a great broad shouldered gelding with a dozen wagons rattling in her wake loaded with the goods that Richard had required. She also carried with her a summons for Richard to appear immediately at court to host along with brother George the Queen's jousting tournament, which would star the Queen's favorite brother Anthony and the Bastard of Burgundy who came not only to tilt with Sir Anthony, but to sign the marriage contract of the King's sister Margaret of York and Charles of Burgundy.

Immediately upon arrival in London Richard established himself at Baynard Castle hoping Edward would permit him to remain. There he found George, his tongue already loose with wine, hoping the same thing. Richard with characteristic directness came right to the point.

"George," he began trying not to be dazzled by his brother's eighteen year old handsomeness and regal air. "You are not in good company."

George looked down disdainfully at his scrawny fifteen year old brother.

"Meaning yourself?" he enquired flippantly.

Richard flushed.

"Of course not! You know whom I mean."

"If you are referring to our cousin the Earl of Warwick, I must remind you that our brother Edward is responsible to him for his high position." George refilled his ornately jeweled cup.

Richard spoke slowly, choosing his words with care.

"It is true our cousin of Warwick has been of great help to our cause. But now he wishes to rule the King."

"Our cause?" snapped George. "You mean Edward's cause."

Richard's eyes widened.

"Isn't Edward's cause our cause?" he demanded.

George turned to his brother angrily.

"Edward's cause has become the Woodeville cause. The strumpet's kith and kin are depriving me — yes and you, too — of wealth and honors that are rightfully ours."

"George!" cried Richard in horror. "You are speaking of the Queen!"

"Are you a milksop and a Woodeville lover?"

"No," Richard admitted, his face deeply troubled. "I like them not. But she is nevertheless the Queen and Edward's choice. There is naught we can do about it!"

"There might be," George spoke darkly into his cup.

Richard's spine tingled with alarm.

"What can you mean?" he asked through lips stiff with fear.

George stomped and blustered.

"If Edward refuses to listen to reason, am I not next in line to the throne?"

"George!" Richard's voice sank to a whisper. "Not while Edward lives."

"Henry still lives and Edward is King!"

"You're drunk," Richard said in disgust, recovering from the shock. "Have you not enough to feed your foolish pride in all that Edward has given you?"

"He has not given me what he has given to that whore's brood!" Richard winced. "Or even to you!" George stormed. "You are just a younger brother and he loves you more than he does me."

Richard shut his eyes and clenched his fists in an effort to dispel the revolting image of his beautiful brother crying in maudlin rage into his wine cup.

They were not destined to hide from Edward's angry eye. The Dukes of Clarence and Gloucester were summoned to immediate attendance on the King at Westminster in all haste.

Using that haste judiciously, Richard with Scogan's expert aid was able to sober George to the point where he could sit his horse. Richard hoped and prayed his brother would not make an ass of himself before the King.

Edward was in a towering rage and demanded an immediate accounting from each of them.

Richard felt a shock. What had he done?

He soon found out.

"Why were you at Carwood Castle without my permission?"

"You gave me permission to leave court, Edward." Richard reminded him.

"I gave you instructions to ride to York to settle a dispute over the Mayor's election."

"This I did, I understood to your complete satisfaction and that of the City of York. Wrangysh is a good man." Richard defended himself. "I further informed you of my intention to travel on to Corfe. This I did."

"Stopping off at Carwood," Edward thundered.

Richard almost hung his head.

"I wanted to see Anne."

"So I am informed, my Lord Duke." Richard resisted an impulse to stop his ears with his fingers. "And do you, like your lily-livered, malmsey sodden, turn coat brother intend to try to marry into the Warwick pie's nest behind my back?"

A wave of anger at this injustice swept over Richard and stifled his voice with the hoarsness of emotion. Ridiculously small before the towering physique of his six foot four brother, Richard stood up to him like a gamecock.

"I do not, your Grace! I was offered the opportunity," the words skipped out in anger, "but I refused in loyalty to yourself."

Looking down on his brother Edward was ashamed. Standing spread legged and unafraid before the regal might of the King, Richard resembled nothing so much as an undersized falcon ready for the chase. His blue eyes were as bright with fury as were those of his brother the King.

"And George?" Edward demanded, retreating slowly.

"George is here to answer for himself," snapped Richard. "Do I have your Grace's permission to withdraw?"

"No, you don't," retorted the King, his anger rising again as he turned on his brother George. "Well, answer for yourself!"

"I have nothing to say," George was impudently sullen. He had thoroughly enjoyed the attack on Richard although it had involved his own courage and habits.

"By the Mercy of God, you had better think of something to say if you want to keep that handsome head on your shoulders."

Both the King's younger brothers blanched.

69

"You wouldn't dare!" George gasped.

"You'd be surprised what I'd dare for England!" shouted Edward.

Richard was reminded that his mother had said just those words.

"George wasn't even there, Edward," Richard started out in defense.

"Not at Carwood perhaps, but he's been sniveling in the ante rooms of the Earl of Warwick listening to his honeyed promises. Don't you know," he turned to George, "the Earl has taken your measure exactly? He'll use you while he needs you, and toss you aside the moment he doesn't. You are only of value to him as the King's brother. When I am no longer King, as the great Warwick seems to wish, you will be worthless," Edward's lips curled in disdain. "Or are you already?"

Stung to fury George put his face under Edward's nose and almost screamed.

"You just don't want me to have Isabel because you, yes, you, the great conquering Edward, couldn't get her." The warning vein began to pulse in Edward's forehead. Richard tried to pull George back but George threw him off like a rag doll. "Maybe you still hope to get her."

The impact of Edward's hand across his brother's mouth sounded loud in the suddenly silent room. George staggered back but did not fall.

"Don't ever let the name of the Lady Isabel cross your lips again in my presence. And as for any idea of marrying her or any other without the approval of the Crown — get it out of your mind! Do you understand, my Lord Duke?"

Realizing that he had gone too far George could only mutter.

"Yes, your Grace." He shook his head to clear his eye sight as he stumbled for the door, not however forgetting to bend his knee to the King.

When they had left him, the King stood long in thought.

"To think that he is the heir to the throne!" He began to throw off his garments. "I'll have to do something about that."

When Richard could collect himself sufficiently from the sordid scene he went in search of his sister Margaret. He found her calmly examining lengths of stuffs beautifully woven in Bruges and sent by Charles as a gift for her trousseau. Although Duke Charles, a close trader, had demanded and gotten two thirds of the annual income of the English crown as Margaret's dowry, he was a generous man and

70

he wanted his bride suitably clad to honor the magnificient court he had inherited from good Duke Phillip. Charles hadn't liked his father, but he did like his court which was a neat balance to his own personal austerity.

Margaret's brow was completely untroubled as she greeted her young brother. Richard hardly knew how to begin. Margaret read the concern in his eyes with keen perspicacity.

"Don't worry, Dickon. I'll be all right."

Richard could only nod.

"He has many good qualities." Margaret sounded as if she were continuing an argument with herself. "He's generous. See?" She held up a really magnificent piece of cloth of gold completely unsuited to her personality.

Richard nodded again.

"He drinks little." Both of them thought of George.

"And I've never heard that he beat his first wife." Margaret tried to joke. It didn't quite come off.

"And Frank?" Richard asked softly.

"Oh, that has already been taken care of," Margaret replied with some heat.

"Taken care of? How?"

"The Queen," Margaret's usually sweet voice was full of venom, "convinced our brother that he would be a nice gift to placate the captious Warwick. Edward married him off to Warwick's niece Anne Fitzhugh."

"Already?"

"Already." Margaret sighed. "She's nice, too." Tears misted the blue eyes. "It isn't her fault."

"I'll miss you, Meg," he patted her idle hands.

"I'll miss you, too, Dickon." She wiped her eyes quickly. They were clear, serene and very blue when she turned on him.

"Don't worry, Dickon," she repeated squeezing his hand. "Charles needs me. I'll be all right."

Dear sweet, motherly Meg. Brave, courageous loyal Meg. Like himself, she needed to be needed.

III

AND THEN THERE WERE EIGHT

Margaret was gone, escorted on the first stage of her bridal journey by the King's cousin and faithful general, the Earl of Warwick and the Duke of Clarence, the King's brother and still his heir. For Edward's resolution to beget his own heir had resulted in yet another royal princess. The wedding party halted for three days in Essex where they were joined by the King and Queen and the Duke of Gloucester. This farewell family party in Margaret's honor had a highly flammable potential which both Margaret and Richard felt. However, all went well and amidst the fond kissings and congratulations of leave taking Richard managed a moment alone with his sister.

"I am more fortunate than you, Dickon."

"How so, Meg?"

"At least I'll be out of all this."

They both looked at George who had managed to behave himself rather well since Edward's outburst but was beginning to get restive again.

"Take care of him, Dickon. He's a bad boy, but our own brother. And I love him."

"So do I, Meg." Richard wondered why this was so, but it was.

"Don't let Edward be too hard on him."

Thinking of the last time the brothers were together, Richard sighed.

"I'll try, Meg. Truly I will."

The last months of 1468 were quiet on the surface, but spring brought out the unrest that lay beneath. Seemingly minor uprisings began to break on the northern horizon and flickered like heat

73

lightning, flashing but not striking. A rebel calling himself Robin of this or that popped up hither, thither, and yon. The Earl of Northumberland, Warwick's brother but still Edward's dogged supporter would put down one Robin to have another rise up at his back. Edward decided to investigate.

Richard was wild to escape the court again and asked for permission to accompany the King, Edward granted it on the condition that he equip and finance his own company. Dismayed but not defeated, Richard borrowed from a friend what seemed to him a fabulous sum which he promised to repay by Easter and set out happily on his first adventures in finance and campaigning.

At Newark both Edward and Richard received startling messages.

A rebel proclamation fell into the King's hands. Damning the Woodevilles and others close to the King, it was obvious who was the author, the Earl of Warwick. Edward advised his followers named in the proclamation to flee for their lives and taking only Richard sought refuge at Nottingham.

Controlling his fury, Edward wrote three letters to the conspirators, Warwick, Warwick's brother George Archbishop of York, and his own brother George.

I pray you come to us in peaceful wise that we may settle our differences to all our good and the common weal of this realm. We hope and trust that you are not of any such disposition toward us as the rumour here runneth.

Richard brought the King his own letter. It was from Anne.

Richard, it began with simple directness, *my lord father has just told my lady mother to pack our boxes in all haste meaning hers, mine, and Isabel's. Isabel does not know this and, oh, Richard, I have not the heart to tell her. With us go Uncle George and your brother George. We go to Calais for what purpose you may well guess. I send you these tidings not to beg your aid, this I know to be impossible now, but that you and Edward may be warned. My father says he will be back this time with a great army. God grant that this reach you in time to save yourselves.*

Farewell,
Anne.

Edward's fury knew no bounds. Tearing his conciliatory notes into a thousand pieces, he summoned his generals Pembroke, Hastings, and Devon to come to him at all speed with sufficient forces to crush the Earl of Warwick, the Archbishop of York, and the King's own brother.

The secretive ceremony on French soil was over in a thrice and Isabel was the Duchess of Clarence. George took her like one of his mastiffs, carefully trained to cruelty, might enter a bitch, snarling, pushing, grunting and slavering. He beat out all his assorted passions of jealousy, meanness, inadequacy, and disappointment on her finally crumpled and unresistant body. When he had finished with her he rolled over and lay panting in gasping sobs within the dark silence of the stifling, curtained bed. Sometime later when the gaspings of his tortured lungs had ceased, he raised his sweating, depleted body on his elbow.

"Isabel," he whispered.

There was neither sound nor movement from her side of the great bed. Suddenly frightened he kicked and tore his way out of the confining curtains. The cool stone of the floor restored his sanity. He reached for the flagon of malmsey ever present on a nearby table. When Isabel regained consciousness he was snoring in drunken gusto at her side.

Isabel dragged her bruised and torn body out of the bed. She wanted to be sick but she grit her teeth firmly against the nausea. She made no effort at silence for she knew from his snoring that George was beyond the reach of sound. She tried to concentrate her reeling senses on the layout of the unfamiliar palace of Humber, Edward's outpost at Calais. She wondered why they had been admitted. Lord Wenlock, the Governor, must be in her father's pay, a traitor to England!

But who is not a traitor to the King these days? she thought.

She tried not to think of her father. Although she had never had cause to love him, until now he had commanded her respect. But he had done this to his daughter just to get even with Edward!

George is a beast, a wild beast!

Isabel clapped her hands across her mouth to suppress the screaming horror rising in her throat. She darted into the corridor and dodging cunningly in and out of frequent embrasures to avoid detection she finally reached her sister's room.

Anne, not yet asleep, heard Isabel's faint scratching on the door. Swinging it open Anne was not prepared for the sight that met her eyes. Her beautiful, gay sister was a mess. The chestnut curls were in wild disarray above a swollen face whose mouth was cut and bleeding. Her gown hung in matted shreds.

"Isabel!" whispered Anne aghast as she caught her limp body. Isabel had fainted again.

Anne heard George shouting as he came. She slipped from her chair where she had sat bolt upright during the long night. She placed Isabel's now limp hand on the satin counterpane and touched the shoulder of the dozing woman on the other side of the bed. Ankarette started awake. Anne touched her fingers to her lips.

"He's coming," Anne whispered into the woman's ear. "I'll meet him in the hall."

Ankarette paled.

"Aren't you afraid?"

"Yes, I am," Anne replied in her direct way. "But if Isabel can stand it, so can I. He can't do worse than that," she pointed to the purpling bruises on the once lovely face that lay on its satin pillow. Anne and Ankarette had done the best they could for Isabel, bathing her gently and putting on one of Anne's night robes that was much too small. Ankarette's gentle hands had touched the torn flesh with an arnica that healed but did not sting and finally had forced a potion between Isabel's bleeding lips that sent her into deep untroubled sleep. Only occasionally during the night watch had she stirred and whimpered when Anne removed her hand from Isabel's. Anne, as young as she was, knew that the hurts to her body would heal in time, the inner hurt would mar her sister forever with its throbbing scar.

She slipped into the corridor and squared her shoulders for the furious onslaught.

"Where is she?" shouted George.

"In there," Anne indicated with her head, her back firmly against the door. "Stop shouting like a maniac!"

Taken back at such orders from this tiny chit of a girl, he did stop shouting. He reached to jerk her aside.

"You can't go in," Anne defied him stoutly, butterflies dancing in her stomach.

"I can't go in to my own wife?" George yelled. "Get out of my way!"

"If you do I'll tell my Lord Father what you did to her!"

"Your Lord Father," George's voice was heavy with sarcasm, "thinks no more of her than he does any other bitch in a trade!"

Anne wanted to run but she held her ground.

"Perhaps that's true," she said scathingly, "I am certain Isabel feels so now. However, the Earl of Warwick expects those who buy his-his bitches to treat them at least as well as high bred dogs!"

In the struggle that followed the return of the Earl of Warwick

76

and his reinforced company to England, the Earls of Pembroke along with Devon, the Earl Rivers and Sir John Woodeville, father and brother to the Queen, were beheaded after summary trials before the Earl of Warwick and the Duke of Clarence.

Unaware of these developments Edward and Richard set out from Nottingham to make contact with reinforcements. At Olney they were met by Hastings with the news of the blood bath. Quickly Edward released all his followers. Hastings who knew where his bread was buttered and Richard who loved his brother refused to leave. Edward clasped them gratefully by the arm.

"We are outmaneuvered for the moment, my Lords. But, fear not! Two can play at this game of guile."

The King was amiable and smiling when he greeted Warwick's emissary the Archbishop of York. Blandly Edward welcomed him and his strong company of horse as if they were his honored guests at Westminster.

"Dismount, Reverend Father. You honor my house. My staff is somewhat depleted, but I think we can manage."

Trying not to be outfaced, the Archbishop endeavored to match the King's tone and failed miserably.

"Your Grace, the Earl of Warwick desires your immediate attendance at Coventry," he blustered.

"Coventry? Ah, yes!" Edward smiled. "Dame Marguerite's favorite hide away. Is she there?" he enquired chattily.

"Certainly not!" the by now completely flustered Archbishop retorted.

"By the Mercy of God, then you'd better fetch her. My Lord of Warwick's is going to need all the help he can get. She's a better general than he is, is that not so, my Lord Hastings?"

The two of them roared with laughter while Richard watched them with hooded eyes. *What was Edward up to?*

"Richard, fetch our horses. We mustn't keep the great Earl waiting," he grinned rakishly up at the outfaced Archbishop. "I am sure he has better things to do than wait on the King."

The King and his company of two were received graciously at Coventry by the Earl with George trying unsuccessfully to hide his great hulk behind the stocky Warwick. They cantered away together in the direction of Warwick Castle with Edward chatting as pleasantly as if they were out on a hunt. Edward's gaze was cooly noncommittal when it fell on Warwick, but there was no mistaking the venom in the blue eyes when they crossed with his brother George's.

"Psst!"

Richard jumped.

The tapestry swayed ever so slightly to reveal a familiar pair of wide brown eyes.

"Anne!" It couldn't be.

"Yes, it is, too." She answered his thoughts.

"Get out of here," Richard snapped. "Haven't you got sense enough to know danger when you see it?"

"It's everywhere these days, so I might as well be here," she replied calmly coming out of her hiding place.

"How did you get here?"

"Oh," she shrugged. "Same as always. I walked."

"Anne, don't tease. You're in danger here."

"So are you, and so, which is more important than us, is the King. We've got to get him out."

"How?" Richard demanded in spite of himself.

"There is a gate in the south wall. I know the guard. He likes malmsey as well as George."

"Well?"

"Well, what, silly? It's as simple as that."

"I suppose it is, if you say so," Richard smiled ruefully. "I wish I had you to solve all my problems."

That evening she was back again.

"He's *that* drunk," she giggled. "Hurry!"

They slid hand in hand noiselessly down the winding stairway. The heavy doorway opened on oiled hinges, she had thought of everything. Except . . . .

"Good-bye, Richard!" she was saying when he drew her after him into the night.

"Anne!" he whispered.

"Yes?"

"You've grown."

"Did you expect me not to," she laughed softly. "You've grown, too."

Suddenly she was in his hungry arms. Her kiss was sweet beyond endurance. She pushed away and smiled softly in the starlight.

"You know, I think I love you, Richard."

"I love you, too, my Pigeon." He wondered if she heard him as she was gone on flying feet.

At the top of the stairway she stopped and leaned panting against the wall. Her breathlessness was not all from running. She touched her lips softly with her fingers trying to remember the feel of his kiss.

Her breath caught in her throat.

"At least I'll have that," she whispered.

She started to turn toward her chamber when she thought of her sister. Isabel ought to have at least that much to cherish through the long years ahead. But how could she manage it? There must be some way. Malmsey wouldn't work on them all. Ankarette? Ankarette was as pretty as a peach and she adored Isabel. Anne smiled softly to herself.

In the matter of a few minutes Isabel slipped through Edward's suddenly unguarded prison door.

"Isabel!"

"Edward!"

She was in his great arms sobbing out all the hurt and pain and loving that they could not share. Edward soothed and caressed her as gently as if she were a wounded bird, as indeed she was. So this was love! In all the years of seeking he had not found it. It was a sort of liquid glow that filled his body with warmth instead of the fire that burned and left him replete but empty. Love, a precious healing thing that had touched him and he had let it go. Slowly their passion grew in mounting waves of joy.

"Isabel," he whispered into her ear. "Does it matter now?"

"No, Edward, my love."

"At least we'll have this." He echoed Anne's words.

"Yes, oh, yes!" Her cry was smothered beneath his lips.

Parting with Hastings after a hasty, whispered conference, Richard headed south down Watling Street, the great thoroughfare that ran to and through London. Hastings headed north and west to gather troops. As the hooves of his horse beat out a steady rhythm on the drought baked earth, Richard's mind numbered off methodically the names of the members of Edward's council. At each castle he gave the summons to assemble at Pontefract Castle in the neighborhood of the stronghold of Middleham where, he guessed correctly, Edward would be sent when Richard's and Hastings' escape was detected. At each stop he commandeered a fresh horse, but drove himself mercilessly on.

He reigned his horse in so suddenly that the beast, his mouth cruelly cut, almost fell carrying his rider with him.

Anne! What of Anne?

Her complicity would never escape her father. Richard was readily acquainted with the deadly consequences of the Earl's cold fury. A small daughter standing in his path would be of slight moment to a father who had used any and every means at his command to climb from comparative obscurity to the giddy heights of exalted position as the wealthiest and mightiest baron in the land, the main prop to the throne.

Prop to the throne? No longer.

Richard tried to analyze Warwick's intentions. King himself? Richard doubted it. Warwick was too canny not to realize that with all his immense popularity, the people would never stand for such a threat to the sanctity of the throne of England. A commoner as Queen stuck in their craws, a commoner as King? Never!

George, then?

Perhaps. But George would not be as easy to handle as Warwick might think at the moment. Once mantled in the robe of majesty, George would most certainly turn out to be an asp in the bosom of his champion. Ruling behind George's throne would be no cinch.

But Anne! What would he do to Anne?

Out of the starry night a pair of fearless brown eyes smiled at him.

Hurry! they seemed to say, *It's done now. Whatever the consequences to us, you must make them work to the glory of England.*

Keeping those brave eyes before him and trying to close his mind to the sweetness of their kiss, he drove himself on into the night.

On a fine day in late September Warwick arose to find an army of several hundred under the command of his brother of Northumberland politely but firmly encamped under the silken tents and gaudy blazons of the Lords of the King's Council.

"My Lord Warwick!" Richard cried before the gate. "The Lords of his Council are come to escort their King in state to his city of London. Pray lower the bridge."

From the donjon Warwick, George and the Archbishop looked down in dismay at the goodly company in battle array. Below them stood the greatest lords in the land. A brilliant sun reflected in the polished steel of their helmets and harness blinded the three standing furious but helpless as Warwick issued the order for the lowering of the bridge. The sun flashing in the gold of the King's hair as he rode out to meet his Lords struck deeply into the Duke of Clarence's smoldering eyes, but not before he saw his brother Edward clasp his brother Richard to him in affection and gratitude. The sullen fire therein burned the hotter.

The Archbishop, ever the opportunist, hastened to present

himself to the King in the full regalia of his office ready to ride the waves of glory on no matter what shore they lapped.

Edward listened to his obsequious excuses with a bland smile playing around his lips.

"My Lord," the King replied for all to hear, his voice bold with new authority, "your thoughtfulness touches us. However, trouble yourself no further, whenever we need you, we shall send for you."

His words and his meaning floated clearly up to Warwick and George.

From the Woodevilles whom Edward had elevated in a canny attempt to free the throne of England from dominance by the barons, the King now turned frankly to his brother Richard as the bulwark of his power. Richard was made Constable of England and given wide authority over the courts by being honored as President of the Court of Chivalry. The just and able manner in which Richard dispatched his duties and used his immense authority assured the King that his confidence was not misplaced.

"Edward," he questioned one of the King's appointments during a private conference on State matters. "You are right to rid yourself of the slippery Archbishop as Chancellor, but to replace him with an unknown Bishop. Is this wise?"

"Stillington is quite capable," replied Edward somewhat shortly.

"Who is he? I'd never heard of him until you elevated him last year."

"Neither had I," Edward snapped dryly. "He'll do." Edward turned to another matter.

"But Edward," Richard persisted, "is it wise . . . ?"

"Enough!" shouted Edward suddenly startling Richard. "I said he'll do. Is that not enough? Do you question the King's judgment?"

"Nay, your Grace," Richard's face was perplexed at Edward's sudden irritation. "I merely wondered . . . . "

Edward's eyes bore down on his young brother.

"There are some things it's better not to wonder about," he warned. "Don't get too big for your breeches."

Richard started to wonder out loud why Edward was in such a sudden tizzy over his inquiry into the qualifications of the Bishop of Bath and Wells but thought better of it and subsided. They turned to Richard's orders and in the excitement of his first independent command the new chancellor was forgotten.

During the busy months that followed, Richard was everywhere consolidating his brother's power. He squelched uprisings, obviously

Warwick inspired, that cropped up like brush fire all over the land. He noted that these uprisings were gaining in Lancastrian flavor and reported as much to Edward.

"Absurd!" declared Edward. "Warwick may be against *me,* but not against York. He'd never break bread with the unclean of Lancaster!"

"Not absurd," Richard ventured to contradict. "The Earl of Warwick is not so much against anything as for himself. Whatever stands in the way of his overweaning ambition is of no consequence." He thought involuntarily of Anne. ". . . to be stuck aside at any cost," he ended slowly.

Where was she? In the busy months he had had no time to find out and no news reached even the sharp ears of Scogan.

"Edward, I must find her," he blurted.

"Her? Who, Dickon?" Edward's mind was full of his own concerns.

"Anne. There's no telling what her father did to her when he found out what she had done."

"Oh, she's all right. Warwick's a devil when aroused, but he'd stop short of fouling his own nest."

"And Isabel?" Richard reminded him.

Edward bit his lip.

"But that was a move to benefit himself just as you've pointed out. That was not a move to punish Isabel."

"If he can do that in cold calculation to one daughter what could he do in anger to the other?"

Edward snorted.

"If you are right in your assessment of his character, he'll save her to use to his further advantage. He wouldn't harm something so potentially valuable to himself. Stop worrying, Dickon," His eyebrows drew together. "Why are you so concerned about that child?"

Richard lowered his eyes.

"Because of what she did for the King," he mumbled.

"Lots of lovely ladies had been helpful to the King. I've not seen you so concerned for their welfare." Edward teased.

Richard flushed, but said nothing.

"So that's it!"

"What's it?"

"You're in love with her."

Richard's heart stood still. His eyes widened in wonder.

"I suppose I am," he replied slowly, "I hadn't thought about it that way."

"Then I'm sorry I brought it up," Edward was all business again. "And you might as well forget it. One brother married to a rebel's daughter is quite enough."

"You're right, of course, Edward."

Edward's eyes softened at the bleak look in his young brother's eyes.

"I can't afford to lose you, Dickon," he put his arm around Richard's slight shoulders. "Your brother Edward needs you — the King needs you."

Richard's eyes misted in gratitude.

"I hope I can fill both needs, Edward."

The problem of what to do with Warwick and George engaged their minds. Edward was so exasperated by now he was ready to make short shift of them both.

"But George is your brother!" Richard was aghast.

"Then let him act like one!" snapped Edward.

"He's jealous," Richard began carefully.

"By God's mercy," stormed Edward, "What more does he want? I've given the whippersnapper half the crown lands. He's richer than I am, and twice as rich as you."

"He wants more, Edward."

"By God, I'm sure he does, but he won't get it."

"Not money, Edward," Richard softened. "Affection from you."

"Well, he's traveling down the wrong road." Edward's face hardened. "He's got Isabel. That ought to satisfy any man."

"She's his wife," Richard conceded. "But he has her love no more than he has yours. He's to be pitied, Edward."

"Faugh!" snorted Edward, but he agreed to the wisdom of inviting his brother George back to court at Christmas time.

"And Warwick's popularity is still enormous. You need his support."

"Well . . . . ," Edward agreed reluctantly.

He would see Anne! If Warwick agreed to come to court for the holiday festivities . . . .

"And I shall hate to have you absent from this family party," Edward did not look at Richard as he fussed with documents on his desk.

"I? But I shall be here."

"No, you won't, my Lord of Gloucester. There are reports of further unrest on the Scottish border. The King needs his mightiest general in the field. Your orders will be ready on the morrow."

The two brothers eyed each other. Edward seated at his huge

desk had brought his eyes to a level with Richard's.

"I understand, your Grace."

"I'm glad you do, my Lord," the King replied in dismissal.

On the surface the country was quiet, the court frolicked in an apparent love feast and on the continent Louis grew restive. If the English people became too happy to fight amongst themselves, they might cast their eyes across the Channel and begin to dream of the reconquest of France.

He must do something about this disgusting state of affairs.

Fine gifts and covert letters which began *Mighty Prince* reached Warwick's eager and willing hands, nibbling at his resolve to return to King Edward's fold. Louis deftly suggested that the great Warwick's failure was due not to any lack of ability on Warwick's part, but to an unfortunate mistake in his choice of lieutenants. Warwick, who had long since begun to look on his son-in-law with a jaundiced eye, was inclined to agree. He was immensely flattered to hear that Louis' picture of the great Earl agreed with his own interpretation of himself.

Louis spun his web happily and sent his friend the Earl a fine pair of matched hackneys. To Louis, who despised people but loved animals, there was no finer gift. The full realization of this and other flattering considerations lessened the impact of the thunderbolt that Louis now hurled in the form of a suggestion that the Earl of Warwick might aline himself with Louis' niece.

Louis' niece! Holy Mother of God! The hated French Marguerite. Even Warwick recoiled at such an alliance.

...would guarantee the alliance of France against Burgundy, Louis wrote glibly.

Hmm! If, at the moment Warwick hated anybody worse than he did the King of England, it was the Duke of Burgundy, Margaret's husband. Forced by Edward to eat crow over this marriage as well as Edward's own, Warwick detested Charles of Burgundy, who had been gleefully aware of Warwick's predicament and had made his awareness known to the seething Earl.

For the lovely Lady Anne, continued Louis, carried away by his own cleverness, *perhaps Prince Edward* . . . .

Warwick began to consider the situation from an entirely new angle. Should Anne marry the hated Marguerite's son, Warwick through his daughters would have one foot stoutly planted in each camp. York or Lancaster he would win. Daughters were not so bad after all. The Earl found himself searching for good points in Dame

84

Marguerite, *Queen* Marguerite, on which he could hang a rationaliza-
tion of his change of heart. At the first, having suckled on hatred of
the House of Lancaster and King Henry VI's termagent wife, he
found little to recommend such a coalition. However . . . .

Even while Edward, trying to act the King rather than the man,
was bestowing new honors on the House of Neville, new uprisings
occurred in Lincolnshire. The estates of the King's own master of the
Horse were pillaged by an old Lancastrian Lord Welles. Edward
determined to investigate the matter personally. George hastily
excused himself on the grounds of a necessary visit to attend to the
welfare of his ailing wife. He rode West promising to join forces with
Warwick to help stamp out the Lincolnshire rebellion.

Edward's eyebrows rose.

"Your consideration for the health of your wife is touching, dear
Brother."

George bent a knee to the King, his face blank, his mind seething.
For this and all other slights . . . .

George's stiff back was hardly out of sight before tidings reached
the King that Lord Welles' son in the names of the Duke of Clarence
and the Earl of Warwick was calling for troops to resist the King who
was coming to destroy the people.

Edward's fury knew no bounds. Hastily trapping Lord Welles he
sent him forthright to the block and formally proclaimed Warwick
and George as traitors. In his blind rage, Edward withdrew the
Earldom of Northumberland from Warwick's brother, who, ever
loyal to the King, had committed no crime save that of being
Warwick's kin.

On campaign in Wales, Richard was aghast when the news
reached him.

"How could he be so foolish!"

Scogan merely shook a gloomy head realizing that Richard was
referring to Edward and not to George.

George's weakness Richard understood, but Edward was the
King!

"A King has no right to be hot headed," Richard worried. "Any
man's loyalty has a limit."

"Save yours, Master Richard."

"He is not only the King, he is my brother."

"So is George," Scogan reminded him.

Richard tried to brush off the thought of George.

"Edward's need of Montagu's forces is more than ever before."

"He'll rue the day," Scogan agreed gloomily. "We all will."

Richard hastening to his brother's aid found his way blocked by Lord Stanley, Warwick's brother-in-law. He made short shift of Stanley's company and in acute alarm hurried on to make contact with Edward.

"Stay, Richard," Edward suddenly sent word. "The rebels have fled."

The channel is ever capricious. Anne held her sister's hand tightly as if to still by sheer will the furies of the April storm and the pains of labor that wracked the tall but too slender frame on the rude bunk.

Blood dribbled from the corners of Isabel's mouth. She had bitten her tongue cruelly in an effort to still her cries of agony and fright.

"Can't you do something?" Anne whispered to her mother who huddled in miserable helplessness in the corner.

The Countess shook her head dumbly.

"You've had two children." Anne felt a stirring anger against her mother who at least shared a responsibility in all this. "You ought to know something."

"Wine," her mother managed in a terrified whisper.

"There is none," Ankarette shook her head. "I've already searched."

Isabel moaned.

"Shh, Isabel." Anne soothed. "We are approaching Calais. You'll soon be in a cool clean bed with a doctor."

Isabel nodded, clenching her teeth but not opening her eyes. Her hand tightened as a paroxysm of pain tore through her body and left her gasping.

"Can't somebody do something?" she whispered faintly. "I don't believe I can stand much more."

Anne motioned to Ankarette, easing her sister's clutching fingers from her own hand she replaced it with Ankarette's and slipped noiselessly from the stifling cabin.

She was thrown headlong into her father's arms. Hastily withdrawing herself and groping for her shattered dignity, she confronted the Earl of Warwick.

"She's going to die if you don't do something."

"What can I do?" The Earl stared back at his daughter a stunned look on his face. "They have refused to let us land at Calais."

"Refused to let us land!" screamed Anne thinking of her promise to Isabel. "Then get a doctor."

"The Earl of Warwick does not beg," her father replied stiffly.

"Not even for the life of his daughter?"

"Child birth is every woman's destiny." The Earl retorted coldly. "She must endure it."

For a long moment Anne eyed her father in cold disgust.

"Holy Mother of God, I doubt that *you* could! I have heard it whispered," her lips curled in scathing disdain, "that the mighty Earl of Warwick for all his roaring like a lion in fair weather is a lamb in foul. Until now I had not believed it."

For a moment she thought he would strike her, but he only said, "Hold your tongue, Child."

"Have a boat lowered," she called boldly. "I'll fetch a doctor."

"You will do nothing of the sort!" shouted Warwick. "Return to your mother and sister!"

"I will fetch a doctor!" Anne shouted back. "Either order a boat lowered or I'll jump overboard and swim. That will not help the already tottering prestige of the Kingmaker!"

But in spite of all her pleadings Anne did not get a doctor.

"Lord Wenlock," she cried angrly at first to the Governor at Calais, "the King will not take lightly to this. The Lady Isabel is the wife of the King's brother."

"I must remind you, Lady Anne, that the King had proclaimed the Duke of Clarence a traitor."

"I am not requesting aid for the Duke of Clarence."

"The Lady Isabel is under a double cloud as wife and daughter of proclaimed traitors."

"Neither cloud of her own choosing," Anne snapped.

Lord Wenlock merely bowed.

"I suppose that also puts me under one cloud. Is that it?"

"Something of the sort, my Lady?"

"Very well, my Lord. We are traitors whether by choice or by inheritance. The lady is also a woman in mortal pain. Does that at least not qualify her for the pity one might feel for a mare in foal?" Her fury was rising again. "Or — a bitch." She fairly spat at him pointing at a greyhound suckling its young on the governor's cold hearth.

Lord Wenlock flushed and shouted for a cask of wine.

"My Lord Wenlock," said Anne bitterly in parting. "If I should ever have the good fortune to face the King again, I shall recommend your Lordship's impeccable loyalty to his Grace. 'Tis a pity you could not have felt so last year when this child was conceived."

They worked like mad, at first to save the child, and failing that, the mother.

"Don't let it die," pled Isabel between her rending gasps of pain.

Anne merely nodded wondering why anybody would want a child of George's.

"It might be Edward's," whispered Isabel before she fainted again.

Anne froze. Fearfully she raised her eyes to see if George had heard.

George was trying to get a cup of wine from the precious cask. He had not heard. Anne sprang on him like a wildcat.

"You-you ... " she cried, beating him about the head and shoulders with small fists.

"He's dead!" Ankarette announced.

Anne whirled. Over her shoulder she heard George's voice muffled with pain. He was staring down at his dead son.

"He looks just like me!"

And you look just like Edward. Anne wanted to shout at him.

Wild rumours swirled around Anne's head unnoticed as she nursed Isabel slowly back to health. Isabel showed an interest in nothing. The lovely color did not return to her cheeks through the idle summer days in Normandy.

One day when Normandy was gloriously abloom with June roses, Anne found Ankarette silently packing her boxes.

"Where are we going?" Anne demanded suspiciously.

Ankarette did not raise her head.

"Only you, Lady Anne."

Anne flew to confront her father. Unannounced she burst upon him in solitary conference with a woman. Astonishment struck her a body blow when a cold, lightly pox-marked face turned to her in annoyance.

Marguerite of Anjou! *Late calling herself Queen of England,* said Edward's bill of attainder. Crazy Henry VI's wife! The dread Dame Marguerite, bugger-bear of all Yorkish children. Her father once defender of the House of York now closeted with the leader of the House of Lancaster. What could all this mean?

The Earl of Warwick eyed his daughter icily.

"What is the meaning of this intrusion?"

Under the spell of shock and long habit, Anne sank in a low curtsey.

"My Lady .... my Lord Father .... I did not know .... "

Marguerite of Anjou's voice was strident as one might expect in a witch.

"My Lord of Warwick, is this unmannerly hussy the gentle, chaste, and obedient child you propose as a consort for my son the Prince of Wales, the future Queen of England?"

"Madam, I beg your humble pardon," his steely glance swept his bowing daughter, "and she will too — for this unseemly performance. It will not happen again! The Lady Anne well knows her place — *and what happens to those who step out of it!*"

"The Lady Anne," remarked Dame Marguerite dryly watching the clouds of anger gathering in Anne's small face as she rose, "seems completely unaware of her position and mine. In the future, child, you will address me as your Grace."

"Why?" demanded Anne.

"Because I am Queen of England."

"There cannot be two Queens of England."

"Nor two kings! My Lord Henry is the rightful King." Her long green eyes burned with the fire of a life's purpose. "We shall destroy the usurper."

"We?" demanded Anne.

"The Earl of Warwick and I!"

"The Earl of Warwick," Anne drew her small statue into its full height and faced her father, "should know as well as his daughter what fate befalls those who step out of their places. I cannot hope that it will happen to you, my Lord Father. But in no manner will I lend you aid in this treason!"

She was gone on swift, silent feel with no by-your-leave.

For a moment Warwick was speechless with rage. Marguerite smiled enigmatically.

"I like her spirit. That is, if it can be bent to suit our purpose," she said.

"The wedding will go forward as planned, your Grace, have no fear."

"Not so fast, my Lord of Warwick. At the moment the bethrothal will suffice. We must not rush the girl."

Warwick's face was bitter.

"Nor you, your Grace?"

"Exactly, my Lord," again the hidden smile. "When you have put my Lord and husband safely back on England's throne — then the marriage. Not before."

Bitter gall. Warwick's face was white. Thus to be badgered by a woman!

"We leave for England immediately after the bethrothal ceremony."

"The Lady Anne will stay with me — to begin the bending process."

The Lady Anne flew to Isabel and confronted her sister with a stormy face.

"So now it's my turn," she blurted.

"Your turn?"

"To be held up, poked, and examined in the market place," Anne's scathing voice rose. Her slight frame shook. "I brought a fair price to our Lord Father the auctioneer!"

Sobbing she threw herself at Isabel's feet and buried her head in her sister's silken lap. Now it was Isabel's turn to soothe.

"Poor little Pigeon."

That made Anne cry the harder. Richard! Until now Anne had remained the child. Even Richard's first kiss had touched lightly but not awakened her womanhood. Now poised upon the marriage block childhood deserted her forever.

"Why can't men be strong enough to settle their own quarrels without walking on women?" sobbed Anne.

Isabel could only pat the bowed head and wonder, too. Her throat filled. Since that first night when George had taken her so brutally and then the death of her child there had been a subtle difference in their relationship. Although it was not in George's nature to say he was sorry, Isabel had known the next time he came to her that in his wild, weak way George loved her. She had nothing to offer in return but she found she could endure his love makings with a certain pity for both of them. For Anne, so small and yet so staunch to be broken thus on the wheel of dynasty was an even greater pity. Isabel's eyes filled.

Anne sat back on her heels and dashed an impatient hand across her eyes. *Women are but empty vessels to be filled with the seeds of dynasty, nothing but a breeding ground for power.* Who had said that? Her father? Hardly. He was not so subtle.

Her eyes flashed as George entered his wife's apartments.

"How can you be so stupid?" she cried, glad for a target on which to vent her frustration.

Startled, George stopped in his tracks.

"How so, Lady Anne?" he asked sarcastically.

"Because you don't know that you are just being used to preen our father's vanity. Oh, yes!" She raged on, "you were to be King and Isabel your Queen — both under the Kingmaker's heel. Now what are you to be? Nothing more than you already were — heir to the throne if I don't beget a Lancastrian brat from the bed of the feeble witted King Henry's even more feeble witted son!"

George's heavy brows drew together. The look in his eyes made Isabel quail in fear. Anne drove on heedless of the menace.

"Why couldn't you have been satisfied with the rightfull position you had with your brother who loves you? No, you had to have what was your due and then your younger brother's too. You're just a spoiled, jealous brat and you've ruined Isabel's life, and mine," she caught her breath, "and your own!"

George turned on his heel and left without a word or backward look.

"Anne!" whispered Isabel. "How could you? In your desire to return hurt for hurt, you have only run up a bill that I shall have to pay. I was on the verge of achieving at least a certain peace with George. Now you have destroyed even that," she ended in toneless despair.

Anne clapped her hands to her mouth, her wide eyes were horrified at her outburst.

"Oh, Isabel!" She cried. "You are the one I would least want to hurt in all the world."

"George!" She dashed after him. "George!"

He paused but did not turn. "I'm sorry," she said to his back, "I had no right to attack you and Isabel because of my hurt."

He neither moved nor spoke.

"Please, George," she pled. "Don't take it out on Isabel. I love her so."

"I love her, too, Anne," his voice with all its natural but seldom used eloquence and charm was full of wonder. "You do have a poor opinion of me, don't you? I won't hurt her."

Anne sighed in relief. She believed him.

"And, Anne . . . . "

"Yes, George?"

"You're right about what you said, quite right."

He was gone on dragging feet.

In spite of Anne's brave words and a sudden new reticence in George, the bethrothal went forward in great pomp at the Cathedral in Angers. Warwick and Dame Marguerite swore to eternal amity on a piece of the True Cross and the struggle for the crown was on again.

Anne watched with brimming eyes as all she had ever known of family sailed away westward across the Channel to wrest the throne from Edward. And what of Richard?

91

Standing in the real shadow of Dame Marguerite, as she had so often stood in childish imagination, Anne looked at the ineffectual youth who was to be her husband. She was glad that she had managed to extract a final promise from George that he would talk to Richard before he travelled further down the road to certain ruin. By Ankarette unbeknownst even to Isabel, she had managed a brief message to Richard.

I have done my best. He is ripe for the plucking. God keep you all.

No greeting no leave taking. That was all. But Richard cherished it against his heart as if it were the tenderest love missile. He felt her warm lips against his own, her slender unawakened body . . . A thrill swept through his own spare frame. A sudden desire to achieve that awakening tore at him like a wild, sweet storm and left him breathless.

Brother met brother as the war clouds gathered. George rode away to the west ostensibly to array troops in Warwick's behalf to bring down "yonder man Edward!" Barons donned harness to fight, for or against, or to sit watchfully at home ready to ride with the victor.

Warwick freed foolish Henry — piously happy and dirty at the Tower — cleaned him up, polished his tarnished crown, and balanced it precariously on his stringy greying locks, then paraded the Lancastrian King in pomp for all to see. At Coventry they poised behind stout walls awaiting Warwick's son-in-law's muster. Warwick was completely unprepared for the news a frightened dusty scurrier stammered out under his master's baleful glare.

"You're lying," Warwick shouted.

"I have it on impeccable authority, your Grace," the dusty squire quavered. "My mother-in-law is a pious woman. She never lies. She saw . . ."

"She saw what?" the great Earl's face was turning purple.

"My Lord of Clarence threw himself on his knees before the King, pardon, your Grace — before that — that man Edward," the squire almost choked over such heresy.

"Go on!" snapped Warwick.

"The King," the unhappy scurrier crossed himself and began again. "Edward raised him and embraced him *right fondly* — those were her very words, your Grace."

"Never mind her very words! What of Gloucester?"

"My Lord Richard," the squire bit his lips in frantic confusion, "the King's young brother . . ."

"Never mind, man, get on with it."

"Gloucester," the man hopefully settled on a compromise, "kissed my Lord . . . kissed Clarence on both cheeks . . . . "

"That's enough," roared the furious Warwick. "You may go."

The man scrambled away gratefully to the huge kitchen where his tale of George's perfidy was received in better grace. Warwick was their good master, but Edward, as yes, Edward, bold, handsome and brave was their King!

Warwick's bitter cup ran over next day when he received a gracious note from George by which Edward had permitted his prodigal brother to ease his honor.

With grace and good love, wrote George magnaminously, *the King in his infinite grace offers the Earl of Warwick and all his followers pardon with divers good conditions.*

The Earl ground it under his heel and dispatched an urgent message to Dame Marguerite to come to him in all haste armed with her son the Prince, his wife, and Louis' spears and gold.

Three suns burned in the April heavens above the field at Barnet as the armies met in a loud clashing of steel and groaning of harness. It was a goodly omen for the three brothers of York, it was said. Riding out abreast, their blazons glinting proudly in the sun, Edward, George and Richard were a study in contrast. To Richard went command of the most critical position, the van. Edward, with George under his watchful eye, commanded the center wing. Hastings brought up the rear guard.

Before dawn on Easter morning Richard aroused his troops and squatted among them to share their cold fare and bolster their confidence. Opaque mist obscured the battlefield. Richard stretched and drew in great draughts of damp air to quell the beating of his heart and the churning of his bowels. His first independent command! Lacking the physique of the warrior Edward, the good looks of George, the experience of Hastings, Richard had nevertheless the will and the courage necessary to a commander.

Tensely he gave the order to advance.

Three hours and the superb generalship of the King's youngest brother destroyed the pretensions of the House of Neville and Warwick. Richard and his weary knights sweated in their steel armor as they rode out of the swirling mists into the sudden silence of death. They were hailed by a giant golden figure under the crown of England and the sun blazon of the House of York. At the King's feet a wrinkled and bloody banner with the Bear and Ragged Staff of Warwick covered two still and crumpled figures. The lethargy of fatigue and suddenly relaxed tensions crept over Richard and left only a deep and painful sadness. He gazed down on the faces of the two Neville brothers, one who professed loyalty only to the image he had created of himself as a Kingmaker; one Montagu, who wanted with all his great heart to be loyal to his king, but could not. The moment that should have been filled with glory was empty as he thought of Warwick whose roof had sheltered him in the only happy years of his life, Montagu who had taught him all he knew of fighting and Anne . . . . His thoughts veered quickly away.

The King raised his visor and smiled in pride at his younger brother.

"You've done it, Dickon! You were superb. Yours is the credit for this day. I shall not forget it."

"Neither shall I," murmured Richard. It might as well have been his own battle axe that had cloven those helmets in two.

"This is no day to gloom, Dickon," Edward's great arm hugged his shoulders with a quick understanding of his thoughts. "Let's on to London to pay homage to the Queen who has at last seen fit to present her Lord with a son!"

This was indeed a glorious day for England. Now all could go home to stay in peace, to beget their own sons or dandle their grandsons before their cottage doors.

Only George's voice did not swell the glad tumult.

Long live King Edward! Love live the new Prince of Wales!

There was no peace on George's bitter face. There would be no peace now or ever for George's restless soul in the long years of harmony for the realm that one brother's generalship and the other brother's virility had brought about. He had swapped a pillow for a post — but what post?

Edward, his brothers at his side, led his army back to London in triumph. The city fathers in scarlet and blue threw open the gates. The three sons of York rode through. The King's face was wreathed in happy smiles for his loyal subjects. The King's brothers — for vastly different reasons — did not smile.

IV

AND THEN THERE WERE SEVEN

But Richard's trial was not over. In the midst of rejoicing and celebration, from out of the West like a poisonous asp uncoiling in cornered frenzy, Dame Marguerite struck.

Richard, ordered back to arms, hardly had time to wonder on his march *where is Anne* before the armies crashed head on at Twekesbury. Richard, again commanding the vanguard, lead the assault. Edward with George in tow, backed up his attack brilliantly and charged the center line opposite Prince Edward, Anne's bethrothed. Dame Marguerite's forces with little more than her fierce spirit to drive them were quickly routed. Shaken by the fierce onslaught of the Duke of Gloucester's company they broke ranks and fled across the bloody meadow.

Suddenly Richard saw a familiar figure in pursuit of a fleeing horseman whose helmet streamed the banner of the Swan. Horror gripped his heart as he spurred his own mount forward.

"George!" he shouted. "Stop!"

The words were flung back into his teeth. He swung himself, cumbersome in his unwieldly armor, down to the ground and reached for his brother. Too late! George's battle axe split the shining helmet and clove the bone with a sickening noise. Driven by fury Richard plucked his brother down from his horse and tossed him to the ground as easily as if he were a rag doll.

"You . . . You . . . " Richard's voice broke with rage.

"No! No!" screamed George trying to scramble away from Richard's glistening dagger. "I but did you a favor."

The blood of fury cleared slowly from Richard's eyes as he looked down on his sniveling brother. It was replaced by the pity of

95

contempt.

"You did me no favor, Brother," he hissed between rigid teeth. "Methinks I would have done you a favor had I used this." Slowly he replaced the dagger in the plain silver scabbard at his belt.

His eyes were caught by the black garbed figure of a woman. Under a black velvet bonnet with its single white ostrich plume, a lightly pock-marked face, laying its bereft soul bare to the world, looked down on the boy whose bright red blood slowly watered the ground.

Richard felt a slight shock. The dread witch Dame Marguerite was no witch at all. She was just another woman who had lost her son.

Richard found Anne in the abbey. *How thin she was!* Her naturally large eyes were enormous. This time there was no eager questioning in their soft depths, only a bewildered emptiness. The months of being dragged around in Marguerite's frenzied and furious wake had taken their toll of a spirit even as strong as Anne's. The brutal transition from childhood to womanhood had been too swift.

Their eyes met and, across a great distance, tried to reach in memory back to the happy days at Middleham. The mists of the past twelve months obscured the view.

"I don't know what to say," Richard began softly.

"What is there to say?"

"You know that although I was the instrument, I was not the personal cause of their deaths, don't you, Anne?"

She understood at once that his groping bewilderment matched her own.

"Why, Richard," she said in mild surprise, "you probably loved and were loved by my father more than I."

Richard could think of no reply.

"At least you had the love of war in common."

"Not love of, Anne," he said sadly, "duty perhaps."

"Whatever you call it, you shared something. He and I . . . " she shook her head hopelessly. "We had nothing."

"He was nevertheless your father, and I'm sorry, Anne."

Anne shook her head. She arose and wandered restlessly to the casement. Out in the abbey fields the brothers were working silently at the planting of their gardens. Spring is late this year, she thought idly.

"My sire, yes," she spoke over her shoulder. "He had no time to be a father."

Evening shadows softened the bare angles of the old abbey.

"And that poor boy," Anne sighed turning back to him. She smiled ruefully. "He hated me as much as I did him. I suppose he thought I'd want to dominate him like his mother did. All I wanted was just to be left free of him."

Richard's voice was hoarse with emotion.

"And were you left free?"

She smiled again and touched his cheek.

"Yes, Richard. At least we have that for which to thank Dame Marguerite."

"Thank God!" Richard caught both of her hands to his lips. She withdrew them gently.

"No, Richard. I cannot stand another hurt."

"Hurt? Anne, don't you know? I want you for my own."

"Edward would never consent."

"Why should he not? You're free to do as you please."

"But you are not."

"I?" Richard's eyes widened in surprise.

"You are the King's brother, of immense importance to the Crown."

"I can still serve Edward as a general with you as my wife."

"Not as well as you could with a European princess at your side. I am no longer of any consequence in state craft." Bitterness crept into her voice.

Richard stepped back aghast.

"Marry another?" he shouted. "Never!"

"You'll do as England requires," Anne told him quietly. "You always have. And I shall understand, Richard." Tears had clouded her clear eyes.

Again Richard heard his mother's voice saying those same words — many years ago. Yes, he had resolved to do just that. He had not then dreamed such a sacrifice would be demanded of him.

"But I don't want your understanding. I want you!"

She was in his arms and bitter months behind were forgotten in the glory of the moment. Anne's immediate response to his hungry kisses sent a thrill of delight pulsing through him. Her body was soft and pliant, yielding against his own for just a moment. Then she drew back, her eyes shining but determined.

"I'll speak to Edward at once," he said huskily, his intense eyes burning with a new fire and purpose.

But there was still reality.

"What will you do for now? Edward needs me to march north

97

against the Scots. He is busy picking up the reins of government."

"Yes, Edward needs you." A shadow crossed her face. She shook off her dread and smiled her heart at him. "I'll go to Isabel."

He kissed her as if he could never have enough. When he had gone the room was suddenly dark and chill.

"Edward, you cannot do this thing!"

The King's eyebrows rose.

"Cannot? Do you speak thus to the King?" Edward began to growl.

"I speak thus to my brother," Richard held his ground stoutly.

"All right, Dickon," Edward was as suddenly all smiles again. "There is none save you who is so loyal."

George was dangling a graceful leg as he listened to the argument. Now he scowled darkly.

"I did not mean it, Dickon. Forgive me." Edward persisted.

Richard was not to be side tracked by his brother's charm.

"It is the duty of the government to dispense justice," he maintained stoutly.

"It is the duty of the government to maintain itself," Edward declared flatly. Richard's scruples were a nuisance sometimes. "And that this government cannot do as long as Henry lives."

"But a man's life. That's . . . that's murder!"

"Was our cousin of Warwick's death murder?"

Richard paled and clenched his fists.

"Warwick fell in fair combat. He was not struck down in cold blood."

"As was young Prince Edward," George suddenly interrupted surlily. "Is that what you mean to imply, Richard?"

"Shut up, George," snapped Edward. "We've more important things to think about than your conscience."

"My conscience troubles me naught."

"Well, it should." The Duchess Cecily entered the discussion suddenly from her seat on the sidelines. "Your crime . . . " In protest George sprang to his feet from where he slouched on the corner of a table. "Yes, crime," his mother continued cooly, stopping him with a haughty gesture, "was the settling of a personal matter and is therefore murder." She turned from one astonished son to another. "What your brother the King contemplates, Richard, is the removal of a menace to the throne. It will therefore be a judicial execution."

"My Lady Mother." Richard's voice trembled in unbelief. "You cannot mean that a man has the right. . . ."

"Edward is a King," Cecily broke in. "He cannot afford to be a man!"

"Henry was a King, also," Richard replied gravely. "Do you think you are God to decide who shall live and who shall die?"

Coldly Edward eyed his brothers.

"I wot not who is God. In England I am King and I say that Henry shall not live. You, my Lord Gloucester are the Chief Justice, you shall carry out my orders."

"I? You cannot mean that, Edward?"

"I command you!"

Richard's face was white to the lips.

"Many things I have done for you, my Brother — and my King — that were not to my liking. This I will not do!"

Edward towered above him.

"Do you dare defy the King?"

"I have no desire to defy the King," Richard stood his ground proudly. "This you well know. I entreat your Grace, if you must do this ghastly deed, to find another for the task."

"Why all the fuss?" George was blandly disdainful again. "Obviously the great General Dickon has no stomach, which I have, but a great conscience, which I have not." He bowed mockingly to his mother whose eyes narrowed although she remained watchfully silent. "I can but add one foul deed to another. Your Grace, pray send me."

Edward looked from one brother to the other. For a fleeting moment of panic he would have turned to his mother and asked her what to do thus salving his own conscience. He was aware that his brothers expressed two facets of his own character. As King, he recognized the cold fact that as long as poor Henry remained on this earth there would be no real peace in England. The Lancastrians would have a rallying point to keep the country in eternal turmoil. As a man he relished the deed no more than did his brother Richard. Henry had done him no personal wrong — Henry had done no man any wrong. Edward clenched and unclenched his ham like hands. Henry had done nothing. Even if his soul should suffer in eternal damnation, what right had he to protect that soul and Henry's useless life at the expense of the welfare of the realm.

"Very well, my Lord Clarence," the King spoke at last. "You shall do the deed tonight. My Lord Gloucester, as Chief Justice of England you shall accompany him and give the order. You are both excused."

The Dukes of Clarence and Gloucester bent their knees to the

King.

On Wednesday morning, May 22, 1472, Richard Plantagenet, Duke of Gloucester, and brother to the King resigned his office as Chief Justice, turned his face toward the North and new trouble on the Scottish border. He had not spoken to Edward about Anne.

V

AND THEN THERE WERE SIX

Richard dismissed his troops with heartfelt words of gratitude for the manner in which they had helped him to secure the border with such dispatch. A late summer haze lay over the northern countryside. Flies pestered Scogan's mule which hung his head and stubbornly refused even to switch his tail.

"You fool," hissed Scogan without heat swatting Mohomet's rump for him affectionately. "You need some protection."

"Won't you be enough, my good Scogan?"

Scogan looked at his master in chagrin. He flung himself to his knees in the dust.

"Surely you know I was not addressing your Grace but this son of a jackass!"

Richard laughed aloud. His laughter carried far in the great open spaces of his beloved North country.

"Get up, Scogan. Of course I know." He smiled gaily at his squire. "Although you have addressed those very words to me in my time!"

"Not since you've become a man, your Grace," denied Scogan rising stiffly.

A shadow crossed Richard's face.

"I like not that title, Scogan." He was remembering his last interview with Edward. "To you I am simply Master Richard."

"Thank you, your . . . Master Richard."

Master and Squire stood together watching a blazing sun set over drought blasted field. *A poor harvest this year,* thought Richard. *These people will need help.*

"'Tis late, Master Richard," Scogan broke in on his reverie, "and

Middleham is far."

Richard's thoughts turned gladly to Middleham, which, forfeit to the crown at Warwick's death, Edward had granted to him in appreciation when James III of Scotland had signified his willingness to negotiate his differences with England. *If you, our dear brother and cousin, will cause the right honorable Duke of Gloucester to desist . . .*

Home! In a fury of haste to prepare it for Anne and be off to London to face the King with his proposal, Richard galloped off into the dusk leaving Scogan kicking Mohomet's sides at first in anger then in resignation.

"And who's to get his supper?" Scogan growled into his stubborn steed's ears. Mohomet laid back his ears and condescended to a leisurely amble.

Before Richard confronted Edward he had to see Anne. Pausing at Baynard Castle only long enough to greet his mother and remove the dust of the journey, he clattered over the cobbles to Cold Harbor.

"George!" cried Richard glad as always to see his brother after the long months that had dimmed the edges of memory of their last encounter.

There was no answering welcome in George's face.

"Well, if it isn't the mighty heir returned to demand his share of the spoils!"

Richard's smile faded.

"Spoils?"

"Exactly! Isn't that what you came for?"

"I came to see you," Richard replied stiffly, "and Anne."

"That's what I thought," George turned his back on his brother and filled his cup without offering the wine to Richard. A tiny flicker of anger blazed in Richard's blue eyes which in the past twelve months had taken on a piercing quality.

"What's eating you now?" he exploded.

"Did you come here to claim the Lady Anne so that you might enjoy the benefits of her share of her great estates?"

"I came here because I love the Lady Anne and wish to take her for my wife."

"Isn't that the same thing?"

"No, it is not!" Richard was now thoroughly aroused. "Where is Anne?"

"Have you the King's permission?" George sprawled in a velvet chair and looked up arrogantly at his brother.

"No, why?"

"The Lady Anne is my ward," George smiled wickedly. "I must in all conscience look after her interests."

"Conscience!" snorted Richard. "At our last tender meeting you denied possessing such a quality."

"Yes, our last meeting. Wasn't that when your dagger sent old helpless doddering Henry to his maker?"

Richard stopped short, aghast at the implication.

"Yours, George, not mine."

"It's only your word against mine. A word here and there to a chosen few . . . England has always wondered about the falcon in the Eagle's nest."

Richard struggled for self control. He ignored the threat.

"I had not heard that you were made the Lady Anne's guardian. When I left she was in the care of her sister."

"There have been many changes since you left, my dear Dickon."

"So I see," replied Richard carefully. "I wish to see the Lady Anne."

"You may not."

"That is for the Lady Anne to decide."

"I make the decisions for the Lady Anne. And I have decided that you shall not see her. Forget her, my dear Brother," he filled his cup again and tossed it off as he rose in dismissal. "She is penniless. The Countess' estates are entirely in my hands. And there they shall remain."

"And the Countess?" Richard demanded sarcastically. "How will she fare?"

"Praying piously," George mimicked touching his fingers together, "in a nunnery where all women who have passed the age of usefullness to a man belong."

Richard turned on his heel in disgust.

"I shall go to Edward."

"Do!" shouted George bitterly at his retreating back. "Run to Big Brother and let him caress his favorite."

"George . . . ," Richard turned back, his anger gone.

George's wine cup caught him just under the ear.

"The vile snake," shouted Edward when Richard reported his interview to the King. "I'll break his back. I'll take everything . . . . "

"Nay, Edward. I want only you to grant permission for me to wed the Lady Anne."

"Why?" demanded Edward suddenly forgetting George. "I had greater plans for you."

"Because I love her," replied Richard simply.

"That is not enough for a Prince of the royal blood."

"It was enough for the King," Richard reminded him.

"That's different," Edward blustered.

"How?" persisted Richard.

"Anne *is* wealthy," conceded Edward looking for a loophole through which to retreat from his adamant refusal. *It will annoy George, too,* he did not add aloud.

"For that I care not, beyond what is Anne's just due. You have already rewarded me well, Edward."

"Then why ask for this?" teased Edward, satisfied that he could make a decision in favor of his favorite brother, salve the council with the bride's great wealth if not royal blood — and, best of all, he smiled again to himself, annoy George.

"This is not a reward for services rendered," Richard drew himself up stiffly. "If you don't grant the permission, I'll . . . . "

"Now, Dickon," Edward warned playfully, "don't spoil it all by threatening the King. Even a favorite brother can't do that."

"Then you'll give your assent?" Richard's crooked smile beautified his solemn face. Edward had seen the new assurance in the piercing eyes. This man would not be denied. He'd better agree before he was defied.

"I'll give her away myself, my Lord of Gloucester!"

Hugging Richard's shoulders with one great arm, as was his habit, Edward shouted in his booming voice that penetrated the thick door as if it were but linen cloth.

"The King desires the Duke of Clarence in attendance at once!"

Anne watched Isabel's face in alarm. The terrible summer and the birth of a daughter had taken their toll.

"Why couldn't she have died and the boy lived," was George's only comment when he beheld his daughter.

"Shhh!" Anne now cautioned George as he stormed into his wife's private chambers over Ankarette's protests. Isabel's sleeping face lay small and pinched on her huge pillow.

"Come outside!" demanded George not bothering to whisper.

Anne rose and complied to keep him from waking her sister who was so badly in need of the moment's rest from the fatigue of labor, a petulant husband, and the hottest summer in man's memory.

"Come with me," George said gruffly when they were in the hall.

He grasped her arm above the elbow and propelled her along roughly.

"Why?" Anne pulled back trying unsuccessfully to free herself from his bruising grip.

"Because I say so!"

"That's not enough," Anne struggled the harder. "Let me go!"

"The King wants you, then. Is that enough?"

"Then free my arm," Anne retorted, her fears allayed. Edward had sent for her at last. Richard had spoken to him! "If the King wants me, I don't have to be dragged."

George freed her so suddenly she stumbled.

"I'll escort you," he announced as she righted herself without his assistance.

"Is that necessary?"

"I'll go," was all he said.

They had not gone far when Anne became suspicious.

"This is not the way to Westminster," she called from the litter that George had insisted on instead of her usual mount.

"The King is at Windsor," George called back not checking his pace.

"Neither is this the way to the barge docks," she screamed now thoroughly alarmed. "Stop this litter!"

The bearers only increased their pace and George did not look back again. Her cries caused little notice in the sorry neighborhood in which they now found themselves. The ways of the gentry were beyond their ken and therefore their notice.

Kicking and squirming but effectively silenced by a beefy hand, Anne was dragged unceremoniously from the litter. Her lips were closed but not her eyes which noted the hanging *Sign of the Black Whale* under which she was propelled. Her mouth was suddenly uncovered but any sign of audible protest quickly squelched by a brutal twist of her arm.

From the rough ministrations of beefy male hands she was thrown into equally beefy, moist, red female hands with a gruff admonition.

"Keep her in the kitchen. Don't let her mingle with the custom!"

The huge kitchen was stifling. Anne jerked herself free and darted for the door. She found her way effectively blocked by the solid figure of the female owner of the beefy hands. The face above Anne's was flushed and steaming with sweat but neither ugly nor unpleasant.

"You're a pretty lass," the face said matter of factly, "though too skinny to pleasure a lusty one like the dook. What does he want of the likes of you?"

Anne feinted to one side. The face only laughed as a meaty hand reached out to pluck her back.

"You might as well calm down, Lass. Twon't be no good to wrassle with me," the face grinned calmly. "You no biggerna the fleas those dirty bastards" she hitched her head good humouredly in the direction of the door that separated them from the custom, "leave in my beds. I could snap you in two just like I do them." She indicated graphically with thumb and forefinger. "But I won't," she conceded grandly, "if ye behave. Don't be afraid. What's your name?" the face demanded as an afterthought.

Anne almost smiled in spite of herself.

"Anne. And I am not afraid." Anne replied stoutly. "I just want to get out of here."

"Well, you can't," the face stated flatly. "My friends call me Venus. You can call me that," she offered. Venus grinned. "It refers to me size not me face."

So the face had a name. And what a name.

"Thank you," Anne smiled. "But you must help me, Venus. Please, I've got to get out of here."

"Now, Lass. I told you you can't. You might as well not fret yourself. The dook gave orders."

"The Duke? How do you know the Duke?"

Venus ignored Anne's question as she hustled her charge into the center of the room.

"Dook or no dook, you have to earn your keep!" Venus looked Anne up and down with disdain.

"Can you cook?"

"No."

"Can you wash?"

"No."

"I was afraid so." Venus shook her head. "How can any one person be so useless?" She demanded of a huge man who, Anne judged by his ladle, must be the chef.

"She don't look useless to me," smiled the chef ogling Anne with delight.

Venus spraddled out her legs and rested her hands on her wide hips.

"Don't you go eyeing her, Will! My Jack will crack your noggin if any harm befalls this lass at your hands."

"That chit," Will roared smacking Venus soundly on the buttocks. "She's too mitey for me. You're more my type."

106

"Humph!" snorted Venus. "You'll be more the type for the grave digger if my Jack catches you rubbing my bottom while the goose burns."

By the time George arrived at the Palace, Edward was in a towering rage and of a mind to issue an act of resumption to the crown of all his troublesome brother's lands and estate incomes. He had reached the point of mentioning the Tower when George strode blithely in kneeling gracefully to the King and meekly waiting to be raised up.

"A very pretty pose," snorted Edward, "and one you'd better assume more often in the future."

"Indeed, your Grace, it has never been my intention to step out of my rightful place."

"By God's mercy," snapped Edward, "if you could but find your rightful place in this world all England would be the happier for it!"

"Yes, your Grace."

Edward eyed George suspiciously.

"I like not your meek demeanor. What are you up to?"

"I, your Grace?" George's eyes widened innocently. "Nothing that is not to the King's pleasure and glory, I assure you. Of what am I accused?" George looked meaningfully at Richard.

"Why did you tell Richard that you were Anne's guardian?"

George's eyebrows rose delicately. His face wore a pained expression.

"Is that what he said?" He shrugged as if to imply *what can one expect*. "My Lord of Gloucester strode into my house demanding the Lady Anne and half the spoils."

Richard's eyes closed in pained disgust.

"And what did you say, my Lord of Clarence?" The King's voice was heavy with sarcasm.

"Did he have the King's permission, is all I asked. Was I not in the right to protect a lady under my roof from molestation against her will — and that of the King?" he hastened to add.

"George!" Richard stepped forward his fists clenched in anger.

"You refused to let Richard see Anne," Edward cut in. "By whose right?"

"As I have just said, your Grace . . ."

"By whose right?" roared Edward.

"In right of my wife," George subsided sullenly.

"Is she aware of this?"

George hesitated a moment.

"No!" he finally replied shortly.

"My Lord of Clarence!" Edward faced his brother George squarely. "You are in no wise to interfere with my Lord of Gloucester's suit in this matter. The crown will decide on the division of the inheritance. Is that clear, my Lord?"

"Quite, your Grace," George went down on his knees again gracefully. "I seek only to please your Grace in all things."

"Faugh!" Edward belched loudly in disgust.

When George and Richard reached Cold Harbor, George offered his brother wine and left him. Richard paced in nervous anticipation of the meeting with Anne now that no obstacle lay in their path. He was in a fever of hurry to be wed and out of London. Home! His thoughts flew to Middleham that he had left under furious preparations against Anne's return to her old home. Her home? Their home now, with the wide windows that he ordered cut in the forbidding walls for stained glass of gorgeous hue to be sent by Meg from Bruges. Beauty and light and happiness for Anne. That was all he asked of life.

"She is not here." Richard had not heard George reenter the room.

The shock almost floored Richard. He sprang at George's throat. George, towering above his brother, felt the steel strength of Richard's fingers and quailed a moment.

"You mad man! What have you done with her? If you've harmed a hair on her head I'll — I'll . . . ."

George tore himself free with an effort.

"Don't threaten me, Brother," he snarled, looking contemptuously at Richard's small statue. "I could grind you under my heel like an ant."

"You fool!" Richard retorted coldly. "I could skewer you here like a chicken before you move out of your tracks!" He slipped his dagger up in its silver sheath and let is fall back with a click. "Why I haven't already done it I'll never understand."

"Because I am your brother, dear Dickon," George scoffed. "And you have a conscience. The lordly House of York rending itself in public would never do, now would it, Brother? *Loyalty binds me* is my Lord of Gloucester's motto."

Richard had had enough.

"Where is she?"

"Since I am not her guardian, I cannot be held responsible for her whereabouts."

"But she was here, you said so."

"When I told her you were looking for her, she left. Perhaps she doesn't wish to accept your attentions, my Dickon." George's eyes swept his unprepossessing looking brother with contempt. "Some wouldn't, you know."

The hooded look of withdrawal fell over Richard's eyes.

"I want to see Isabel"

"My lady wife is unwell."

"George, I don't want to fight with you — if I can help it. But if I don't find Anne, I will. Get out of my way!"

George stepped aside and made his brother a mocking bow.

"By all means, dear Dickon. Consider my house at your disposal."

The days drew into weeks while George firmly denied, in spite of Richard's pleas and Edward's dire threats, any knowledge of or responsibility for Anne's whereabouts.

"She was here when I slept," declared Isabel her eyes bright with fever and worry.

"Who else was here?" inquired Richard when he finally managed, with Ankarette's connivance, to get in to her.

"No one. Anne was relieving Ankarette to give her a few moments rest."

Ankarette who was usually as well informed as Scogan had heard nothing. Exhausted by constant vigil at her lady's sick bed Ankarette had slept long and deeply knowing she could trust Isabel, whom she loved with a devotion akin to adoration, to Anne as she could to no other.

Torn between the desire to kill George himself and the effort to keep Edward from doing it for him, Richard's agony of mind was further increased by physical discomfort. Scogan had taken to long absences from his master's side just when he needed his healing hands on his troublesome shoulder or his healing words on his troubled mind. His squire would return as quietly and as unexpectedly as he had departed, offering no explanation but merely picking up his duties where he had left off and carrying them out with his usual efficiency. His garrulous tongue suddenly ceased its wagging. This further irritated Richard who counted on his servant as his sole source of companionship, news, and entertainment. Richard swore and raged at Scogan when he could catch him nearby, taking out on his squire all his frustrated feelings that he dared not vent on George for fear of losing his self control and doing him real harm.

"You might just reply," stormed Richard after his angry words

109

had buffetted Scogan's ears with no apparent results. "And what are those for?"

Richard indicated some worn and faded garments laid neatly out as Scogan usually did for his master after a bath and message.

"Put them on, Master Richard," was all Scogan replied.

Something in Scogan's voice caused Richard to obey. The two exchanged no words as Scogan threw a plain cloak around his master's shoulders.

"The nights grow chill," he commented shortly.

Unquestioning Richard followed Scogan out into the November night. He raised his eyebrows when Scogan indicated that they would walk. They rose still higher when Richard noted the degrading of the neighborhoods through which they passed. He only rested his hand the tighter on his dagger and made no comment.

The noise that issued from the *Sign of the Black Whale* was raucous, but good natured.

"Tis here the wine is good and strong, Friend," commented Scogan clapping Richard soundly on the back. "There's other entertainment as well." He snickered meaningfully.

Richard opened his mouth to protest but caught the warning look in Scogan's eyes just in time to mumble what he hoped would pass as a suitable reply.

"Let's at it then, Friend."

Completely bewildered but catching the spirit of excitement in Scogan's mysterious conduct, he returned his squire's hearty blow with such enthusiasm that Scogan, caught unawares, stumbled against the door jamb. Grinning, the two entered the *Sign of the Black Whale* arm in arm like two boon companions seeking an evening's entertainment.

Scogan proceeded to get uproarously drunk and Richard was just about to yank him up and drag him home to severe chastisement when a huge woman with red, beefy hands entered the common room from the steamy kitchen. Richard saw Scogan stiffen. "Venus!" he roared joyously. "And it's about time."

The woman grinned and headed for their table in its obscure corner.

"Well, if it be'ant, Perkin the game cock. Whose yer friend?"

"Him?" Scogan shrugged and turned his back squarely on Richard. "Will or Henry or some such. He's a likely companion for a night's revel. Drinks well, wenches well, and talks little."

"He's even scrawnier 'n ye be," she eyed Richard who thought it safer to keep his mouth shut. He merely bobbed his head at her and

110

tried to look as drunk as he had thought Scogan was. "What'll it be tonight?"

So this was where Scogan had been passing his time! He watched his servant in amazement. Where had Scogan put all that wine? If he had it inside himself, Richard had certainly underestimated his faithful squire. Suddenly wondering what Scogan was up to, he began to enjoy himself. This was better than the mummings and disguisings that were to be featured at court during the approaching Christmas season. The mummers never put on so finished a performance as Scogan was turning out at the moment.

Venus — Richard grinned to himself — was as impressed as Richard by Scogan's arch advances. She backed away slightly from his exploring hands looking around for her lord and protector, the mighty Jack. When he failed to show, she inched her way back to their table. Scogan boldly propositioned her for the evening.

"You!" she roared in pretended contempt at Scogan's size which was little more than Richard's and about half her own. "Ye be so puny I might lose you in my great bed!"

"I'd have no trouble finding my way back to you," Scogan guffawed, "if you tossed me off."

He smacked her rear a solid blow and apparently downed another cup of the strong, sour wine.

"First, let's sample the fare before we decide," Scogan rose uncertainly and attempted to propel Venus toward the kitchen.

"You know the custom beant allowed in the kitchen," Venus shook him off, her grin fading.

"C'mon," Scogan persisted. "If you be worrit about that Jack of yours, I fixed that."

"Ye be a sly one," declared Venus, "but ye can't fool my Jack."

"His body may be twice mine but I've got twice his head for wine." Scogan nodded his own head owlishly to prove it.

Venus still hesitated.

"My friend pays well," Scogan suggested hitching his head at Richard.

Venus eyed Richard speculatively. Taking his cue, Richard tossed on the table a small bag of gold coins that Scogan had added as an afterthought to his costume. Its pleasant clinking sound carried the argument. Venus headed for the kitchen with the two in tow.

When the heavy door swung to behind them cutting off the noise from the common room, Richard would have cried out if Scogan had not trod on his toes. Across the steamy cook room Richard saw Anne, her arms white to the elbow, kneading dough. Scogan must

111

have managed to warn her with a look for her hands never missed a stroke as the two men wandered from one pot to another tasting and smacking their lips as if they were bent on testing dishes to be set before the King. Scogan kept up a running stream of critical comment until he reached a steaming pot of green turtle soup that Will was stirring lovingly. Scogan maneuvered deftly to place himself between Venus and Will leaving Richard between Venus and Anne. Gaily he wrenched the ladle from Will's hand and dipped up the steaming brew. Without warning he slipped and fell sprawling, throwing the boiling liquid in his ladle directly in Will's face and carrying the pot down with him. Scalding soup splattered on Venus' bare legs where she had pulled her kirtle up under her belt to protect it from just such accidents. The howling, screaming confusion covered Richard as he flung his cape around Anne and pushed her through a back door that he had located with his eyes when he saw what Scogan was up to.

Rain sluiced down in torrents covering the uproar as Richard and Anne raced down the slippery alley.

"Hurry!" was all Richard said. "I must get back to Scogan."

A disapproving face under a virginal white coif answered Richard's frantic tugging at the bell of St. Martin's cloister. He saw that the door was about to be slammed in their faces.

"Please!" he begged. "Take the lady in."

"Have you wronged her, sir?" the prim voice demanded.

Richard lost his temper. He thrust Anne's shivering body into the protesting arms of the startled sister and shouted over his shoulder as he raced off through the rain to succor Scogan.

"In the King's name I command you to take her in."

Sister Agnes who was not as prim as she looked and relished any relief in the sanctified monotomy of her cloistered life, removed Anne's sodden cloak and eyed Anne's flour caked arms.

"The King indeed!" She grumbled as she led her trembling charge to the mother superior.

Anne's romantic story had enlivened the love-starved life of Sister Agnes through the Christmas season and well into a bitter cold February before the family conclave managed to pacify George and gain his consent to a marriage that threatened to rob him of a part of his immense wealth. Edward's mood matched George's in ugliness.

"But, Edward," pled Richard in private. "It is not in the interest of the country to have the Royal family at each other's throats. Let him have what he wants."

"And then, by God, he'll want the throne next," stormed Edward. "Will that be in the interest of the country? I won't do it."

"Then let us keep the Warwick lands in the north and hold Barnard Castle for the Countess. That's all we'll need."

"No! He shall agree to an equal division of property or I'll throw him in the Tower."

"You've threatened that before. You know you won't."

One stormy scene followed another while more time passed with Anne in sanctuary at St. Martin's and Richard chafing to get her out and to turn his back forever on London. Finally, in desperation he went to his mother.

Cecily clad herself firmly in the mantle of York and travelled the cold and slippery streets to Cold Harbor.

"Where is George?" she demanded.

George had all his very real charm, which he rarely used of late, ready for his mother.

"You are a fool!" she snapped looking up at her second son whose handsome face remained unmarred by his habitual petulance and heavy drinking.

"Is that the way to greet a favorite son?" George smiled in teasing geniality. Momentarily his likeness to Edward was remarkable.

"How can anyone so gifted with natural charm be such a . ... a . . . ." Cecily spluttered. "You are very charming when you like. 'Tis a pity you don't like more often."

"Pray let me make you comfortable, Madam. Then you may upbraid me to your heart's content."

"Comfortable?" Cecily shivered in the grim vastness of the great hall. "You've done nothing to improve this mausoleum. No wonder the Countess never liked to stay here."

"If I made it more comfortable perhaps she might like it and come to stay. I care naught for my mother-in-law's company at such close range."

"Whom do you care for, my Son, besides yourself?"

"You, my charming Lady Mother."

Cecily's eyes narrowed.

"I came not to bandy sweet words with you!"

"Then why did you come, Madam?"

"What do you hope to gain by your attitude toward your brother Richard's marriage?"

George's face darkened.

"Just what is my due, Madam."

"Your due!" flared Cecily. "To keep you from rending England in turmoil with your eternal grasping ways, Edward has almost beggared the crown. He could resume it all and that is just what he is of a mind to do."

"At brother Dickon's suggestion, I suppose."

"That's why you are a fool! It is only your brother Richard that stands between you and the Tower. The King's patience is exhausted."

"Never fear, my Lady Mother. The House of York would never do that to its own."

"Take care, my Son, that you count not too strongly on that. Even the House of York must protect its own interest as you have good reason to know."

"Henry VI was a Lancastrian."

"Henry VI was a menace to the peace of England. I am warning you not to take his place."

Even George lost countenance.

"You don't mean . . . ."

"I merely mean you had better take what Edward offers you and be content."

Cecily was equally short with her son the King. Reluctantly he agreed to let George have the lion's share of the Warwick and Beauchamp lands leaving Richard and Anne Middleham and various manors in the north that they loved and Barnard Castle in trust for Anne's mother, should she come out of sanctuary.

Cecily stood by proudly while, at least on the surface, peace and tranquility was restored to her house. The three sons of York joined hands in brotherly amity and plans went forward for Richard's wedding.

"And the Pope's dispensation?" George could not forebear to inject a tiny cloud into the peaceful horizon.

Richard's patience was gone.

"I will consent to no further delay. With the King's permission, Anne and I shall wed at once. The dispensation can come later. Edward?"

"Did I not promise to give her away? You shall be wed Dickon, the church will or nil. The Pope's curse will not kill a fly!"

"Take care, Edward!" warned Cecily. "That His Holiness never hear of such blasphemy."

"Today let us rejoice, my Lady Mother, tomorrow we can light a candle and pray the harder."

Spring came early in the North. Its light through the glorious panes of colored glass that now softened the austerity of Middleham Castle's thick walls was reflected in the hearts of Richard Plantagenet, youngest brother to the King, and his Lady Anne. Through long, lazy summer days Richard and Anne rode over their estates improving the plight of the drought ridden herder and farmer and making friends for the Duke of Gloucester, Lord of the North, and his brother the King of all England. Clear moonlit nights were filled with the glory of their love. Sparkle and gaiety returned to Anne's brown eyes, color to her cheeks, and the eager questioning to her lips. For the first time in his twenty years of violent living, Richard knew the healing grace of a love that answered all the needs of his awakened body and a deeply flowing affection that erased the pinched and questioning look that had already begun to age his narrow face.

England basked in its first fully peaceful year of the century. The three sons of York were truly touched by the golden sceptre of Fate as each in his turn produced a son; two Edwards and a Richard. The King sought to honor his youngest brother; Richard sought to honor his oldest brother; Isabel suggested that they bless their first son by naming him for the King. No one thought to honor George.

Suddenly George remembered that a Lancastrian Parliament when he and Warwick had imprisoned the King back in 1470, had passed an act declaring him the heir to the throne after Marguerite's Prince Edward. King Henry VI and Prince Edward were both dead. Who then was the rightful King?

Away up in the North Richard felt the rumbles of George's bitter musings. Across the Channel brooding spitefully over the hated Edward's popularity, and the general peace in his country that might cause England to cast an eye on former French conquests, Louis XI felt the waves of George's new discontent lapping on his shores. Snatching joyfully at any straw to stir up discontent in England, Louis cozened George, a poor substitute for the mighty Warwick 'tis true, but better than nothing.

Edward moving watchfully about his kingdom felt the uneasiness and summoned Richard to his side.

"The time is ripe to invade France," Edward told his brother. "I have word from Meg that Louis is making passes at Burgundy."

"Methinks he is also making passes at George." Richard added.

Edward shook his head in disgust.

"What ails him, Dickon?"

Richard shrugged.

"He was born with a bitter taste in his mouth."

"Holy Mother of God," Edward growled. "I've poured half the sugar of the realm down his gullet trying to sweeten it. What more can I do?"

"Give him a command in the army against Louis," suggested Richard. "He's a capable soldier if he tries."

"George is capable of many things *if* . . .," snorted Edward.

Suddenly the King's face was wreathed in a happy smile.

"I like that, Dickon. It will put both Louis and George in a damnable spot. Yes! I like it well." Edward looked at his brother with new respect.

"You are eternally a source of surprise to me, my Lord Gloucester. You have proven yourself a general without peer. Now in statecraft you rival Louis' slyness!"

"I did not mean to be crafty, Edward. George's pride is in continued need of being bolstered. This could be a way to do it."

"Crafty or no, it's a masterly suggestion. It will effectively quiet Louis' and George's plotting and create an outlet for the feeling of unrest — thanks to brother George's wilted pride — that I sense around the country side."

"Money?" asked Richard practically.

"Benevolences," grinned Edward. "Should not my subjects feel benevolent toward a king who has freed them of civil war for the first time in fifty years?"

Richard squirmed, one never knew just how far to go with Edward.

"Is that just, Edward?"

Richard's blasted conscience again!

"Is what just, Dickon?" his exasperation was evident in Edward's voice.

"Requesting money of your subjects you have no intention of repaying."

"A benevolence is a gift not a loan." Edward said shortly.

"You know that isn't so, Edward." Edward's eyebrows rose but Richard disregarded the storm warning. "No subject would dare refuse the King."

"He'd better not," snapped Edward. "There isn't a man in England who wouldn't profit by my reconquest of the lands in France that pious Henry lost us. Over weaning piety is just a cloak for weakness," Edward warned his brother.

Richard flushed.

"You well know I am neither pious nor weak," he flared in

sudden anger. "Justice is not necessarily piety and this *you* should heed."

For a moment brother glared at brother, eagle at falcon. Then Richard was aghast at his own temerity. He fell on his knee in genuine regret.

"Pardon me, your Grace, I spoke in unseemly haste."

"Nay, Dickon, get up. 'Tis I who attacked you falsely." Edward stroked his own cheek thoughtfully. "I suppose even a king is not above advice, if it's good." He suddenly recalled himself and looked down at Richard who still knelt abjectly before him. "But this is not good." He pointed a long finger. "You tend to the men. I'll tend to the money."

Council, broached on the subject of the invasion, assented happily thinking of past glories to be regained to say nothing of increased trade. The people, broached on the subject of money, assented not so happily, thinking of the huge debts with his London merchants already run up by their King. Edward knew them all by name, their children, and more important their wives. Ah! It was difficult to refuse their genial and handsome King anything. Their gold jingled as it poured into the crown coffers and was counted scrupulously by the treasurer, Thomas Grey Marquess of Dorset, the Queen's son by her first marriage.

When he declared the amount sufficient, commissions of array were issued to the Dukes of Clarence and Gloucester who hurried off to gather men to the King's banner and take leave of their wives and sons.

"Don't fret, Richard," Anne soothed her husband's troubled brow.

"He is so small!" Richard worried, peering into his son's cradle.

"But we are small, my Love. How could our son be otherwise?" Anne tried to hide her own fear from Richard.

Richard subsided but the fine line of worry that had begun to furrow his forehead between his eyes cut the deeper as he noticed the listlessness of his child. Little Edward unlike his giant uncle in every way except his Plantagenet goldenness, even cried without enthusiasm.

Richard's crooked grin appeared as he drew Anne to him and tried to soothe her uneasiness as she had done his.

"Aye! I was as puny. All my mother could think to say of me to our father after enthusiastic accounts of the rest of his healthy brood was *Richard liveth yet!*"

Anne tried to join him in his laughter. Much later she whispered smiling softly against his bare neck.

"This one should be stronger."

Richard crushed her against him again in speechless wonder at the glory they had shared.

"My Love," he whispered finally into her soft hair.

She did not hear him for she slept and when she awakened in the morning light, he was gone to champion his brother's cause against Louis of France.

Again the brothers glared at each other across the widening abyss of their different interpretations of integrity.

Richard smote the table with his fist.

"You can't do this, Edward!"

The King pounded with his own ham like hand.

"Who are you to tell me what I can and can't do? I am the King!" he snorted.

"That's just why you can't do it!" Richard shouted back. "The King can't go back on his word."

"What word?"

"You promised your subjects when you extorted their money that you were off to conquer France."

"I promised only to lead an army against Louis. And I didn't extort their money, they gave it freely."

"You *extorted* it," Richard held his ground, "to reconquer our rightful possessions in France, not to make a splash and come home empty handed."

George swung a well turned leg from his perch on the table and gleefully watched his two brothers one after the other pounding it to pulp. He was glad for once he was not the object of their hassle. The thought crossed his mind that his brother Richard was a good champion to have.

A smooth voice cut across his thoughts and Richard's anger.

"Hardly empty handed, my Lord. Louis has agreed to pay us seventy five thousand crowns to withdraw our forces and an annuity of fifty thousand crowns yearly as long as the truce lasts."

Richard turned suddenly to face the man who addressed him, unconsciously including himself in the royal We. Sir William Hastings had shared an intimate life with Edward, always at elbow with more wine, more women, more witty stories to beguile the King who was deserting the Queen's bed more frequently for other sympathetic and less demanding companionship.

118

"Us, my Lord Hastings? I understood Louis was paying his tribute to the crown."

Hastings colored slightly but maintained his equanimity.

"There are other projected grants to the Lords of the Council," replied Hastings mildly. "In which you yourself, my Lord of Gloucester, will share quite handsomely."

"That is a bribe! I will not accept it!"

"As you will, my Lord," replied Hastings without rancor, "as to the rest of us, what matter if it bring peace between France and England and wealth as well?"

"How much of this gold will find its way into the pockets of the common man of England who financed this expedition?" demanded Richard.

"Who cares, my Lord? They'll have their trade."

Richard looked frantically to his brother for denial of these words of heresy toward the English people. But his brother at Hastings' shoulder merely returned his stare coldly.

Quietly a little bit of Edward's glory faded in the eyes of his young brother. For the first time they parted in anger without apology from either side. In his sticky web of diplomacy, Louis sat back in relief and raised the salt tax.

There was no new and stronger child for Richard and Anne that year nor the next. And sorrow dealt them yet another blow. Word reached them at Christmas time in the snow bound fastness of Middleham that Isabel had died in childbirth. She had lingered just long enough to name the babe Richard.

"Oh, Richard," wept Anne bitterly in his comforting arms. "Why couldn't it have been mine?"

But little Richard lingered scarcely into the bitter January of 1477.

VI

AND THEN THERE WERE FIVE

Richard found George wild with grief and swearing vengeance whether on fate in general or someone in particular was not clear. It came as a shock to Richard that George with all his willfulness had really loved Isabel, the only person he had so honored besides himself. There was no mistaking the depth of his older brother's grief. George broke down and wept while Richard at first stood by, uncomfortably at a loss how to meet his brother's surprising emotional but genuine breakdown. Little by little, the constraint between them eased and in two short weeks they built a companionship such as Richard in his very real affection for this brother had always imagined possible. True, there was not the deep love and respect he felt for Edward and his mother, nevertheless there was a tenuous bond of friendship that had always existed for Richard but had been hidden from George by his jealousy. They rode, they hunted, they talked away the cold nights before a roaring fire. Richard even joined George in his frequent cups of strong and heady malmsey although Scogan was careful to see that his Master's was well watered. During these quiet hours together Richard caught a glimpse of his brother as he truly was — handsome and eloquently charming, weak and shallow. George's giant body housed a small soul in desperate need of affection to bolster a feeling of inferiority. This inadequacy George tried to hide from himself by his temperamental outbursts and wild attempts at worldly power. Richard saw it all and gave his affection gladly. His own small frame which housed so great a soul he offered as a buffer to protect his brother from the disappointments and disillusionments of a ruthless age.

Across their tranquility a shadow fell from beyond the Channel.

121

In the bitter January snows, Charles of Burgundy had fallen in the siege of Nancy.

"Poor Meg!" Richard thought with regret for his sister Margaret who had built a solid life, so like her sturdy frame, of calm happiness. Charles the Rash, as some had called him, with Margaret's quiet strength to lean on, was become since his marriage to Richard's sister, Charles the Bold. It was a good life, without glamour 'tis true. But glamour demands a terrible toll.

Suddenly Richard longed for Middleham.

"Poor indeed!" snorted George. "Our sister Meg could buy us all in the market place. She'll be the greatest heiress in Europe. Who ever thought that dull, fat Meg would outdo the sons of York on the road to glory?"

But there was no bitterness in his heart toward Meg.

"I wasn't thinking of money," declared Richard slowly.

"Well, she's well quit of that stubborn, stuck-up Charles," declared George flatly. He had never forgiven Charles for laughing uproarously at his discomfort when George was the butt of Duke Phillip's jokes so long ago in Burgundy.

"Maybe Meg doesn't agree. They became very compatible. Now what does she have?"

"Money!" replied George flippantly. "What else lasts?" A shadow darkened his face. "Nothing else does."

"Neither will money if you don't handle it right."

"Are you accusing me of mishandling my wife?" There was an edge to George's voice. He had drawn too deeply on his wine cup Richard saw with chagrin.

"I didn't know you were thinking of Isabel," Richard began gently.

"Will I ever be able to think of anything else," George cried out, hurling his cup against the wall. Richard touched his shoulder in sympathy.

"I'm sorry, Dickon, I didn't mean it," George murmured contritely. Richard's eyes misted at the use of Edward's pet name for him that heretofore George had handled only with bitter sarcasm.

"I know you didn't, George. It's all right."

George was always sorry for his wild hurting ways. Richard wondered if he could always make it all right for George.

"I wish she'd come home," George said childishly. "Meg, I mean."

"She won't, George. Why don't you go for a visit?"

"Perhaps I will." A new light flickered in George's eyes but was soon gone. He poured himself another cup.

Before he even reached London to answer a summons from the King at Westminster, news came to Richard that George, in a drunken rage of loneliness, had decided to make his vengeance particular. He seized Isabel's woman Ankarette whom he had always hated because she tried to protect her mistress from his rages. She was accused of poisoning his wife. Taking the King's justice into his own hand, George had her tried and executed forthwith in his own right as Duke of Clarence.

Edward's bellow of rage filled the halls at Westminster.

"Let him go to Margaret for a spell," Richard suggested when he could make himself heard.

"Let him go," roared Edward, "I'll drive him out of England with my own hand, or better still . . .," the fingers of the King's huge hands flexed as if to fit themselves around a throat.

"Edward!" The Duchess Cecily did not shout, but her penetrating voice had the same effect. Edward ceased his raving and tried to focus his eyes rationally on his mother.

"It is unseemly," she reprimanded him coldly, "for the King to shout his family troubles abroad for all the realm to hear. Besides, take care that your rage harm not yourself. You are too fat, Edward."

It was true. Richard had been shocked at the subtle change in his brother. Still magnificently handsome, Edward was becoming gross. His face was too ruddy, his eyes too paunchy. The touch of his own fingers left a white mark on the King's face that was slow in receding.

"Madam," Edward replied to his mother regaining his self control with an effort, "when any man other than the King sets himself up to deal out the King's justice, and that by intimidating a jury, it ceases to be a family affair. It is time that man were brought before the courts and himself called to account for his misdeeds."

"Now, Edward," began the Duchess. "You can't. . . ."

"Madam, I respect you as dowager head of the House of York and as my mother. But you and Richard cannot forever protect the Duke of Clarence. He will have to pay homage to the King of England — not because the King is his brother, but because the Crown is the age old symbol of power, as you remind me daily yourself, Madam. Without its awesome hold on the loyalty of the English people, where will they be?"

There was a pregnant silence.

"Torn to bits by civil war," Edward answered his own question, "or parcelled out piece meal to European powers. Louis, for example. Is that what you want?"

The silence continued. Richard was again touched by Edward's grandeur. At the moment he was every bit a king. The pudgy man was cloaked in the mantle of the ruler.

"No, my Lady Mother," Edward's voice gentled somewhat. "You would be the last to wish to see what your lord my father paid with his life to bring to England destroyed by the petulant arrogance of one man. Is this not true?"

For the first time Richard heard his mother's proud voice muffled in uncertainty.

"Yes, my Son, in that you are right." Cecily's clear eyes were lowered. "But he is nevertheless your brother — and my son."

Richard was reminded suddenly of Marquerite of Anjou standing on the bloody field at Tewkesbury looking down on another Edward, a mother rather than a Queen. Perhaps this Edward was remembering too, for he passed his arm around his mother's bent shoulders and turned her face gently up to his.

"All right, Mother. This time let him go as Dickon suggests." He smiled ruefully. "You remind me constantly that the King cannot afford to be a man, and then you make it difficult for me to be so."

Margaret in her own loneliness was overjoyed to welcome her favorite brother George. Having no need to be jealous where Meg was concerned — for Meg gave her rich affection in abundance and there was none to share it — George put himself out to be charming. Looking to the future Meg made a proposal.

"George, this is my step daughter, Mary. Mary, my dear, I am certain that you will enjoy the company of my favorite brother the Duke of Clarence."

And she left them alone to the compelling forces of nature and the attraction of their magnificent physiques. For Mary of Burgundy was as beautiful as George was handsome. She was moreover wealthier than Margaret and heiress to the Dukedom of Burgundy. If not exactly a crown, it was a magnificent coronet.

George was immediately attracted.

Mary was not. She had already seen Maximillian of Austria and, having inherited Charles' boldness as well as his dukedom, she intended to do as she pleased.

But Margaret might have prevailed had not Edward immediately put up a howl.

"This looks like the answer to a prayer." Richard commented.

"The devil's prayer maybe," Edward stormed at Richard whom he had recalled to his side before Richard had hardly had time to dismount at Middleham and clasp Anne in his dusty arms. "George at home is menace enough. Rolling in all that money and living cheek to jowl with Louis of France? Never. As long as Burgundy can hold out against France, England is safe from them both. Brother George is no match for Louis."

"But Meg is." Richard reminded him. "She hates his guts," he added coarsely.

"Like you?" Edward grinned and was suddenly grim again. "That's why I need Meg just where she is — alone. Where George is concerned, I'm never quite sure of Meg. She's always looked at him with one blind eye."

"Then will you forward Sir Anthony's suit? I understand the Queen has put her brother forward as a candidate for the Lady Mary's hand."

Edward closed one eye and snorted.

"That will never do, either," he declared flatly.

So at least Edward was becoming aware that the rapaciousness of the Woodevilles was also a menace to the power of the throne. Edward's great vitality might be a check to their greed while he was alive, but God help England if. . . . Richard shied away from the thought but the King's physical appearance worried him. His girth had increased in the last few weeks in spite of Cecily's warning. His naturally high color had taken on a purplish tinge.

Richard welcomed a sullen George peremptorily recalled to Court. Try as he might he could not reestablish the comradeship they had enjoyed after Isabel's death. George was in an ugly mood. He discounted the fact that Mary of Burgundy would not have had him anyhow and laid the blame for his blasted hopes squarely at the King's door. Or was it the Queen's? George hated Elizabeth Woodeville with a passion that even for George was strong. He had always felt that she stood between him and his brother's affection, that she pushed her greedy family between him and his rightful honors. He had felt some such jealously for Richard, but he knew deep down in his heart that Richard loved him and would never willfully cause him hurt. About Elizabeth Woodeville's feeling toward him, he had no illusions. The Queen returned George's hatred with venom. George had been a party to the execution of her father when he rode with Warwick against the King. The Queen had not yet evened the score.

Richard had noticed the almond shaped eyes under the silver gilt hair as the Queen covertly watched the Duke of Clarence. Suddenly Richard felt cold. Had not the Queen brought about the execution of the brave Earl of Devon because of his foolish words to Edward against her suitability as a consort? Edward had been furiously angry, but Elizabeth Woodeville was not impressed. Her hold on Edward was a strange one. Still beautiful and erect and more important to Edward's lust, highly sexed after bearing him six children, she was able to meet the driving needs of Edward's great body with a vigor that no other, not even his new and gaily fascinating mistress Jane Shore could quite equal. In a sense, while Edward strove to free his mind of her harping greed, she kept him her physical slave.

Richard shuddered and went in search of George whom he found closeted at Cold Harbor with Bishop Stillington. Their whispered conference ceased immediately upon his appearance.

"Dickon," cried George in feigned welcome. "You honor my house. Here's wine to warm you although the spring is unseemly hot."

"Yes, my Lords," the Bishop agreed obsequiously. "I understand the plague has struck the city early and hard."

Richard sensed something he could not understand, a feeling of menace unassociated with the dread plague.

"The King has petitioned permission for the court to eat meat on fast days to keep up their strength. Methinks he will retire to Windsor until the wedding." The Bishop chatted on with homey intimacy sipping his cooled wine daintily.

Richard thought gladly of his young namesake now four years old. Richard of York the King's second son to be wed to little Anne Mowbray. A good marriage. He hoped Edward would do as well by his namesake, Richard's own son. For a moment, he thought with pain of the empty cradle at Middleham. His and Anne's great love had produced nothing more to fill it, and though their son Edward *still liveth*, he thought wryly, as had been said long ago of himself, he had not waxed strong as they had hoped. Riding tired him too quickly, lifting a battle axe made his face flame with the strain. Richard sighed and brought his thoughts sharply away from Middleham.

He tried to outsit the Bishop, but the old man's loquaciousness finally drove him home without a private word with George. On his way back to Baynard Castle Richard was brought to wonder about Stillington again.

"Why did Edward ever pick such a garrulous, empty headed man as Chancellor?" Richard demanded of his mother after reporting the conversation.

"He's done no harm in the office." Cecily's eyes narrowed slightly.

"Nor any good that I can recall."

"Edward removed him in time," the Duchess reminded him.

Richard stopped, suddenly short.

"Why did he do that if the man had done no harm?" he wondered aloud.

"The King has his reasons," was all Cecily had to say.

Edward was obviously robing himself to go out with Hastings. The Queen made an arrogant movement of dismissal that was apparent to all but Hastings.

"My Lord," Elizabeth Woodeville's impatience was scarcely cloaked.

"Your Grace," Hastings was all geniality blandly ignoring the Queen's obvious desire to be rid of him.

"Edward!" the Queen's voice had the effect of a stamping foot.

Edward lowered his right eyelid and examined his wife who had again entered his private chambers unannounced. A tiny shock struck through his groin. Hastily he turned to Hastings.

"Wait for me outside," he ordered.

"Madam," he rebuked Elizabeth when Hastings had bowed himself out, "that is scarcely a garment in which to visit the King unless he is alone."

"We are alone aren't we, Ned?" Her moist mouth widened in a studiedly provocative smile.

Edward knew full well she was up to something but that did not prevent his senses from stirring.

"What is it, Elizabeth?" he demanded impatiently trying to rid himself of her thrall. "My Lord Hastings awaits."

Elizabeth's face darkened a moment. Her dislike of Hastings was as mutual as his of her and second only to her dislike of George. However, she thought looking critically at Edward's swelling body and heightened color, Hastings might be useful one day. Take care in this quarter. But George! George was a useless stumbling block to be ground under heel like that brash and smart aleck Desmond.

"The French Ambassador has become attentive to one of my ladies."

Edward wondered who might be termed the aggressor in such a suit.

"So? And what has this to do with the Queen's visit to the King in such a whorish gown? Perhaps you should have lent it to this lady."

"Cease, Ned. There is no need for you to be coarse."

Edward's eyebrows rose. He grinned maliciously as the pulsings in his body were increased by another glance at the provocative garment.

"You have created the need, Madam."

"Stop teasing, Ned."

"Shall I show you I am in a far from teasing mood?" He made a stride in her direction. Deftly she put the table between them.

"The Ambassador whispers in my lady's ear."

"Damn the Ambassador!" Edward's foot kicked the heavy table aside as if it were a toy.

"Not all of love," managed Elizabeth just before Edward's mighty arms cut off her breath and his lips crushed hers to silence.

Elizabeth freed her mouth but not her body.

"He says that George whispered to Louis that he wanted Mary's hand only as a means to seize his brother's throne," she gasped pushing his face away. Edward dropped Elizabeth as if she burned his hands. She staggered against the post of his great bed.

"Faugh!" exploded Edward. "You come like a strumpet to my chamber to undermine my brother?"

"It is *he* who is undermining *you*." Elizabeth panting pushed the silver gilt hair out of her eyes. "He told Louis that since this plum failed he has still another that will rock the realm and settle you for good."

Edward stopped stock still in confusion. His blood that she had fired to boiling point would not cease its pounding and let him think.

"Ned!"

Edward's bemused eyes turned full on Elizabeth. Her alabaster body gleamed in the candle light, the filmy wisp that had scarce concealed its voluptuousness lay crumpled at her feet. With a low growl he reached for her and swiftly covered her nakedness with his own.

"Have you need of any whore tonight?" her eyes glinted triumphantly into his.

His only answer was a thrust that caused her to moan with delight.

Richard had already left London, when George was summarily sent for and accused by the King — in the presence of the Lord Mayor of London — of undermining the laws of the land by taking the King's justice into his own hands.

"But you have already pardoned him for that," raged Cecily who had sprung immediately to action as the gates to the Tower clanged shut on a defiant George.

"I have pardoned him for nothing, Madam. I have tried to forget his misdemeanors but he will not let me. Now I'm through."

"But you promised me," shouted Cecily for once beside herself.

"Need I remind you, Madam, as you have so often reminded me, that it is unseemly for the Duchess of York to shout her troubles abroad for all the realm to hear?" Edward's voice was coldly sarcastic, a tone he had never dared use to his mother before. Cecily heard it and a tiny fear flickered behind her eyes.

"You have brought the troubles of our house into the public eye by casting your brother, the Duke of Clarence, a prince of the royal blood into prison. George is a stone in the foundation of York, a weak one I grant," she warned him direly. "If you destroy him you will destroy a grain in the sanctity of the crown. Your sons will inherit the avalanche that will tumble down around all our ears!"

"You cannot frighten me."

Cecily regarded her son with narrowed eyes.

"You are already frightened," she declared. "So *that's* it. George knows! Richard told me that Bishop Stillington was at Cold Harbor."

"Does Richard know?" Edward demanded.

"I have not told him and I do not think George would." She shook her head, her mouth set bitterly, "I told you no good would come of your union with that gilt haired strumpet."

"Madam!" shouted Edward, "you speak of the Queen!"

Now it was Cecily's turn to address her son in cold contempt.

"Some would say not."

"Have a care, Madam. Women have also suffered in the Tower."

Cecily drew herself up in all the dignity of her regal bearing.

"If you dare to threaten a hair on the head of the Duchess of York you will find yourself torn to shreds by the very people who have fought to keep you on the throne. You are nothing but a frightened man to speak thus wildly."

"On the contrary, Madam. I have taken your advice at last. I am no longer a man, I am the King. And the King I shall remain — and my son after me."

"You need not fear that I shall tell your secret after guarding it all these years. But never forget that I am protecting England, not you!"

Cecily swept toward the door.

"However," she turned and pointed a long finger at the King, "I know who is behind this. If harm befalls a hair of George's head, let her know that it is *she* among us who will have cause to be afraid. As you once warned the Earl of Warwick, let it not come to a test of might between us!"

Wagons rumbling at first day awakened Richard. For a time he lay afraid to open his eyes and find himself back in London with its intrigues, broken loyalties, and family strife. Tentatively, he reached out a hand and groaned in relief as it came in contact with Anne's soft hair.

She sprang instantly awake.

"Richard," she cried softly in real fear. Her soft fingers caressed his cheek and etched the fine lines forming so early at the corners of his eyes. "What is it? Are you ill?"

He caught her hand to his lips and rolled over to prop himself on an elbow.

"No, my Pigeon. Praised be to God I was never better now that I can touch you."

He bent his head and drew strength and joy from the sweetness of a long kiss. Anne cuddled her small body against him and sighed sleepily.

"Lie down, it's early yet," she giggled happily. "Noah can't have got on his costume yet. And that impressive beard! That takes hours to give it the proper biblical dignity that befits the father of the race."

"The miracle players and the good men of York might resent such a flippant attitude toward Father Noah as just a trifle blasphemous on the lips of the Duchess of Gloucester, wife of their good lord," Richard teased nibbling at her ear.

"That tickles," Anne shivered in delight. "It's boring, Richard. I wish we didn't have to go."

They lay still a moment while noise of the preparations for the Corpus Christi festival rose from the streets of York.

"Edward would enjoy it," Anne spoke wistfully.

"I wish he could have come with us."

"Richard, I'm afraid," Anne whispered. "He tires so quickly."

"Now that summer is here and Scogan can take him in hand, all will be well," Richard promised holding her close. "Today let's forget it and be gay and young again. Please, Pigeon."

Anne smiled up at her husband.

"One more kiss like that last and I shall be as gay and as young as

130

a bride."

Richard bent his head to her.

The day was long but Richard and Anne managed to delight the people of York who took them instantly to their strong hearts. The fame of the Duke of Gloucester as a man of justice and wisdom had spread far and wide in the few short years that he had resided at Middleham. He was known gratefully as the Lord of the North, the King's right hand man. His wife's gentleness and charity kept their door wide open to any in need. Now they honored their Lord and his Lady by inducting them into the Corpus Christi Guild with great pageantry. The Duke and Duchess of Gloucester walked in the procession between walls hung in glad welcome with splendid tapestries and doorways strewn with flowers among the rushes by the citizens of York.

On their return to Middleham Scogan was awaiting them with a troubled look on his face. Richard's heart sank. He squeezed Anne's hand. He had had his heart set on living out his days in peace with Anne guiding the men of the North, whom he loved and who loved him, to peace and prosperity for their own happiness and the ultimate good of the Crown. This he would do for Edward and England — his mother's domineering face swam before his eyes — but no more.

"I don't want to hear it," he now said gruffly to Scogan.

Anne dismissed Scogan with a glance that said, *Later.*

Scogan nodded in understanding and left them to greet their son who had prospered truly under Scogan's loving tutelage. A faint color tinged his cheeks and a sparkle enlivened his usually dull eyes.

"See, Father?" little Edward cried proudly, tugging at the string of a small bow that Scogan had lovingly fashioned for him.

Richard caught his son to him and held him close.

"I see, my Son. One day you'll be a great warrior like your uncle, the King."

Impatiently Edward squirmed free of the embrace. He grasped Scogan's hand to tug him off to new adventure.

"Shall I be the King's right hand man like you, Father?"

"Indeed you shall, Edward," Richard smiled gratefully at Scogan while Edward pulled the harder on Scogan's hand.

"Come Scogan!" Edward shrilled. "The enemy is without. They'll storm the wall if we don't make haste."

"Hold them but a moment, Master Edward," commanded Scogan, "while I gather up the reserves."

Edward was off gaily to defend the castle against the enemy.

131

"And now, Master Richard," Scogan's smiling face was solemn again, "I would not let the scurrier bring it to you at York. I hope I did no wrong."

Remembering the deep happiness of his few hours alone with Anne and the days of rejoicing with the good people of York, Richard shook his head as he read his mother's message. His eyes were full of weariness as he handed the letter to Anne.

"You did no wrong, Scogan. You are thoughtful in everything that concerns my comfort. I am grateful."

Anne's eyes were despairing as they met her husband's.

Come at once, the Duchess was calling across the miles. No salutation, no signature. The situation must be desperate. What had George done now?

"I will not go!" Richard turned his back on them and walked slowly to the casement. June sunlight sparkled on the fertile fields of Middleham. Contented workers within the bailey were cultivating their garden plots, and gathering the fresh vegetables that Richard, whose simple appetite revolted against the rich meats and heavy sauces of the court, loved. Further out beyond the walls, herders tended their flocks on green pastures that Richard had helped them to irrigate from the river Ure.

"Will you go with me, Anne?"

She had known that he would go, that he could not refuse the call of duty. Nevertheless her eyes closed tightly to hide their pain.

"And Edward?" she reminded him softly.

"Scogan will watch over him."

But Anne was shaking her head sadly.

"Nay, Richard, Scogan must watch over you. You need him most."

"I need you," he cried.

"The King needs you," she replied throwing her arms about him from behind and resting her cheek on his back. He did not move. "It will not be long, my love, until you are back with us."

Richard sighed.

"It is ever thus."

The summer boiled on endlessly as did the family harangues, but finally it passed as does all evil. Touched by an early frost, England flamed in the brilliant glory of its great forests.

And still the Duke of Clarence lay at the Tower while the strain began to tell on them all. The Queen's narrow eyes warned the King while the obsequious Hastings tried to beguile him. The Duchess of York hovered like a storm cloud. Richard caught in an undercurrent he could not fathom, travelled restlessly back and forth from Windsor to the Tower. George in whose arrogant eyes a flicker of real fear had suddenly leapt up, pled with Richard.

"Make him see me, Dickon!"

"I've tried, George," Richard shook his head in dismay. "He flatly refuses."

"But he must, Dickon! He must!" George tore at his brother's sleeve. "I've got to tell him, I didn't mean it."

Richard was appalled as he looked at his once stalwart brother like whom he had always wanted to be. The handsome face was sallow and unshaven, the bright gold locks limp and unkempt, the eyes near wild with fear. The fastidious Duke of Clarence was disintegrating before his younger brother's eyes.

"Didn't mean what George?" Richard asked in what he hoped was a soothing voice.

But George flung himself away and drooped disconsolately in the single chair that added no comfort to the bleakness of his quarters.

"I've got to tell Edward," he said dully. Suddenly he sprang to his feet and plucked at Richard's sleeve again. "Dickon!" he cried a gleam of hope animating his wild eyes. "Get to her. Tell her to call him off, she's the one who's behind this. Edward would listen to me if she would let him, he always has," he ended pitifully.

Yes, thought Richard. *Edward has always listened before to George's eloquent and contrite excuses for his misdeeds. Why won't he now? What evil lies between them of which I can gain no inkling.*

The Duchess of York, he was sure, knew more than she would tell. George was holding something back. Each cried out to him to check the King's vengeful wrath.

"How can I help you," Richard replied hopelessly, "when I don't know what's going on? Call *her* off you say. Call off whom?"

"That strumpet who calls herself Queen," George flared in a sudden return of spirit. "She's behind all this, she's always stood between me and Edward. She's out to get me like she got the Earl of Desmond for an idle word against her!"

George was weeping great noisy wracking sobs. Richard closed his eyes against the sickening sight of the pitiful wreckage of the wild spirit that was his brother.

"George," he touched his brother's heaving shoulder gently, "I'll help you in any way I can but you'll have to tell me . . . . "

"No," George jerked himself away. "I must tell Edward. Don't you see if I tell you, he'll never believe me."

Suddenly George crumpled to his knees before his brother who eyed him in horrified pity as he grovelled at his feet kissing his hands while tears streamed down his dirty cheeks.

"Help me, Dickon, before it's too late. Tell her I'll never say a thing if she'll just call him off!"

"Get up, George," Richard tried to raise the brother who was twice his size. "You've no need to grovel to me. You know I'll do all I can. I'll see the Queen at once." He sighed helplessly. "If I knew what I am asking for . . . . "

"Just get him to talk to me, Dickon. I can fix it up if I can just talk to him."

"All right, George." Richard soothed. "I'll see the Queen and Edward again. Let your man tend you and sup well. I'll be back."

Richard had noted that no retainer of the Duke of Clarence was at his side. He was tended by unknown appointees of the King, men who were wholly Edward's and knew full well who buttered their bread. It was definitely not the Duke of Clarence. Richard's face was deeply troubled as he turned toward Windsor. What was behind Edward's sudden and adamant stand against his wayward brother?

"If you are come from the Duke of Clarence, I do not wish to speak of the matter," Edward declared coldly.

Richard cast his eyes about. Hastings' face at the King's shoulder told him nothing. Did he detect a slight leariness in his eye when the Chamberlain glanced at the Queen? When the Queen's long eyes rested on Richard they looked through him as if he did not exist.

"May I speak with your Grace alone?" Richard ventured.

"No," replied the King flatly. "Whatever you have to say has been said. There is nothing further to be gained by another interview. I am occupied with preparations for my son's wedding and have no time for idle considerations."

"Idle considerations!" cried Richard his anger rising. "Since when is the fate of the King's brother an idle consideration?"

For the fraction of a second Edward hesitated.

"Ned!" the Queen's voice cut across his uncertainty. "My Lord the Comptroller wishes to discuss his accounts. The hour of his appointment is already passed. If my Lord of Gloucester will excuse himself . . . . "

"Edward," Richard achieved a calmness of voice with an effort as he pointedly ignored Elizabeth Woodeville, "if you refuse to talk to George now, it will rebound to your eternal shame."

"Take care, my Lord of Gloucester," thundered the King, his hesitation wiped out by the Queen's glance, "that your persistence bring not down our wrath on yourself."

For a long moment their eyes met and held across a widening breach.

"Take care that you bring not down the wrath of God on your soul." Richard turned on his heel and was gone. The Queen's eyes bored into his retreating back.

Richard poured out his remorse to Scogan.

"I handled it badly, Scogan. But it's like fighting in the dark. Who is the enemy?"

Scogan was as deeply in the dark as his master. His probings below stairs had gleaned him nothing.

"Now the Queen will refuse me an audience," Richard paced restlessly up and down shaking off Scogan's ministering hand.

"Mistress Anne will scold me, Master Richard, if you grow any thinner. Eat! You'll need all your strength for what lies ahead."

"That's just it, what lies ahead?" he mused somberly. "And what lies beneath it all?"

But Richard was wrong about Elizabeth Woodeville. The Queen sent for him.

"What has the Duke of Clarence told you?" she demanded when he presented himself before her. Determined to control his temper and if necessary for George's safety to meet guile with guile. Richard replied quietly.

"Nothing, save that he wishes to speak his own defense. He begs that your Grace will use her great influence with the King to hear him out."

"In what matter?"

"George says he will speak only to the King."

Did he detect a note of relief in her voice?

"The Duke of Clarence has committed acts that are prejudicial to the safety of the realm. No amount of pleading can save him now."

"Will you plead for him, Madam? At least ask the King to hear him?"

"Nay, my Lord, a good wife meddles not in her husband's business."

Richard caught frantically at his self control.

"Not even when it may mean the life of a member of the royal family?"

"Not even then, my Lord." Elizabeth Woodeville was obviously enjoying his discomfort.

Richard was consumed with rage at this woman, whose insatiable demands had undermined the greatness of his brother Edward to benefit the horde of locusts that were her family. Would she now destroy his soul? He was convinced that George had guessed correctly. Whatever it was, she was behind Edward's adamant attitude.

"Madam," the cold fury was apparent in his voice. "If you foster this crime, you will bring the opprobrium of the ages down on yourself."

"You mean the opprobrium of the Duchess of York and the Duke of Gloucester, do you not, my Lord?" She laughed contemptuously. "And of what consequence is that? You are determined that the welfare of the soul is more important than that of the body. I disagree. You continue to be a good general to the King's body and let his soul rest with this God you continually harp on."

"And if the general should desert the King?" his voice was husky with loathing.

"The Duke of Gloucester would never desert his brother."

Her mocking laughter followed him down the corridor.

Richard had not seen Harry Stafford in years. Now as Duke of Buckingham, first peer in the realm, Harry was jerked from the obscurity of Brecon into the limelight to pass judgment on the Duke of Clarence, brother to the King, for treason of a high and aggravated order. Only the King in council accused his brother. The council acquiesced uneasily but in full knowledge that the Duke of Clarence was the instrument of his own destruction. Ironically as the young Duke stood before the hushed members of Parliament, Harry Stafford's resemblance to the man he now judged was startling. The blood of Edward III flowed strongly in both.

"Death!"

The word rang in his ears as Richard blindly left the chambers and wandered on foot through the sodden streets of London. The mood of January 1478 was befitting the tragedy that beset the House of York. Month after weary month of pleading for his brother's life now ended in a public sentence that must be carried out. There could be no turning back. On Edward Plantagenet would lie forever the responsibility for the death of his brother, between Edward and Richard Plantagenet would lie forever the shadow of a weaker brother whom with all their greater strength of will they could not sustain. The House of York was not the bulwark of the realm that Richard had been led to believe. It was rotten to the core. Down around his ears Richard's illusions came tumbling. He staggered and would have fallen but for the gentle pressure of a firm hand beneath his elbow.

"This way, Master Richard."

Richard's eyes focussed slowly on Scogan. He tried to smile but succeeded only in making his teeth chatter. Scogan could not pick him up after the blow his brother Edward had dealt him as he had done so long ago when his brother George had tripped him. Gently he cast his fur lined cloak across his shoulders and led him homeward. Dociley as he had done in childhood Richard followed his squire.

Richard found George in a state bordering on madness.

"Dickon," he babbled wild with fear, "you've got to stop him! He can't do this to me."

Richard raised his brother from his knees and led him to the lonely chair.

"I'm afraid he can, George," said Richard bitterly.

George shook as if with the ague. His cheeks were grey, his eyes sunken, his magnificient body thin to emaciation. Gradually the shaking ceased and a sly look replaced the fear in his dull blue eyes.

"You *can* stop him, Dickon," he whispered grasping at Richard's arm.

Richard felt a shock.

"How?" he demanded.

George raised his wine cup jauntily with a touch of the old arrogance.

"Malmsey! The drink of kings," he laughed shortly, "and worthless dukes. It drowns sorrow, why not fear?" He turned a cunning look on Richard.

"You know I'm a coward, don't you, Dickon?"

"Don't George." Richard pled. "You'll meet death bravely as you would on the battle field."

"No, my dear Brother. Perhaps you could — not I. One son of York is rotten to the very core."

"Please George . . . . "

George stopped him with an impatient gesture. "Nay, at least let me talk! If I have disgraced the House of York with my wildness in life, I shall bring down endless shame upon it when I am brought to the block. Yes, the Duke of Clarence, the King's brother and first peer of the land will kick and scream and cry out his terror. His screams will echo through the streets of London and out across the great realm of England — and in the King's heart."

Richard bowed his head and ground his fists into his eyes.

"It will not be a pretty sight, Dickon."

"What did you do, George?" Richard asked hopelessly without raising his head.

For a long moment George's eyes were held by the single simple jewel in Richard's velvet cap.

"Nay, this I will spare you, brother." In embarrassment, George touched Richard's bowed head. "To give such knowledge would but put your head beside mine on the block. And I find, Dickon — too late as always — that I love thee."

Richard's narrow shoulders shook.

"Richard," George's voice was suddenly devoid of all emotion, "you've always tried to help me. Help me now."

Richard raised his head.

"Anything, George, that I can do."

"You cannot save me from . . . death, this I know. But you can save me from disgrace on the block."

"I don't understand."

"Do it now." George pointed to the silver dagger at his side.

Richard sprang back in horror.

"No!" he cried. "You cannot ask such a thing!"

"But I do. You promised to do anything you could to save me."

"This I cannot do."

George's hopeless look haunted him that sleepless night.

Yet Edward delayed. An expectant hush fell over London. Richard found his way barred when he visited the Tower. He paced away the sleepless nights. George's accusing eyes dogged his frantic steps.

"He's afraid, Scogan, and they won't let me see him. I must help him. But how?"

In answer, Scogan, who knew of George's last request, held out a tiny vial to his master.

"It is tasteless, Master Richard, and causes no pain. The King will allow the Duke of Gloucester to send his brother a parting gift of his favorite malmsey."

Richard's face was terrible as he struck the ampule from Scogan's hand.

"Get it out of my sight!" he rasped through clenched teeth.

Finally Council would wait no longer. Respectfully they reminded the King that a sentence passed and approved must be carried out. The Speaker before the Bar of the Lords, requested that whatever was to be done, be done immediately.

"It would be a kindness, Master Richard," persisted Scogan as

Council met.

"And transfer the guilt to my own soul," cried Richard in anguish.

"It · is not like you, your Grace, to think first of yourself," Scogan reminded him gently.

"I am denied admission to his presence," Richard argued as he fingered the vial.

"Trust that to me, your Grace."

"Are you sure there is no pain?" Richard still held back.

"None, Master Richard."

Slowly like a man himself condemned Richard returned the vial to his squire and bowed his head, his arms limp hung between his knees.

"Scogan," Richard whispered. "Tell him . . . tell him . . . . "

"I'll tell him you sent it, Master Richard," Scogan's voice was full of compassion. "That's all he'll need."

That night for the first time since his marriage to Anne, the flux took over draining Richard's body and leaving him depleted of any hope or feeling.

Three days later Richard rode northward turning his back forever he hoped, on London. In his pouch he carried the licenses to found two colleges, one at Barnard the Castle he had saved for Anne's mother, one at Middleham, with priests to pray for the King and Queen, his own wife and son, the souls of his deceased brothers and sisters — and for his own soul.

Few would have recognized the anguish wracked face of the Duke of Gloucester. The small body seemed shrunken. Pale eyelids hooded the pain in lackluster eyes that now peered rather than pierced.

VII

AND THEN THERE WERE FOUR

Across the Somme Louis glared at Margaret Dowager Duchess of Burgundy. Meg glared back without her usual complacency. Louis disliked all women. True, he had loved his mother and felt a certain affection for Charlotte, his wife. But they were his. Margaret was definitely not his, nor did she intend for Burgundy to be. Along with his great fortune, Meg had inherited Charles the Bold's hatred and distrust of the Sovereign of France.

Louis, disgusted that a mere petticoat stood in his path of aggrandizement, put his fertile brain to work and began to stir up trouble in Scotland to distract Edward while he, Louis, worked on Edward's sister Margaret.

The Scots raided and burned the border castle of Bamburgh. Like lightning Richard, quickly appointed by Edward Lieutenant General in the North, struck across the border with an enthusiastic band of his men of York. That put an end to that. The Scots retired licking their wounds. Louis shrugged his shoulders and began to try to cuddle up to Edward.

Margaret of Burgundy crossed the Channel for the first time since her marriage and gave her brother a piece of her mind.

"I wish to remind your Grace that you sold me to Burgundy in order to keep Burgundy in the English interest," she told Edward scathingly, "now I'll thank you to mind your own business and let me mind Burgundy's."

Margaret's prosaic good looks had become great beauty in the twelve years of marriage to a man who came to love her deeply and to trust her judgment as he might have that of another man. Richard, recalled to London for her visit, felt proud of his handsome sister who now held her ground before the King. Meg was tall and regal like their mother. Richard instantly recognized a stability in his sister which might be found lacking in his mother's intensity that sometimes bordered on fanaticism.

Looking from his sister to his brother, Richard could not feel the same pride. Edward was now frankly fat and even a mite slovenly in his attire. Since George's death word had reached Richard far away in the North of Edward's increased debauchery. His enormous energies, depleted by lust, flagged quickly. Great plans ended in weak endeavor.

"Your solemnity does not fit the occasion, my Lord Duke."

A pair of merry green eyes laughed into his.

Richard's polite reply was lost in the strains of the music that accompanied the dancers who thronged the great hall at Westminster in honor of the visit of the Duchess of Burgundy.

"Do you not dance, Sir?"

The voice was soft and charming the face piquant and naively friendly. Richard felt instantly attracted in spite of himself.

"Poorly, Madam," Richard ventured a brief crooked smile.

"That's better," the lady approved. "Shall we try?"

The smile and the music were both compelling. Richard found himself drawn into the figure responding readily to the lady's deft directions. His enjoyment was troubled momentarily when he caught Hastings' mocking eyes upon him. Did he imagine it or did his partner share a brief nod of understanding with the King's Chamberlain over his shoulder as they met and bowed in the figure? If so, the encounter was quickly forgotten. Richard gave himself up with rare pleasure to pure enjoyment of the rhythm of the dance.

"Even Richard is not proof against her wiles," Margaret remarked with lifted eyebrows when they met in their mother's house after the ball.

"Against whose wiles?" Richard asked pleasantly still under the influence of the music which he loved·and a pair of gay green eyes that had beguiled although they had not stirred him deeply.

"Mistress Shore's."

Richard froze. Gone was the remembered pleasure of an evening spent in the company of the King's favorite and most blatantly flaunted mistress.

"Don't take it so hard, Dickon," Meg relented with a fond smile. "We know you are not susceptible. You take everything too hard. It did you good to relax. Perhaps it will bring you to understand what she does for Edward who escapes his harping wife for her understanding gaiety."

Understanding? Richard was suddenly remembering the covert glance Jane Shore had exchanged with Hastings. He wondered if Edward who shared almost everything with his boon companion Hastings, also shared his mistress with him. Nay! Not knowingly. Even Edward with his complete disregard for moral standards would stop short of that. Disgust curled Richard's lips.

"He should have thought of that when he went to the bushes for that harping wife," exploded Richard in sudden bitter expression of the festering hatred that he had carried in his heart for Elizabeth Woodeville — he could not think of her as Queen — since George's death. This visit to London with its glimpse of his handsome, beloved brother once mantled in glory, now disintegrating before his very eyes, had intensified his feeling of loathing to an alarming point. "He had a lawful wife, he should keep him to her — in spite of who she is," he could not forebear to add. His chagrin at being himself so easily duped by a pair of green eyes added to his anger. He longed for Anne and the clear, cool air of Middleham. Why had he ever consented to come back to the intrigues and rich foods, both indigestible to his plain tastes, of his brother's court?

"Don't be so puritanical, Richard," his mother commented. "All men are not so fortunate as you in their nature, nor in their wives."

"Are you condoning Edward's licentiousness, Madam?"

"You are as angry with yourself as with Edward, my Son," Cecily reasoned mildly, "that you were not as proof as you thought against a pair of pretty eyes. Frankly, if I had a choice," Cecily's voice also betrayed a touch of bitterness, "I find the Mistress Shore less harmful."

The puritanical streak in Richard was offended at his mother's admission. Besides . . . .

He took the memory of the exchanged glance between the King's mistress and the King's most trusted friend back with him to Middleham.

Even in his beloved North, Richard could not entirely escape the vicissitudes of being the King's brother. George's jealousy was replaced by that of the Earl of Northumberland with whom he shared the Government of the North in the King's name. Henry Percy had never forgiven Richard for opposing Edward when the King had taken the Earldom from Warwick's brother and returned it to the Percy family. That the people of York gave their whole hearted loyalty and affection to Richard, completely ignoring Northumberland, did not help the situation any. Richard knew that the Earl's loyalty was questionable, and, in spite of Richard's tact, Henry Percy knew that he knew it.

Together, however, they forged the military power of the North in readiness for Edward's projected full offensive against Scotland to be led by the King in person. While Richard and Northumberland marshaled their forces and awaited the King's coming, Edward's health worsened and soon he was forced to admit to himself and to his brother that Richard must conduct the campaign without him.

"What shall I use for money?" Richard inquired practically.

"Benevolences," replied Edward shortly.

Richard winced at the hated word.

"Don't cross me now, Dickon," Edward begged tiredly seeing the look of disapproval cross his brother's face, "I have no longer the will to argue. Just do as I say, or rather, let me do as I will."

But when the King announced that he also intended to recall the tax he had levied for the abortive war with France and subsequently returned at Richard's urging, Richard was driven to protest vocally.

"You can't do that, Edward!" Richard cried.

Edward blustered and glowered.

"You persist in telling the King what he can and can't do. Would you be King in my stead?"

"Nay, Edward, you know not. But this is unwise. Already the realm is rife with discontent," he drove on unthinking, "because of the greed . . . . " he stopped short. Even the King's right hand man cannot tread the inner sanctum of the King's family.

"Well?" demanded Edward. "You were saying?"

"Nothing, your Grace," Richard tried to hide his confusion.

"You are thinking of the Queen and her limitless and insatiable brothers and sisters," Edward replied flatly for him.

Richard said nothing.

Edward sighed heavily.

"They are a plague of locusts but if it were not they it would be some other faction."

"What of the older nobility? Do they not resent your partisanship?"

"Meaning yourself, for example?"

"No, Edward, not myself. You have given me more than I have ever dreamed of having. But there are others who fare not so well."

"So? And who can complain of Edward the Fourth's generosity?"

"Hastings for example."

"Hastings!" exploded Edward. "In all England is there another

144

who is closer to the King?"

"Nay," replied Richard surprised at the slight prick he felt that this was so. "My Lord Hastings is honored above all men by the King's friendship. I spoke of more tangible things — lands, honors of rank."

"And are these tangibles you speak of more important than the King's favor?"

"Not for me, Edward, but then I have the tangibles."

"And would you swap them for the King's favor?" Edward asked his brother, carefully scrutinizing the narrow care worn face.

"Gladly would I trade them all, your Grace, for such a boon." Richard was surprised at the intensity of his emotion. Since George's death his great love for Edward had lain dormant buried under the disillusionment of the King's defection. Now it rushed back into his hungry heart. Where had they lost the way? Could he but turn the clock back and begin anew in the sunshine of their youth! Now looking at the wreck of his beloved brother, he knew that youth was gone for them both forever. His eyes stung.

Edward smiled and for one brief golden moment all the beauty of that lost youth with its vigor, bright dreams, and high hopes was his again.

"You really mean it, don't you Dickon?"

Richard could only nod.

"Listen, Richard!" Rarely did he call him so. The genial smile was replaced by a serious pleading. "You could readily take Will Hastings place, but could he yours? Could he win the trust and friendship of the North as you have done for me? Could he subdue the unruly Scots? Could he mete out the King's justice with the impartial hand that you have done?" Edward paused and drew his ponderous body up in all its imposing height. He was still a magnificient figure of a man with eyes of intense purpose which now bored into Richard's. "Could he bear the government of the realm on his shoulders as you shall have increasingly to do? The answer to all is *Nay*, Richard. A Hastings can beguile the King's idle hours it is true, but only Richard Plantagenet can save this country we both love from chaos."

Suddenly he slumped exhausted into his mammoth chair. Alarmed Richard rushed to his brother's side.

"I am no longer fit, Dickon. I shall leave my responsibility to this great kingdom in your hands. Take care of my son, Dickon, and stamp out the seeds of discord that will spring up when I am gone."

"Cease, Edward," Richard pled. "You are over wrought. You

shall guide your son's steps to the throne through many years to come."

Edward smiled wanly.

"We both know that isn't so, don't we Dickon?"

Richard bowed his head unable to speak. He felt his brother's hand heavy on his shoulders.

"Let nothing happen to what I have done for England," Edward whispered. "There is much I have not done, but what I have accomplished, no man can say was not for England's good."

As he rode northward across Edward's England turning his glad face homeward, Richard thought of all that Edward had accomplished in little over twenty years of rule. His brother's achievements were very real. At his coming to the throne, Edward had found a realm torn and ravaged by civil war and the inner conflicts of the great barons who wished to rule the King. Of the twenty years the last ten had been unruffled by inner turmoil with the exception of the machinations of the feckless George. By his marriage to a commoner, Edward had reckoned to lessen baronial threat to the power of the throne, and to strengthen the bond between King and subject. His reckoning was astute although his choice had been bad. The turbulent North had been brought quickly under control by the wise government of the Duke of Gloucester whose Council of the North was becoming famous at home and abroad for its impartial justice. Edward had shown his brilliant ability as a diplomat by, if not outwitting the wily Louis, at least holding him at bay and milking him of a pretty penny while he did so. The wool merchants, of whom the King had become a not inconsiderable one in his own right, were devoted to their King who, even in the blaze of his own personal glory, never forgot to forward their interests. Edward was a King whose subjects knew him personally, had shared his board and society. Now as his hand slackened on the reins and at the same time grew more oppressive, his people grumbled but did not cease to love him.

Neither did his brother Richard who could not agree with him in all things yet wondered what other man could have done as much.

Richard was welcomed at York with wild joy. In his pouch he carried an exemption for the city from the hated tax. Although he could not dissuade Edward from his intent to raise by taxation money for the Scotch campaign, their Lord of Gloucester had succeeded in having his Yorkshire men who had fought so bravely and given so freely of their goods excluded from the levy.

Preparations went forward but still the King did not come to lead the campaign. Finally because his troops were getting restive, Richard decided to take the offensive with Henry Percy. As soon as he received word of Richard's intent, the Earl sent peremptory orders to the men of York to array themselves and meet him at Northallerton on Monday following ready to march against the Scots. Grumbling at the haughty tone of the summons the men of York hastened nevertheless to obey. Upon the heels of this order came a message from Richard who was unaware of the Earl's unauthorized levy. The Duke of Gloucester requested his friends and retainers at York to join him on the following Thursday at Durham. Joyfully the Yorkshire men feasted an extra day and set out on Tuesday to obey the summons of their good lord. The furious Earl of Northumberland cooled his heels at Northallerton while Richard was unaware of the offense that he had not created but for which he got the credit in Henry Percy's jealous mind. Richard's banner of the White Boar flew over a great army that burned Dumfries, stormed to the very gates of Edinburgh and returned the mighty stronghold of Berwick — that Marguerite of Anjou had traded to the Scots — to a proud King of England who forthwith wrote jubilantly to the Pope.

We thank God, the giver of all good gifts for the support received from our most loving brother, whose success is so proven that he alone would suffice to chastise the whole kingdom of Scotland.

The King called for a great celebration at Christmas time to rejoice at this good fortune and to reward the brother who had brought it all about.

Harry Stafford's eyes glittered at the magnitude of the King's gratitude. Huge grants of authority in the West marches and border country were made to Richard and his heirs. To bolster this enormous power he received the Castle of Carlisle, and all the King's lands and manors with their fees, rents, and profits in the country of Cumberland. This constituted an immense hereditary prerogative that Parliament was quick to confirm in appreciation of the Duke of Gloucester's signal service to King and country.

The young Duke of Buckingham for all his great inheritance in Wales was no longer the wealthiest lord in the land. The Duke of Gloucester had far surpassed him. Harry was second to Richard in both wealth and rank.

"You see, Dickon," smiled Edward. "You have nothing to fear from any quarter. You are independent."

That such an appanage might become in the wrong hands a menace to the power of the throne was seemingly apparent to no one save the Queen. Quickly she prevailed on the King to set up an independent household for the Prince of Wales at Edward's castle of Ludlow with her brother Anthony Woodeville, Lord Rivers as his governor and Lord Richard Grey the Queen's second son by her previous marriage as one of his councilmen.

"To secure the loyalty of Wales," the Queen reasoned demurely, "and to forward his education in the art of goverance."

Edward's eyebrows drew together.

"What better tutor could you have chosen, Madam?" growled Edward who despised the foppish Anthony with all his grand learning and poetry writing. But he acquiesced, too fatigued with advancing illness to contest her will.

The Queen bowed gracefully to her lord. Why should she not? By playing her cards well she had run up an impressive score: one son and heir to the throne safe in the fortress of Ludlow and securely under the influence of her family, Thomas Marquis of Dorset, first son of her former marriage in charge of Edward's treasures in the Tower, a brother Admiral of the fleet, and her bevy of sisters wed to great estates such as that of Harry Buckingham. As she rose her eyes met Richard's over the King's head. There was no mistaking their message. Of her opposition, only he remained. Richard could not suppress a shiver of apprehension.

Nothing to fear from any quarter Edward had said. Richard was suddenly in a fever to take his wife and son out of this atmosphere.

Parliament elected Edward's under secretary of the Treasurer and Richard's friend John Wode as Speaker then adjourned after commending the martial exploits of Henry Percy of Northumberland and Sir William Stanley, captains to the Duke of Gloucester in the successful Scottish campaign.

Richard was wild to be gone, to take his wife and son out of this explosive situation back to the security of the territory that Edward had granted him. The boiling tropic atmosphere of the court was too rich for his blood. He longed for the cooling breezes of the moors and the touch stone of friendship he had forged in the North.

When he rode out, Harry Stafford accompanied him with a great retinue to visit Harry's sister Joan at Buckingham Castle in Norfolk. Richard found himself glad of his loquacious company. Although the road they traveled was far out of Buckingham's way, Harry proclaimed himself glad of the opportunity to renew acquaintances and reminisce of their youthful days at Middleham. Under the spell of Harry's charming eloquence Richard did not realize that Harry's amazing resemblance to George in looks as well as manner was responsible for Richard's instant response. Casting aside his habitual

148

reticence Richard laughed and joked. He unfolded like a flower under the sun of Harry's personality.

But Anne felt uneasy. She had noted Harry's likeness to George and correctly assessed its influence on her husband. She was remembering also that in those very days of their youth which the two men were recalling with delight, Harry had not been happy but miserable in a jealous petulance that also reminded her of George. Seeing Richard so carefree, Anne tried to join in their merry making but her smile was forced.

At Northampton they parted with many promises on Harry's part to renew their discussions on the spot. He would join them presently at Middleham as soon as he could return to Brecon and set his affairs in order after the visit to his sister.

Richard beguiled the rest of the journey for his little son with gay stories and promises of the life of high adventure they should live from now on at Middleham. Far above the strifes and discords of London and out of its restraints and restrictions, they could live in peace and happiness. He and Scogan could resume their fascinating activities with the joyful addition of his father's constant presence. Only occasional visits from such delightful cousins as the Duke of Buckingham would keep them abreast of affairs and relieve the delicious monotony of their days. Father and son smiled at each other. Only Scogan noticed that Anne did not share that smile.

Before they could even formulate this pattern of serene existence, their dream castles came tumbling down about their ears.

In mid April a scurrier covered with sweat and dust galloped into the court yard of Middleham Castle with the stunning news that Edward IV King of England and France and Lord of Ireland had died at table on April ninth of an acute attack of indigestion. By his will, Richard Duke of Gloucester was declared Protector of the Realm and Guardian of the King Edward V during his minority.

Louis of France already a victim of two strokes of apoplexy shivered in his furs at Plessis-les-Tours and cackled with glee. Now while England was occupied with the cross currents of a minority rule, France would gobble up Burgundy — and the hated Duchess.

BOOK III

THE KING'S UNCLE

VIII

AND THEN THERE WERE THREE

Buzzards have their meat marked even before it falls.

The King has left all to your protection — goods, heir, realm, Hastings had written. *Secure the person of our sovereign Lord Edward the Fifth and get you to London.*

Richard hesitated awaiting official notice of his authority. There was no word from the Queen. To Earl Rivers at Ludlow Richard wrote courteously.

My Lord, I commend me right heartily to you and to our own Sovereign Lord Edward V whom God have in his keeping. As Protector of this realm according to the will of our late King Edward IV and Uncle to our Lord Edward it is my desire to honor our sovereign by entering London with him. In this matter I heartily pray you to inform me by what route and when the King will travel to his capital city of London.

His messenger clattered out across the drawbridge in the direction of Ludlow. On his heels arrived a second message from Hastings.

The Queen and her kindred have taken over the direction of affairs, Hastings wrote wildly. *Only by the most desperate means have I succeeded in limiting the escort of the young King whom the Queen desires to have march in battle array. Haste ye and fail not to secure the presence of Lord Edward at any cost.*

Anne watched the fine etched lines of care return to the beloved face. Edward clung to his father.

"You promised, Father!"

"I know, my Son," Richard tousled the fair hair sadly. "But I also promised the King, my brother, to watch over England."

"We don't need England, Father. It's nicer here."

Richard smiled wanly.

"Indeed it is, but this is a part of England, too."

"Scogan says you are Lord of the North and need bow to no man."

"Scogan talks too much!" Richard retorted sternly, reminding himself suddenly of Meg. Poor Meg! She'd have her battles to fight, too, now that Edward no longer stood between her and Louis.

As he paced the battlements at Middleham anxiously awaiting news from London, his son's hand clutched tightly in his own, Richard again considered his brother Edward's magnificence which he had always acknowledged, his might which he had never fully realized. While Edward's great figure strode the halls of Westminster Palace, they had all been protected in some way from impending evil. Now what?

He dashed below forgetting his son who cried out unheard,

"Wait, Father! Don't leave me!"

To his brother's Council he wrote a simple letter declaring himself ready to stand in the shoes his brother had left him. As he had been loyal in war and peace to Edward so would he be to Edward's son. If their silence meant they were debating his authority, he asked them to consider his rightful position according to the law and his brother's will.

Edward's shoes were very large. Could he fill them? He wondered silently.

Anne wondered aloud.

"Must you go, Richard?" she whispered into his ear after she had satisfied his sudden desire. With Anne alone he knew where he stood. She was always ready in his need with a response that made him humble in its devotion.

"I must, my love," he whispered back holding her tightly against his heart.

"Alone?" she cried in fear.

"Nay, my Pigeon. Harry has written to offer his loyalty and support. Holy Mother of God, I shall need it."

Anne lay still.

"Have a care, Richard."

"I shall, my love," he answered after a long and yearning kiss, never dreaming that it was Buckingham rather than the Queen who caused her unease.

They met where they had last parted two short months before. Buckingham's effervescence reassured Richard until new dispatches

154

from Hastings were put into his hands. The situation was even more grave than he had anticipated.

"He sounds a trifle wild," remarked Harry as Richard relayed a message from the Lord Chamberlain that the Woodevilles intended to ignore Richard's appointment as Protector and scotch his power by having Edward crowned before the Protector reached London.

Richard wondered if Hastings were standing by him or against the Queen. Certainly if the Queen's party won out there would be an end to the wide swarth of glory Hastings had cut during his long years as King's favorite. Elizabeth Woodeville would make short shift of a man who had stood closer to the King than his own wife, who had led the King from her bed to that of Jane Shore.

Richard passed a worried hand across his brow. He felt a warning churn in his bowels.

"There is no doubt that the Woodeville vultures have moved in to pick the late King's carcass," he remarked dryly. "The young King is already at Stoney Statford."

"What?" shouted Harry Buckingham, springing to his feet in real alarm. "That is a day's ride miles closer to London. We must make haste." Buckingham began to throw on his battle harness. "Why didn't you let me bring a large retinue as I requested," he rebuked Richard.

"Stay, Harry," Richard soothed him. "Do not fly off the handle. We must not stir up trouble by arriving in London bristling to do battle. If we do, we may find someone to do battle with."

"I am of the opinion that we have already," Harry snapped officiously. "Richard, your complacency may cost us the kingdom."

Buckingham's use of the royal *us* did not escape Richard, but he thrust it quickly into a closet of his mind and slammed the door as the graceful figure of a man garbed in more opulence than King Edward with all his magnificence had ever affected entered the room.

"My Lord Rivers," Richard inclined his head in cold courtesy to the Queen's brother. "We were expecting you."

"We were not expecting my Lord of Buckingham," Anthony Woodeville replied haughtily, ignoring Richard's greeting. Another royal *We* thought Richard wryly.

"Nevertheless, I am here." Harry Stafford and Anthony Woodeville took each others measure forgetting Richard momentarily.

"The King?" Richard inquired calmly.

"The King lies at Stoney Stratford," Rivers tried to stare Richard down.

"Why so, my Lord? Our rendezvous was here."

Rivers looked the small erect figure of the King's uncle up and down contemptuously. He bowed mockingly.

"The King was mindful of the comfort of his beloved uncle. Our considerable forces would have over run the town of Northhampton leaving no room for yours, my Lord Gloucester." He paused and glared at Harry. "And certainly nor for yours, my Lord Buckingham."

"This considerable force of which you speak, my lord Rivers," Richard interrupted blandly. "Is that intended as a warning?"

"Take it as you may, my Lord. The force is there."

"And the warning no doubt." Richard's eyelids hooded his eyes which seemed to look through Anthony Rivers to some point beyond. Rivers resisted a desire to look behind himself.

"It were more mete that the King remain at Northhampton," said Richard softly. "You shall dine with us in his stead."

"Nay, my Lord. I must attend the King."

Rivers found the door blocked by a huge Yorkshire man wearing the insignia of the White Boar.

"Wrangwysh," ordered the Protector. "You will escort my Lord Rivers to the quarters assigned to the King. You will see to his comfort and return him here to dine with my Lord Buckingham and myself at six o'clock. Is that clear?"

"Quite clear, your Honor," Wrangwysh grinned happily at River's chagrin. "This way, my Lord."

"Just a moment, Wrangwysh," Richard stopped him. "Can your men handle my Lord River's *considerable force*, do you think?"

"Two to one, your Honor," replied Wrangwysh gleefully taking a practice swing with his pike, "two to one."

Richard nodded in complete satisfaction. Wrangwysh had accompanied him against the Scots.

The village of Northhampton had scarce settled its head for the night when Anthony Woodeville crept cautiously down the split log steps of the inn and made his way noiselessly across the common room. Slowly he eased the leather latch off its hook and slipped his body through a narrow crack into the moonless dark.

"I could not sleep either, my Lord," a cold voice cut across his stealth.

The hooded eyes of the Duke of Gloucester swam into view out of the velvety, fragrant spring darkness. In the light of Wrangwysh's lantern there was no mistaking their purpose.

"Arrest him, Wrangwysh!"

"I told you so, Richard."

"You were right, Harry." Richard's shoulder drooped with fatigue and disappointment. "It is hard to believe."

"Nothing is hard to believe of the Queen," said Harry bitterly.

"True," agreed Richard remembering a night long ago when Harry was only twelve. Harry was remembering too as they rode together the fifteen miles to Stoney Stratford.

The dawn was barely breaking when they clattered over the cobbles of Stoney Stratford. But the King was already mounted. The boy's eyes widened in alarm when he saw the uncle he had been carefully taught to hate in his year under River's tutelage.

"I thought you were my Uncle Rivers," little Edward faltered, tears filling his eyes.

Richard's own eyes misted as he recognized the fear in Edward's voice. He and Buckingham quickly dismounted and did obeisance to their sovereign.

"Edward," he spoke kindly. "I am your uncle, too, your father's brother. When your father the King died, he left you and your kingdom in my charge until you are old enough to rule alone. Do you accept his wishes?"

Edward looked about him. Even his young eyes could understand the situation that confronted him. The blazon of the White Boar completely surrounded the retainers of Earl Rivers.

"I suppose so. If my father the King willed thus I shall have to agree. But why not my Uncle Rivers?" he asked piteously.

"Come, Child," said Richard gently thinking of his own son, "and I shall try to tell you."

Later at Northhampton where they returned to await the reaction of London to the Protector's coup, Richard tried to reassure Edward with the gay tales that his own Edward loved so dearly. The young King watched him with unsmiling eyes.

"You aren't so bad," he declared suddenly with the quick adaptability of youth.

Richard smiled remembering that Anne had said the same so many years ago.

"Am I supposed to be?"

"My uncle Rivers said that you were . . . ." Edward colored in confusion.

"Now you see that he was wrong in that also."

Edward nodded gravely.

"In that, perhaps," he agreed reluctantly.

London was jubilant.

Gowned in their best scarlet heavily trimmed with fur, Mayor and Council met the King's procession as it wound down the hill from Barnet and on toward London. The burgesses in bright violet robes were in notable contrast to the lord Protector and the Duke of Buckingham who, clad in the somber black of mourning, flanked the fair young King in his tunic of blue velvet, the color of his Plantagenet eyes. The cheers of thousands crowding the walls and streets were accompanied by the glad peals of church bells.

The jubilance was universal. Woodeville unpopularity had reached fever pitch — hated by the Commons for the profligacy of the Queen's two older sons, by the Lords as brazen upstarts, and by the people at large who placed the responsibility for the death of the former King's brother squarely at their door. Fully aware of all this, the Woodevilles had made a bid for the King's person and lost, glory be to God! Hail the Protector — and, of course, the little King.

Remembering the good Bishop of London's kindness to himself when Edward had deposited him there as a little tyke on his return from exile in Burgundy, Richard led a now thoroughly bewildered King to the Bishop's Palace for safe keeping until quarters suitable to his rank could be decided upon. Westminster was out of the question.

"Where is my mother?" demanded Edward.

"At Westminster," Richard replied with a sigh. Here was another difficult explanation he must make.

"At the Palace? Then why am I not there?"

"Listen, Edward," Richard did not have to stoop to get on a level with the King's eyes. His twelve year old nephew was nearly as tall as he. "Your mother, the Queen, has taken your brother Richard, your five sisters, and the Marquess Dorset with her into sanctuary, not into your father's palace."

"But why?"

Richard looked helplessly up at the Bishop's kind face and at Buckingham's animated one. Buckingham the eloquent took over.

"Your Grace," he was carefully deferential while his attractive smile could not fail to draw the boy's confidence, "the Queen is afraid of the anger of the people."

"Why should the King's mother fear anyone?" demanded the King, his habitual arrogance returning with his confidence.

"There is no reason, your Grace," smiled Buckingham, "unless she refuses to abide by the late King your father's will. The lady Elizabeth is in sanctuary of her own choosing."

"Then she shall come out," Edward stamped his royal foot. "We command it."

Both Richard and Buckingham were startled by the regal outburst. The shy, frightened boy was suddenly become the King.

" 'Twill be well thus," replied Richard quietly. "If we can accomplish it."

"Will the Lady dare defy the King?" Edward began to strut in his blue velvet before the amused eyes of the Uncle. The Bishop and Buckingham were not amused.

"We shall see, Edward," said Richard putting a friendly arm around the boy's shoulders unconsciously imitating his brother Edward's gesture.

Edward shook off his uncle's arm and spread his legs like his father was wont to do. The petulance of his face, however, was entirely Woodeville. Richard's smile faded. The fine line of worry cut deeply between his brows.

Neither at the command of the boy King her son, nor at the urgent request of Council would Elizabeth Woodeville budge. Richard, worn out with the excitement of the past weeks and the pressure of mounting problems, sought a moment's respite with his mother. He found Cecily seated in the casement where Richard had first found Anne and as he found his mother all too frequently since George's death. There was a waiting, listening air about her that made Richard uneasy. It was as though she were expecting someone to ride out of the North as Richard had waited for his brother Edward. Who? His father, George? Richard's scalp, prickled as his mother turned empty eyes on her one remaining son.

"Richard!" She passed her hand over her eyes as if to clear her thoughts.

"Yes, Mother," Richard replied gently. "Are you unwell?"

"I, unwell?" Cecily snorted with a sudden return of her dynamic personality. "Of course not, Richard. You know I'm never sick!"

It was true. Richard at thirty was amazed at his mother's enormous vitality and regal statue. After bearing twelve children and burying eight of them, the Duchess Cecily was still the touch stone, nay, the very bulwark of the House of York. Baynard Castle was thronged day and night with the followers of York. Here great decisions were made, always in the presence of the Duchess and after her opinion had been respectfully sought.

"Has that strumpet decided to act like a Queen and come out of hiding?" Cecily demanded at once.

"Nay, Mother, not yet."

"Nor will she until you force her hand," Cecily warned. "The hand that handles her must be gauntleted not gloved."

159

Richard's head drooped on his hands.

"Why won't she? No one has a mind to harm her."

"Nor has she a mind to be a docile dowager Queen hidden behind the shoulder of a king and a protector. She and her scavenger family would rule the King."

"That she can't do," Richard declared. "Neither the Council nor the people will stand for it. But she and her daughters can in full honor enjoy the deference and acclaim due the King's family."

"That she won't do," Cecily retorted. "But she must let little Richard out. How will it look to the Kingdoms of Europe that the next in line to the throne of England is hiding in fear of his life. Are we barbarians that such should be so?"

Richard had wished a thousand times that he could be out of it all and back in the peace of Middleham. Now the taste of the clean air of the moors was strong in his mouth.

"I would go home and leave it to her," he said wearily. "What matter who rules?"

"Richard!" cried his mother aghast. "You are not your father's son if you speak thus."

"I don't want to be Father's son," cried Richard defiantly springing to his feet. "I want to be myself."

"For shame! That the last son of York should even so think. The responsibility of this kingdom rests on your shoulders. You cannot afford to be a man."

"Nay, Mother, say me not that. I am not the King, thank God, and I will always be just a man."

"You are more important that the King," persisted Cecily. "You cannot desert the sacred trust your brother left you."

Richard slumped again. He knew her words were true. He must forever be the King's man and never his own. His eyes were full of sadness as he looked at the domineering woman who stood proudly before him.

"You, who have born twelve children, were you never just a woman?"

The situation grew tense.

Hastings had expected to have the young King pressed into his ready hands with the undying gratitude of the Lord Protector. It had been the Chamberlain's intention to govern the boy King to his own complete satisfaction and great comfort while the Protector ruled the land. Hastings cared not a fig for the power and cares of government beyond that of the King's person. Prestige at court and a certain wealth were all his little soul required. His stand against the Woodevilles was purely in his own interest. They alone threatened his position with the King — or so he had thought.

Now another and more formidable obstacle presented itself in his path. With a shock, Hastings realized that the Protector intended to execute Edward's will literally. Richard would rule England in the King's name and interest and would also govern the King's royal person until he could govern wisely on his own. Lord Hastings was to retain his position on the Council, his lands, and honors. He was not to be this King's companion.

Richard began to notice that meetings other than those he supervised at Baynard Castle were taking place.

"He's also taken Mistress Shore to his bed," Buckingham regaled him with the city gossip. "'Tis also said she sees the Queen."

Richard, as was his blunt nature, confronted Hastings squarely with this gossip.

Hastings tried to bluster his way out.

"This matter is my private affair," he remarked haughtily, "and does not concern yourself."

"What does concern myself and the safety of this realm are your plottings with my Lords Rotherham, Morton, and Stanley. Does this mean that you are birds of a feather?"

"I understand you not," Hastings shrugged.

"You understand me very well, my lord Hastings," Richard spoke between his teeth. Unreasoning anger was getting control of his caution. The image of Hastings as the underminer of his brother's health and defiler of his greatness clouded Richard's usually clear judgment. And now Hastings betrayed that brother's personal friendship by taking his mistress before his master was yet cold in the grave. Resentment boiled over. "Rotherham is discontent because he has been replaced by John Russell as Chancellor, Morton is a born intriguer in self interest, Stanley is an opportunist. They are queer birds with whom the Chamberlain of the Royal Household chooses to fly. I warn you to quit their company, my Lord, or hold your meetings openly in Council."

"Quit the lady, too, my lord?" retorted Hastings sarcastically. "Perhaps my lord of Gloucester is envious. The lady in question is kind of heart. I might arrange . . . . "

Fury exploded in Richard.

"Get out," he shouted.

Make haste, Beloved, wrote Richard that evening. *I have great need of thy presence. At least with thee I can find surcease. Give credence to what Scogan will tell thee of events in this place. He will care for our little Edward if he be not strong enough for the long journey. In any case our son will be better off in the free, clear air of the moors. There is no clarity to anything here. Against thy coming I have leased and am making ready Crosby Place that we may in this turmoil have a home of our own, a retreat from the stress of government. I never realized what Edward stood up to. His great will and personality were equal to the task. Am I? The answer is without thee, nay. With thee, perhaps. Delay not!*

Thy
Richard

With many misgivings Anne complied. Richard's anguish was apparent to her in the very loquaciousness, so foreign to Richard, of his letter. In spite of Scogan's reassurances her heart was heavy as she parted with little Edward, so wan and listless since Richard had left him. His eyes had momentarily taken on new life when he saw the gifts with which Scogan came laden from his father, a silver dagger to match Richard's own, a pair of matched hackneys for Scogan and his charge to explore the moors beyond the walls of Middleham, and, best of all, a tiny jeweled hour glass.

Before you have turned this many times, my Son, I hope to be back to race with you in Wensleydale. I send you Scogan, and beg that you will spare me your mother for a little. Methinks my need at the moment is greater than your own.

For two whole days after Anne's arrival on June fifth in London, Richard gave himself up entirely to their mutual need for each other. A touch of the magic of their first union was upon them. Under its influence Richard's soul, torn with suspicions and disloyalties that his own nature could not understand, was healed somewhat. Anne's own cheeks, which had become as alabaster pale as their son's, bloomed again in a new ecstasy of youth and love.

Then Richard turned gladly to the field of action on which he could be completely at ease. In Lord John Howard he found an able and loyal lieutenant. Howard set out after Edward Woodeville, the Queen's brother who had absconded on the Queen's order with the fleet and the King's treasure which had been conveniently in her son Dorset's hands. Instructed to clemency by Richard, Howard undermined Sir Edward by offering the King's pardon to all sailors who would desert him and return to English shores. The sailors returned promptly and gladly. Sir Edward did not. With a good tidbit of Edward's personal fortune jingling in his pockets, he escaped to

Brittainy to be welcomed by a myopic, balding young man with great pretentions, one Henry Tudor.

At Richard's shoulder committed only to his loyalty to the Protector stood Buckingham. Loudly he let it be known that he was Richard's friend, with all the force of his position as first peer in the realm after Richard, his immense wealth, and his winning sunny personality that nicely complemented Richard's austere solemnity. When Richard faltered, Harry was there to sustain, when Richard wearied and lost heart, Harry was there to encourage, when Richard became utterly disgusted with the cross currents of court life, Harry was ever ready with witty and beguiling stories to lighten his humour. Harry was the foundation stone of his sanity and — Harry was very like George. To Richard, always hungering for affection and approval, this close companionship filled a gap that George had not, although Richard had longed for him to.

In appreciation for these services to himself and his obvious loyalty to the King, and in realization that some one must help bear the brunt of governing the Marches as he had done for Edward, Richard made to Buckingham, under the King's seal and approval of council, vast grants of authority in Wales and the West Marches. Although he did not beggar the crown by land grants, nor did he make Buckingham's appanage hereditary as was his own in the North, Buckingham became a virtual viceroy in his home county of Wales.

He showed his appreciation by doubling his efforts in Richard's interests. What Richard willed, Buckingham helped to bring about with the eloquence that Richard so sadly lacked. Richard was a business man, Buckingham a man of the world. They complemented each other's talents for the good of the realm.

Buckingham was present when William Catesby sought Richard's ear. Catesby was a newcomer to the Council whom Hastings had brought forward. Now he was obviously distressed and ill at ease.

"My Lord . . . my Lord . . . ," he stammered glancing uneasily at Buckingham.

"Speak up, Man," Richard reassured him. "What I should know so should my Lord of Buckingham."

"This is very difficult to say, my Lord," Catesby excused his hesitation. "My Lord Hastings has been good to me."

"Hastings?" Richard was instantly on the alert.

"You are aware," Catesby colored slightly, "of his relationship with Mistress Shore?"

Richard nodded curtly.

163

"Through her he is in contact with the Queen."

"This I know, too," snapped Richard. "What of it?"

"They are planning to unseat the young King — and your-self — and place his younger brother, who is completely under the Queen's control on the throne."

"No doubt," snorted Richard. "And how do they plan to accomplish this deed?"

"Without the Protector, my lord Hastings thinks to control the council and the Queen. Morton whispers in his ear."

"And my Lord Stanley."

Catesby shrugged.

"He wants to bet on the winning horse."

"You know all this for a certainty."

"I am in my Lord Hastings complete confidence." Catesby flushed darkly. "And I am betraying that confidence." he added unhappily.

"But in the King's interest," Richard reassured him.

While his anger was still hot within him Richard summoned the Council.

As the members gathered Richard hastily dispatched a batch of letters Northward in the pouch of Sir Richard Ratcliff. In his hour of need it was characteristic that Richard should cry out for help to his personal friends of the North rather than to demand as Protector support of government troops against the rebels.

We heartily pray you, he wrote to Wrangwysh at York, *to come unto us at London in all the diligence ye can possible after the sight hereof with as many as ye can defensibly arrayed, there to aid and assist us against the Queen, who doth intend to murder us and the Duke of Buckingham in order to disinherit you and all men of honor in this realm. Fail not, but haste you to us hither.*

To Thomas Wrangwysh, when his Lord Richard said *in all diligence,* he meant at once. Scarce had the members of Council begun to make their way to the White Tower of the Tower of London than three hundred Yorkshire men were hastily donning harness in order to put themselves under the banners of the Earl of Northumberland for the March southward.

At ten o'clock on the morning of Friday the Thirteenth of June, the usher closed the heavy doors of the great council room on a cross current of tensions. Richard's face was grim as he seated himself at the head of the table. His hooded eyes, cold and brooding, passed over the expectant faces that closed in around the brilliantly polished board. To his left and right sat Howard and Buckingham, staunch in their loyalty. John Morton, Bishop of Ely, one time Lancastrian and arch plotter of all England, looked in feigned calmness at the Lord Protector. How had Edward managed to embrace this sly denizen of the art of intrigue into his Council and keep him quiescent if not whole heartily loyal? How indeed, had Edward managed many shifting loyalties in this kingdom of individualists. Edward's great prowess as a ruler was again brought to Richard's mind with a shock. The Bishop of Ely correctly read the distrust in the Protector's eyes and marked it down for future reference — if there were a future! Stanley the slippery opportunist prospering on the periphery of great events ever ready to ride in for the kill on whichever side. Richard's spine tingled. Stanley was also the third husband of the mother of Henry Tudor, the upstart pretender patiently biding his time in Brittainy with his small eyes narrowed for better discerning events across the channel. Stanley's narrow dark face split by a long sharp nose was uneffected by the cynical smile that cracked his thin lips. Of the future he had no fear. If there were a future for anyone, the Stanleys would always be there. They kept a foot in every camp.

Hastings! The taste of gall was bitter in Richard's throat. With eyes still bemused by the charms of Edward's woman, Hastings dared to presume that he himself was more loyal to Edward's memory than Edward's own brother! The thought was intolerable. In Richard's eyes Hastings read that for himself there was no future. He paled suddenly.

"My Lords," began Richard abruptly his eyes still on Hastings. "It has come to my attention, and to that of certain other gentlemen here present, that there is an active conspiracy amongst us, against the government of the Protectorate."

"Amongst us?" cried loyal John Howard, shocked to the core.

Thank God for the John Howards of the world, thought Richard devoutly.

"Yes, my Lord," Richard rested his chin on his hands. "While you, my Lord Howard, were busy clearing English seas of the traitor Edward Woodeville, others here seated, were equally active in plotting with that traitor's sister, Elizabeth Woodeville. It is their desire to secure the person of our young King through the murder of the Protector, appointed by our late beloved King Edward, and my Lord Duke of Buckingham, without whose loyal aid the Protectorate would have failed in its incipiency."

"But who would dare?" began John Howard still incredulous.

"My Lord Hastings, perhaps you can answer my Lord Howard's question."

Hastings sprang to his feet.

"The Lord Protector wishes to seize the power unto himself," he shouted hotly.

"May I remind you, my Lord, that I have no need to seize the power, as you say. That power was lawfully granted me by our late Lord Edward the master whose will as well as whose bed you, my Lord Hastings, his most trusted friend, have been so quick to betray." There was a moment of strained silence.

"My Lord Hastings, has been assisted in his efforts by the Lords Rotherham, Morton and Stanley. These men I hereby accuse . . . . . "

Stanley sprang to his feet and rushed to Hastings who had drawn his dagger and stood crouched as if to spring.

The usher flung open the doors shouting *Treason* at the top of his lungs.

The chamber was crowded with men at arms. In the scuffle that ensued Stanley went down from a mighty crack on the head. Hastings stood defiant between two guards who looked to Richard for orders. Richard's questioning eyes swept the remaining members of council. Following Buckingham's lead they nodded to a man. Only John Howard, a man of dedicated purpose but slow anger, hesitated a moment before he inclined his head with the others.

Richard nodded wordlessly to the guard who dragged Hastings, his defiance all gone, from the chamber.

Anne shopping happily in the street of the drapers for stuffs to brighten the austere walls of Crosby Place, heard the proclamation.

By the authority of the royal Council and the Lord Protector William Lord Hastings has been summarily executed on Tower Green this thirteenth day of June the first in year of the reign of our sovereign Lord Edward V after being detected in a plot to destroy the Lord Protector and the Duke of Buckingham. In order to forestall riotous attempts to free him, Lord Hastings has been immediately sent to the block for the weal of the realm. The government is secure. All citizens are required to go peacefully about their affairs.

Anne stumbled as she made her way blindly homeward. She found him alone in the gathering gloom.

"Why did you not tell me, Richard?" she asked gravely across the room. "You must have known what you intended before you left me."

He did not raise his head to look at her.

"Had I told you," his voice was thick with misery, "I might not have been able to do the deed."

"Need the deed have been done at all?" she asked softly.

He sprang to his feet and faced her for the first time. He was shocked and frightened at the transparent paleness of her face, the dullness of her eyes.

"Would you have me jeopardize my position, nay, my very life, by letting the traitor live?" he cried.

"Was it your position as Protector or your position as Edward your brother's loyal supporter that Lord Hastings attacked in your mind."

Richard's eyes widened in horror as Anne turned to leave him.

"Nay, Anne!" he cried in anguish reaching out for her. "Desert me not also!"

"No, Richard," she said sadly turning into his arms. "I shall not desert you. Take head that you desert not yourself."

Now the Council led by the Duke of Buckingham directed Richard to secure his nephew and namesake from Elizabeth Woodeville's clutches in order to put a period to her plottings.

"But I cannot violate sanctuary," Richard protested although he saw the wisdom of the move.

"He is but a child. He cannot have sought sanctuary of his own. His mother keeps him there."

"No matter," Richard was adamant, "he is under the protection of the church."

"Protection against what, Richard?" John Howard reasoned.

"Verily, I know not," Richard shrugged unhappily. "There is none who wishes her harm . . . ," his mother's face flashed unbidden across his consciousness, " . . . that I know of," he ended in confusion.

"Tell her this."

"I?" demanded Richard. "Nay, I am scarcely the one to tackle her. After what has transpired she may have a concealed dagger in her bosom." He smiled with grim humour.

"Little Lord Richard must come out to his rightful place with his brother," they told him firmly.

Alone and ill at ease he faced the Queen for the first time since his brother's death. There was no mistaking the implacable hatred in her eyes.

"You are very sure of yourself to dare to come here," she told him coldly. He noted the almost imperceptible crack in her imperiousness and hastened to use it to advantage.

"There is no need for us to quarrel, my Lady," he reasoned

167

courteously. "Our interests should at long last lie in the same channel. You are the King's mother, I am his protector . . . . "

"And ruler," she snapped.

"At your own lord's commission," he reminded her gently.

"He ever loved you above all other," she cried. "Even his own son."

"Nay, Madam," he protested. "It was because of his great love for his son that Edward left him and his kingdom in the hands of one in whom he could place implicit trust."

"Could he not trust his own wife?" Elizabeth Woodeville's green eyes narrowed to venomous slits.

Richard tried to tread the uncertain ground with diplomatic tact.

"A woman could scarce keep this great land of ours in good order, Madam. Because of his great love for you, Edward could not leave such a responsibility on your shoulders."

"Faugh!" the Queen spat out. "That's poppycock and you know it. A woman can do anything she's of a mind to do."

Looking at the Queen and thinking suddenly of his mother, Richard was inclined to agree. Now he ignored her outburst.

"Come out with little Richard and let me look after you in your rightful position as members of the royal family."

"Never! At least not while Harry Buckingham stands whispering in your ear."

"Buckingham?" asked Richard surprised. "What has he to do with you?"

"Need you ask?"

The almost forgotten night so long ago when Elizabeth Woodeville had cast the child Harry into her lecherous sister's bed returned to Richard's mind with a shock.

"He has not forgotten," she interrupted his thoughts. "I might be safe with you in your stupid sense of loyalty to your brother, but Buckingham owns no loyalty except to himself. I warn you, though why I should I know not, have a care of the fancy Duke of Buckingham. He will cozen you to your sorrow."

"Those are strange words coming from one who has just plotted my life," Richard was stung to answer.

"Why should there be any love between us?" she demanded. "You ever sought to win Edward from me."

"Nay, Madam, you were my brother's wife. As such I respect you."

"Nevertheless your hatred of me is as strong as mine for you!"

"I am not come here to discuss our personal feelings for one

168

another," Richard's rising anger made him impatient. "I came to demand that you stop sulking like a child and come out to the royal chambers in the Tower where Edward awaits you."

"I will not! Who are you to demand of the Queen?"

"The dowager Queen, let me remind you."

"Are you also reminding me that yours is the power and not mine?"

"As you will, Madam. In any case if you will not come with me, let me take Richard to his brother the King."

"No!"

"It is as I warned you," Richard reported to the Council. "She will not hear to it."

"Then fetch him out!" As usual Buckingham was the spokesman. Richard examined Harry in the light of his interview with the Queen. There was charm, there was reason, there was loyalty — and there was the daily more startling resemblance to George. He dismissed the Queen's warning from his mind.

"No, this I will not permit," Richard was courteously firm.

"The situation is intolerable," John Howard was genuinely perplexed. "What say you my Lord Archbishop?"

Thomas Bourchier, Archbishop of Cantebury thought long before he replied.

"The Lord Protector is right. We cannot violate the laws of the church. However, perhaps I can handle her. At least, let me try."

Where Richard, the young King, and the Council had failed, the gentle archbishop succeeded at least in part. Richard Duke of York taking the Archbishop's hand confidently left his mother in sanctuary at Westminster and joined his brother Edward V in the royal apartments of the Tower. They were seen together daily playing at darts on the Tower Green.

With Anne's words still sounding in his ears Richard ordered the release of Stanley and Rotherham. Morton was another matter. At Buckingham's suggestion Morton was put into Harry's custody. Richard's conscience was just beginning to ease a little when he found Bishop Stillington, the loquacious, standing on his door step. The Bishop's face was serious, his usually loose tongue strangely at a loss how to begin. Recalling his last personal encounter when he had found Stillington closeted with George immediately before his arrest, Richard felt both impatient and uneasy.

"Well, my Lord Bishop," Richard addressed him shortly. "What is your business? I am extremely occupied."

"As you well know, my Lord," Stillington began. "There is a growing disaffection among the members of Council since the later — the late — ."

"The death of Lord Hastings," Richard finished crisply for him. "How so, my Lord?"

"Some say there will never be peace in this realm as long as a Woodeville sits on the throne."

"No Woodeville sits on the throne of England. Edward is a York."

"The boy's mother is a Woodeville," Stillington reminded him. "And that brings me to another matter."

"Get on with it," snapped Richard feeling his temper beginning to rise.

"Others say that the reign of Edward V begins like that of Richard II. The parallel is very strong, my Lord," Stillington rushed on seeing the rising irritation on Richard's face. "Thomas Humphrey of Gloucester, uncle to the boy king, just as yourself, was murdered in order that others might control the king in their own interests and to the detriment of the realm. Chaos ensued and eventually Richard II himself was murdered and his house replaced by that of Lancaster."

"Your history is sound, my Lord, but why recite it to me? I was reared in its knowledge."

"One would not like to see history repeat itself," Stillington's voice was solemn.

"While I live no one will harm the King!"

"And if you do not live?"

"We have suppressed that plot. The government is secure. The Queen has released the Duke of York."

"There will be others — as long as a child sits on this throne and the Queen continues in her attitude."

"My Lord Bishop, I have no time for riddles. Pray get to the point. I am certain that you came not here to give me a lesson in history."

"That is precisely why I came, my Lord," Stillington seemed surer of his ground. "To point out that minority rules are always disastrous. England needs a strong man on the throne to replace the mighty Edward, your brother."

"Those are bold words, my Lord. Their bearing on the situation escapes me."

"Edward V is the heir of Edward IV's body. You, my Lord, are the heir of his great spirit. Some say you should assume the throne."

"Preposterous!" shouted Richard springing to his feet to face the Bishop who had remained standing. "Edward V is the legal heir to the throne, and I am sworn to uphold him."

"Edward is not the legal heir to the throne and you are not sworn to uphold a bastard!"

It was out. The Bishop sank shakily into a convenient chair and panted as a horse winded from the race.

For an incredulous moment Richard stared down at the man as he tried to assimilate what he had said. Suddenly he snatched him from his chair and held his heavy body up with one thin arm.

"Are you aware of what the penalty of treason is, my Lord Bishop?" Richard hissed between his teeth.

"Stay, my Lord," Stillington managed to extricate his garment from Richard's clutch. "I am not a fool that I would make such a statement without proof."

"You are a fool to make it to me! What proof could you show for such a monstrous lie?"

"If it is a lie, my Lord, why did my Lord Clarence die in the tower?"

Richard froze. His eyes looked at but did not see the fat Bishop before him. He was seeing again his brother George.

What have you done, George? he had pled with his brother to tell him.

Nay, Dickon, I will spare you this. To tell you would but put your head beside mine on the block . . . , George had said.

His eyes focussed suddenly on Bishop Stillington who, although he was without talent or prestige, had been made Chancellor by Edward fifteen years ago. Stillington had been removed without apparent cause shortly before George's death, Stillington had been arrested immediately after George's death, Stillington had been with George just before his arrest. Richard's eyes narrowed with fury. He reached again for the Bishop who was about Richard's height but twice his weight and snatched his pudgy face close to his own.

"So! You were the instrument of my brother's destruction and now you want to destroy my other brother's son. Get out," he roared, "and mind your foul tongue lest you find yourself in Hastings' shoes!"

But Richard was upset enough to seek out his mother at Baynard's Castle.

"It is true, my son," Cecily sighed, glad to shift the ugly secret to other shoulders. "That strumpet was never his wife."

Richard thought his mother had taken leave of her senses.

"What proof can there be and why was such a thing not revealed before now?"

171

"It cost the one person to whom it was revealed his life."

"George?"

"Yes, Richard. George."

"You mean Edward destroyed George to protect his own skin."

"Elizabeth Woodeville destroyed your brother — and my son," Cecily's voice shook with emotion. "Edward could never withstand her. She tricked him into an illegal marriage, she bled the strength of his body to satisfy the lust of her own and the wealth of the realm to the gratification of her avaricious family." Cecily rose and paced back and forth like a lioness caged away from her cubs. "Elizabeth Woodeville killed your brother George by her cunning just as surely as she killed your brother Edward by her lechery. Her spawn have no right to the throne."

"Mother!" cried Richard meeting the wild look in her eyes. He grasped both her arms above the elbow and shook her until her rigid body relaxed and slumped against him. He lowered her gently into a chair and knelt at her knee. "You are overwrought, Mother. Her children are your grandchildren."

The fire returned to Cecily's eye and she sat bold upright.

"No child of hers is a grandchild of mine! She took my sons . . . ," the irrational look returned, "and God will take hers!"

Aghast Richard summoned a servant and ordered warm wine. When he had settled Cecily against the cushions and dismissed the servant, he sank to the floor at her feet and rested his back against her knees.

"Tell me about it," he said as calmly as he could.

When she had finished, darkness had fallen in the room. Although it was June, Richard felt cold to the core. Forgetting to summon her servants with rush lights, Richard left her brooding in the gloom.

Anne's eyes questioned him across the room.

"What is it?" she asked him when she had seen the look on his face and quietly dismissed her attendants.

"Why have you no fire?" he demanded his eyes seeming to look through her.

"Fire? The night is stifling."

"I am cold," he answered brusquely. "Have a fire lighted at once."

When the fire roared on the hearth Anne placed a chaste silver cup in her husband's hand while he sat hunched in shivering misery before the flames. He did not notice that his wine was unwatered but gulped the fiery stuff and let the cup drop unnoticed to the floor. It clattered noisily to Anne's feet where she sat quietly pretending to sew while she waited for the inner storm that shook Richard's frail body to subside.

"Anne," he spoke as if from afar off. "We are lost."

She waited saying nothing. Her sewing slipped unnoticed from her nerveless fingers to join his cup on the floor.

In a flat didactic voice he poured out his tale.

"Edward entered into a precontract of marriage with Lady Elizabeth Butler shortly after he came to the throne. He did it, of course, just to have his way with her. However, in the eyes of the church his marriage to Elizabeth Woodeville is illegal."

After she had recovered from the shock Anne spoke softly but firmly.

"In the eyes of God, they were married for nearly twenty years."

"The church is God's chosen representative on earth and the church says they were not wed," he persisted dully.

"Was the church chosen by God or by itself?" Anne's voice was slightly contemptuous. "Edward and Elizabeth had eight children."

"All bastards," he interrupted.

Anne sprang to her feet her eyes flaming.

"What are you saying?"

"That little Edward is not the rightful king."

"Who then has a better right?" she demanded scathingly.

Richard hesitated. For the first time he faced his wife squarely.

"The Council is of the opinion that I should take the throne."

The long silence drew itself out interminably. Anne felt faint whether from the stifling heat of the fire or the appalling revelation she could not tell.

"And in your opinion?" her voice choked out the words.

He lowered his eyes.

"I must bow to their will."

"Nay, Richard," she sprang to him. "Beloved," she cried softly holding his head against her breast as he so loved for her to do. "We must bow to no will save our own. Please, Richard," she pled earnestly trying to look into his eyes "let us fly this place and go home to our son. We promised, Richard, we promised," she was sobbing softly and hopelessly.

He would not meet her eyes.

"Nay, Anne, I cannot. The country needs me."

"I need you, our little Edward needs you, the men of York need you. Is this indeed not enough?"

"For me, it was ever enough, my love, but not for England."

173

"England or Edward?" she cried in anguish.

He bowed his head against her in wordless misery.

"Then we are indeed lost," she whispered releasing him.

During the momentous days that followed they scarce spoke. In their rare moments alone Richard often found Anne's questioning eyes upon him. He could think of nothing to say. Events moved with relentless inevitability making the retreat he longed to make daily more impossible. How could he make her understand that he could not let his personal inclination stand in the way of duty? He must restore Edward's glory in the eyes of England, he must protect England. *From what?* he sometimes asked himself in confusion. The Woodevilles, Henry Tudor? The silver voice of Buckingham in one ear and the accustomed voice of the authority of the House of York housed in his mother's person in the other gradually obscured his self examinations. He was swept along on the river of popular demands toward the harbor of the throne — or was it shipwreck? Sleeplessness plagued him. The lines deepened on his dark face. What were the worried eyes that peered more anxiously into the future seeing?

Anne called for Scogan.

Do for little Edward what you can, she wrote sadly realizing that their son could not stand the long journey. *Your master needs you.*

Scogan rejected the plea. Anne showed his faithful servant's answer to Richard.

Perhaps I can help Master Edward, Scogan wrote. *Only God can help Master Richard now.*

Richard stood long looking at the words.

"He is wiser than I," Richard's voice was full of pain and sadness.

And so it was that Edward was not present at the splendid coronation of his father as Richard III, King of England and France and Lord of Ireland. Neither was another Edward playing at darts in the Tower Green with his brother Richard, namesake of the new King. Thomas Wrangwysh stood proudly by with his men of York under the banner of the White boar while the glittering Duke of Buckingham the King's most avid supporter bore the King's train and the white wand of the High Steward of England. In his loyal hands John Howard, created Duke of Norfolk, bore the jeweled crown. Lord Stanley, his mean narrow face expressionless — hadn't he known he could always land on his feet like a cat? — bore the Lord High Constable's mace. The Earl of Lincoln, the King's sister's son with the cross and ball preceeded his mother Elizabeth Duchess of Suffolk who walked alone in state. Who was carrying the Queen's train? Margaret Beaufort, third wife of Lord William Stanley and mother of Henry Tudor.

Thus was the first official move of King Richard III an effort to reconcile the shifting loyalties that he had inherited along with his throne. As he walked on the broad ribbon of red cloth toward Westminster Hall, Richard tried to reconcile himself to the choice that had been forced upon him. In dispossessing his brother's Woodeville heir to reinstate the House of York, was he not more loyal to Edward than Edward had been to himself? The hot July sun flashed on the golden cartwheels of Buckingham's rich blue velvet gown and momentarily blinded him. Or was he but groping to retrieve his brother from the Elizabeth Woodevilles and Hastings and Jane Shores that had stolen his greatness from him? Richard looked to his wife for reassurance that this last was not so. Fragile and lost in the heavy robes of state, Anne answered him only by repeating his question with her enormous brown eyes now deeply sunken in her small face.

"Can you?" they tormented him.

By justice and good rule, I'll justify it, his heart cried out to her, *in your eyes, Beloved, as well as those of my subjects.*

Richard threw himself into the task with the fervor and the intensity of will that had driven him in his boyhood days at Middleham. For his own sake he set himself to rule by merit. What had he told his brother Edward so long ago?

It is the duty of the government to be just.

And what had been Edward's reply?

It is the duty of the government to maintain itself.

By justice he would command the loyalty of all his subjects and maintain his government by merit. By mercy he would justify to others — and to himself — the one breach in the foundation of his own character, the setting aside of his brother's son. He must touch the hearts of his subjects and satisfy those hearts that he was their Sovereign Lord.

He began by lecturing his judges.

"All men are to be treated as equals under the law. Justice is to be meted out accordingly without fear or favor."

To set the example he summoned one Sir John Fogge who was a Woodeville relative and thus a deadly enemy, from sanctuary and taking his hand called on the people to do likewise with their enemies for the peace and good of the realm. To some, such a novel idea opened a vista of future harmony that was dazzling to contemplate.

"Long live King Richard!" they shouted.

To others it was merely foolhardy.

"A man ahead of his times," they commented privately raising skeptical eyebrows.

Lady Katherine Hastings, he took under his own protection assuring her the enjoyment of her late husband's estates. Edward, Earl of Warwick, George's son, became a ward of the King's own household. He was sent with his sister Margaret to Richard's lovely castle of Sheriff Hutton to be cared for by John de la Pole, Earl of Lincoln, son of Richard's sister Elizabeth, Duchess of Suffolk.

Rotherham, Hastings fellow companion, was pardoned as Stanley had been. Morton, at Harry's own request was entrusted to Buckingham's sharp eye, Stanley, Richard kept in his own entourage.

Thus Richard sought to resolve the conflict in his soul and to establish a firm foundation of personal loyalty for his rule.

Standing with his arm around Anne at the East casements of Westminster Palace, he gazed silently out on the London that Edward and other kings before him had known for centuries. Fertile fields and farms still touched its walls, the pageantry of the church thronged its narrow streets, filthy in spite of royal decrees to the contrary. London, a sprawling giant with the mighty Thames as its life line, become through the efforts of the House of York — Richard's House — a city of great consequence on the outer perimeter of the known world. Scorned as barbaric by the fastidious Venetians, hated as competitor by the mercantile German Hanse towns, feared as greedy aggressor by the quarrelling French, eyed with envy by the colonizing Spanish, an individualistic thorn in the side of the Pope at Rome, London was yet a source of awe to Continental visitors who were amazed to find it the busiest and richest of towns. Edward had made it bustle with world affairs. It was now the permanent home of Parliament, the mecca of ambassadors, a great warehouse for the depository of rich goods from all over the world.

Richard sighed and tightened his arm. He had never liked London for these very reasons. Now he was touched with a certain feeling of pride.

"It has beauty," he said softly.

"Yes," agreed Anne, whose thoughts were at Middleham. She sniffed as if to inhale the clean air of the moors, instead her nose wrinkled with distaste.

"We'll change all that, Pigeon," Richard squeezed her again laughing playfully at her expression.

Anne smiled back at her husband and tried to share his mood.

"You can't change everything," she warned gently.

They stood silent again watching the city go by.

"Richard, I want to go with you," Anne said at last. "I don't want to stay here alone."

"Alone? Why, Pigeon, Harry will look after you for a few days and then my mother will be here until you leave to join me at Warwick."

The mention of Harry as always sent a shiver of apprehension through Anne.

"But that's nearly a month," she persisted. "Besides, I don't trust him."

"Don't trust whom?" Richard's eyes sharpened suddenly as he released her and stood back for a better look at her.

"Harry."

Richard's eyes widened in amazement.

"Why, Beloved, he's the staunchest supporter we have. If it hadn't been for Buckingham we might . . . . "

"If it hadn't been for Buckingham," she burst out turning from him, "we might be happily at Middleham with our son and out of all — all this," she ended lamely.

"Ah, Anne," he drew her back against him and kissed her soft hair. She relaxed into his embrace aching for the lost freedom of Middleham where they could share unworried the bliss of their love. "Buckingham is my friend."

"Have you forgotten his behavior at Middleham? He was a petulant spoiled brat with no friends but himself!"

"He has grown up since then."

"Has he?" Anne asked turning to face her husband.

"You do him an injustice, look what he has done for me."

"And how has he profitted? What Harry has done, he has done for himself. I warn you, Richard, you have made Harry Stafford second in power only to yourself. He will be your undoing."

"Ridiculous!" Richard was rarely impatient with Anne. "Harry would not harm the source of his power. You say yourself that he is always acting in self interest. A man doesn't strike the hand that feeds him."

"Have you forgotten my father?" Anne reminded him.

"That was different."

"How so?"

"Warwick wanted to rule the king."

"And what does Buckingham want?"

"He has all he wants. I have just granted him the rest of the

Bohun lands."

"Are you sure he has all he wants?"

Accompanied by a splendid retinue Richard wound his way out of London on a tour of his kingdom as had done all the kings of England since time began. His subjects must know their King personally. What Richard lacked of the physical attraction with which Edward had so charmed his people, he made up in the earnestness and sincerity of his instructions to his Lords.

"See that your own counties are well guided and that no extortions are done to our subjects," he counseled. "Uphold the right of our mother church and protect our people of whatever degree or station from oppression. Keep the highways free of crime and use such authority as you rightfully possess to such an end that each of you may be named a very justicer."

Richard was tired when he reached Gloucester after a stimulating but fatiguing few days at Oxford. The university delighted him and he regretted to leave its peaceful atmosphere of learning, but he pushed on to his rendez-vous with Buckingham and news of Anne.

Gladly Richard took Harry's hand and felt the warmth of his smile. Somehow just being with Harry seemed to fulfill Richard's personality. He often wished he could be expansive like Harry, drawing the world to himself by a mere smile. Now he relaxed and let his friend's loquacious charm still the uncertainties and anxieties that beset him whenever he dwelt too long within himself.

"And Anne?"

Buckingham's face tightened.

"The lady Anne was not much with us," he said at last.

Richard sat upright in alarm.

"Is she ill?"

"Nay, your Grace." Richard shook his head in unconscious dislike of the title as Harry continued. "She seemed well enough. She pled the duties of redecorating the royal apartments."

"Oh," sighed Richard in relief. "And my lady mother?"

Buckingham was all animation again.

"The Lady Cecily is an amazing woman. I found her company stimulating."

Richard laughed.

"Stimulating is a mild word for my mother. She would have made a good king."

"Indeed she would, my Lord." Buckingham cleared his throat as he twisted his wine cup in heavily jeweled fingers. "She lets nothing stand in the way of statecraft."

"She is the very bulwark of our house," Richard said proudly. "But news, Man. How goes it in London?"

"In London all is well, Chancellor Russell is an able man. In the south however, rumour runs that there is some unease."

"Why so?"

"Richard!" Buckingham ceased his pacing and drew up a chair. Richard noted idly that it was the first time Harry had addressed him with his christian name. He raised his eyebrows as he noted the unwonted seriousness of Buckingham's usually animated face.

"Well?" Richard sighed hating to leave the pleasant intimacy of the moment to return to business.

"You must be well aware that the sons of Edward pose a menace to the peace of England and the security of your throne."

Richard lay suddenly still against the pillows of his chair waiting for he knew not what. A faint chill touched his spine. There was a warning churn in his bowels.

"I am aware of no such thing," he said finally.

"But, your Grace, surely no one knows better than yourself that a deposed monarch has no place in this world. That is a simple conclusion that any ursurper has to face."

Richard sprang to his feet, his face white with fury.

"Ursurper? That is a strange word from the same lips that so ardently and recently pled the legitimacy of the right of Richard III."

"Nay, your Grace, forgive me." Buckingham's voice was anxious although his sunny smile was a trifle thin. "I mischose my word."

"So it would seem, my Lord." Richard's eyelids drooped over cold eyes. "As a matter of fact, you mischose a number of your words. It were best that they had all gone unsaid."

Was there a look of alarm in the usually smiling eyes of the Duke of Buckingham? Richard's rising anger gave place to unease. He waited.

"Your nephew," Buckingham persisted, "was nevertheless a king. The people will not forget it as long as," the graceful man, pacing again before Richard, so like George in looks and manner, swallowed hard, "as long as . . . ." He came to an abrupt halt and looked apprehensively down at his King.

Richard stared back his eyes blank.

"As long as what?" he demanded finally in a soft voice.

"You know the people of England put great store in the sanctity of kings," there was something frantic in Buckingham's voice.

"Your qualms in this matter are somewhat belated, my Lord," Richard remarked dryly.

"England will not stand for two kings," blurted Buckingham.

"England has but one King, need I remind you, my Lord Buckingham? Richard III whom your Lordship has so zealously championed — until this moment — is the only Sovereign."

"Richard," cried Buckingham falling suddenly to his knees and clasping Richard's hands. "I am still your most faithful champion. That is why I am warning you of what must be done!"

Richard, to whom physical demonstrativeness was distasteful even from Buckingham, withdrew his hands.

"Warning me of what?"

"That Edward, and Richard, too, must be withdrawn."

"Withdrawn from the Tower? That I intend to do. You well know I plan to send them to the care of Lincoln at Sheriff Hutton with George's children."

"Nay, that will not suffice. Withdrawn from life was what I meant."

Unbelief, revulsion, anger crossed Richard's face. His frail body shook in a paroxysm of trembling. Buckingham's eyes widened. He thought the King would strike him.

"My Lord Duke of Buckingham," Richard was panting for self control, "such words or even such thoughts from anyone other than yourself would mean the block!"

Buckingham blanched and fell back.

"What I have done, I have done as I, the Council — and primarily yourself — considered the best for the realm." The knuckles of Richard's hands whitened as he clasped them to still their trembling. "Edward's sons, although they are bastards, are nevertheless, my brother's sons and my nephews. They are my wards and no harm shall befall a hair of their heads!"

"Henry IV and your own brother Edward were not so idealistic," Buckingham warned. "They knew they had to be rid of Richard II and Henry VI and they did it. A king cannot afford such qualms."

The ugly scene so long ago when Edward had decreed that poor foolish Henry must go — and his mother had concurred — crossed Richard's mind. He bit his lip to keep his teeth from chattering.

"You were not so gentle with Hastings," Buckingham's persistent voice was in his ear.

"Hastings was a traitor and met a traitor's death! Edward and Richard are but children. They have done no harm!"

"Only the harm of birth. You must be rid of them, Richard."

In sudden fury Richard struck Buckingham full across the face.

"Say not such things," Richard's warning voice came hoarse between rigid lips. "Nor think them. Who dares to, I will declare a traitor such as Hastings."

Buckingham was well aware that he meant it.

On the morrow when Harry knelt to take leave of his Sovereign, Richard raised him with his own hand.

"We were both hasty, Harry." Richard did not smile although his voice was friendly. "Let yesterday's words — and thoughts — be forgotten."

"They are already forgotten, your Grace."

But Buckingham's face was grey without its usual sunny smile as he rode westward away from the rising sun with Bishop Morton his prisoner in tow his own wily face a study in craftiness.

Richard turned his eyes north toward Warwick and the anticipated meeting with Anne, but some of the gladness was gone.

His joy at the sight of her, however, quickly dispelled the fatigue of the gruelling state journey and the misgivings that had nibbled constantly at Richard's mind since his parting with Buckingham. For two days they sought the privacy of Warwick Castle with only their personal retainers. Here they tried to forget the present and reach back into the serenity of first love. At last Richard sighed and reluctantly declared himself ready to meet the Spanish ambassador that Anne had brought in her train. He attacked the business at hand with new hope and a clear eye. Thus it was that a week passed before they sat alone again.

Richard was relaxing in the balm of Anne's quiet happiness at his presence. For a time he watched her nimble fingers at their needlework. His eyes drooped. He was almost asleep when she spoke.

"Why did you suddenly decide to send Edward and Richard to Sheriff Hutton? I thought they were to remain in London until your return."

Richard started awake. It took a moment for his mind to clear and her words to sink in.

"What did you say?" he whispered.

Anne smiled at her husband's bemused face.

"I'm sorry, Beloved, I didn't know you were asleep. You need your rest . . . ."

Richard sprang from his chair and grasped her arms. Her face paled in alarm as he shook her.

"What did you say?" he shouted.

"Your fingers are hurting me, Richard."

"Answer me! What did you say?"

"I asked you why you sent Edward and Richard to Sheriff Hutton prematurely. Are you ill?"

"Who told you?" he demanded ignoring her question.

"Sir Robert Brackenberry of course, the constable of the Tower. Who else? He felt he could trust me to assure you he had done as you requested for their safety. He told no one else."

"As I requested?"

"Richard!" Anne was now thoroughly frightened. "What is the matter?"

"I wish I knew, I wish I knew!"

He turned on his heel and left her without further words.

It took Richard's messenger a week to gallop to London over roads soaked with sudden summer thunderstorms. Both rider and horse were fagged by the gruelling journey when Robert Brackenberry's reply at last was in Richard's hand.

On the night before his departure to join Richard at Gloucester, the constable sent word, the Duke of Buckingham had conveyed Richard's order to him that the Duke be permitted entry into the royal apartments of the Tower in order to remove the King's nephews under cover of darkness to unknown quarters. This because the general unrest in the south might pose a threat to their personal safety. Brackenberry, though uneasy, had not seen fit to question the authority of Buckingham as High Constable of England. Had he done wrong?

Richard hastily sent assurances to his constable in whom he had complete trust.

Bide thy time and tongue until I can ascertain the truth in the matter.

Richard's messenger had a fresh mount but scant rest before he galloped up the road toward Sheriff Hutton, sparks and mud flying from his horses hooves.

For a time the rains ceased and the royal procession wound its way on northward in more physical comfort. For Richard there was no comfort of the spirit. Hunched in the saddle of his favorite mount White Surrey he rode silently on through Conventry to Leicester. For a brief moment wry humour lightened the brooding darkness of his face. An insolent letter awaited him from his fellow sovereign Louis XI who took time out from his efforts to bribe the saints to let him enter heaven to write briefly.

Monsieur mon Cousin,

I have seen the letter that you sent me by your Herald Blanc

182

*Sanglier and thank you for the news you've given me, and if I can do
you any service, I'll do it very willingly for I want to have your
friendship.*

Adieu, Monsieur mon Cousin.

Richard grinned. Had ever a monarch been so cavalierly
welcomed to the ranks of kingship! He could not forbear to reply in
kind.

Monsieur, mon Cousin,

*I have seen the letters you sent me by Buckingham Herald
whereby I understand you want my friendship in good form which
contents me well enough.*

After a mild assurance that he had no intention of breaking any
truces signed by his brother until they ran out — hardly half a year
yet he thought with a grin — he warned Louis that his subjects were
greatly provoked by French piracy which was against the spirit of the
said truces.

*Therefore in order that my subjects may not find themselves
deceived by this present ambiguous situation, I pray you that by my
servant this bearer, one of the grooms of my stable . . . .*

"That ought to make him scream," chuckled Richard as he
dictated to his secretary John Kendall.

. . . you will let me know in writing . . .

It was Kendall's turn to chuckle.

"Let him wriggle out of that," he murmured to himself as he
added Richard's final words, as insulting as Louis' own.

*. . . your full intentions, at the same time informing me if there is
anything I can do for you in order that I may do it with good heart.*

Tongue in cheek Richard seized his secretary's quill and finished
with a flourish.

And a farewell to you, Monsieur, mon Cousin.

Richard found little else to amuse him as the tension increased
under the strain of awaiting the return of his scurrier from Sheriff
Hutton.

The news that reached him at Nottingham was worse than the
tension of uncertainty.

"Edward's sons are not here," Lincoln sent word. "What goes?"

On the heels of his reply to Lincoln — *I know not what goes.
Guard your tongue while you await my coming* — Richard sent a
runner to Brecon in Wales.

*On pain of our displeasure wait upon us immediately at
Pontefract Castle.*

But when he reached Pontefract, Richard did not find Harry

awaiting his pleasure or displeasure. Nor did the Duke of Buckingham send his Sovereign any message. The only word Richard's scurrier brought back was a rumour allegedly emanating from Bishop Morton escaping his erstwhile jailer in the direction of the channel that the usurper Richard III had murdered the sons of his brother in order to secure his precarious hold on the throne.

Anne ordered the fires built higher and tended her husband in silence. What was there to say? Richard huddled shivering in his fur cloak. They had never been a pair to chatter idly, so now Anne tried to comfort him merely by her presence. If she left him for a moment he became fretful.

"You know it isn't so, don't you, Anne?" He spoke once with such sadness that Anne ran to him and knelt at his feet stroking his pinched face with a thin hand.

"Of course, Richard," she whispered. "Grieve not so, beloved."

He took her hand in his own and stroked it noticing its thinness with the edge of his mind.

"Although I did not with my own hand, I caused it by my actions."

"Nay, Richard," Anne pled, "do not torture yourself. You did what you — and the Lords — thought was best for England."

"There is no place for a deposed monarch to rest save in the grave," he said in a far away voice. He continued to stroke Anne's hand but his eyes peered beyond her into what? The future? The past? "And now he who had the best cause to be true, is a traitor — to *me*, Anne, who loved him!" Richard's voice was full of pain. He sprang to his feet and paced restlessly back and forth snapping his dagger up and down in his sheath. "Is there no loyalty any where? My motto makes a mockery of me! *Loyalty binds me.* Does it bind no one else?"

He ceased his harried pacing and looked down at Anne's bowed head.

"You warned me against him, didn't you, Pigeon, and I wouldn't listen." Anne didn't raise her head. "I am a poor judge of character. Perhaps I saw in him only what I wanted to see." Richard took up his pacing. The dagger clicked off the rhythm of his steps. Anne raised her eyes full of pain and sorrow but made no effort to speak. She knew that Richard was talking to himself, trying to still the anguish in his soul. "He was so like George. I thought he would be as I always wanted George to be." His voice broke. His frail body collasped into his chair. "In trying to seek solace for myself, I have doomed Edward's sons. I am forever cursed!"

184

Anne sought miserably for the right thing to say. Was there any thing right to say?

"It is too late to look back," she told him tonelessly. "The time for choice has passed us by. Perhaps Edward's sons are no more but there is still England and you are her King."

Perhaps if she could not console him, she could drive him to seek release in work.

"There is much to be done, Richard, you cannot afford to wallow in personal grief."

"Even you? You sound like my mother. I suppose she is right. A king has no right to be just a man."

"For me, you will ever be a man — my man, Beloved. But also, I can no longer claim you solely as my own. You have a far greater destiny to fulfill than just that of husband —" she hesitated, thinking of the delicate child that would join them on the morrow, "and father."

"I would that it were not so," he reached out hungrily for her. "Don't leave me, Anne," he whispered into her hair.

Anne sighed and nestled closer to him.

"Not yet awhile, Beloved," she said but not aloud.

Until this moment Richard had not been able to bring himself to declare his own son as heir to the throne. As week after week of fruitless seeking yielded no clue of the fate of Edward's sons and Buckingham continued to elude him, Richard suddenly sent to London for the rich garments and hangings that had been turned out for his coronation. Thus he sought to honor his friends of York by investing his son as Prince of Wales in their city. The citizens of York welcomed him wild with joy that their friend and Lord of the North had become their Sovereign. They loaded his table with white demain bread, tuns of fine wine, great bream from the river Ouse, and swans by the cart load.

The excitement was too much for little Edward. Manfully he walked in the long hot procession almost staggering under the weight of his magnificent robes of state. Gritting his teeth he knelt during the tedious ceremony at York Minster.

"Father . . .," he whispered finally in a small voice. Clutching at Richard's hand the new Prince of Wales sank in a dead faint. With grim determination and the iron will he had inherited from his father, Edward had held on until the recessional reached the outer perimeter of the immense crowd thronging the steps of the Minster. Thomas Wrangwysh with a curt order drew up his men in a stiff line that hid the King of England from his subjects as he swept up his

185

little son and heir into his own arms.

Across the crumpled figure Richard's eyes met Scogan's troubled face.

"I'm sorry, Master Richard," Scogan shook his head sadly. "He needs more than I — or any man — can give."

"No!" cried Richard in anguish.

His small burden stirred. A pair of blue eyes brilliant with fever smiled up into his own.

"I'm sorry, Father," the child murmured.

Remembering back across the years how his brother had saved him from the fatigues of his knighting, Richard clasped his son tightly to him and strode homeward.

On the morrow word reached the King that the Duke of Buckingham had lent his name to the sporadic uprisings that broke out in the Lancastrian strong holds of Wales and the southern counties.

"Giving aid to Henry Tudor's cause!" Richard commented to Anne in amazement. "I thought his ambitions were more personal."

With her usual insight, Anne hit on the probable cause of this astonishing development.

"Bishop Morton most likely assessed Harry's shallowness at a glance." She colored suddenly.

"As I should have done," Richard remarked grimly noting her confusion.

"Nay, Richard, blame not yourself over much. You are not a man of intrigue. The Bishop is a past master in that art. I'll wager that Harry honestly thought he was strengthening your cause — and of course his own — by . . .," she wet her lips, "by eliminating Edward's sons, if in truth this is what he has done."

"How could he do such a thing without consulting me?"

"Because he knew in his heart that you would never consent, but thought that, faced with the accomplished fact, you'd have to condone it."

"Condone murder?" Richard groaned. "And that in my own family? What monster . . . ."

"That's just it," Anne interrupted earnestly. "When he found you would not, he listened to the wily Bishop.

" '*Cast your deed on him,*' he probably whispered in Buckingham's ear.

" 'And be the King myself' was Buckingham's most likely smug reply, 'Who has a better right?'

" 'Not so fast,' the sly Bishop would most certainly say, 'Though none has a better right, it's might that counts. Henry Tudor has the House of Lancaster, and the hatred of the House of York, at his back. What have you to offer? Better another kingmaker, my Lord Duke, than the block, is it not so?' "

Richard regarded his wife in wonder.

"Women will never cease to amaze me," he declared with a smile realizing that in her apt mimicry, Anne had probably hit on the real facts of the case.

"Thus," Anne continued, "the Bishop will make you out just that — a monster to be driven from the throne and replaced by his own candidate who, in gratitude will grant him a cardinal's hat."

"I shall make you my chancellor, Madam. Such masterly deduction I have never heard!"

"How else can you explain it?"

How else indeed? It was, however, hard for Richard to believe that Buckingham had been false.

Richard gave Buckingham one more chance to clear himself. When this elicited no response, he left Anne to return to Middleham with Edward and taking Scogan went in search of Harry himself.

When he reached Lincoln, Richard learned that Buckingham had indeed betrayed him. Calling all his personal retainers together Harry was heading up what was evidently a well planned rebellion. The disappearance of Edward's sons was merely incidental. Anne had been wrong at least in that.

Coldly Richard sent out orders that the Duke of Buckingham was to be apprehended as a traitor. Aided by renewed rains, the disinterest of Richard's subjects in Buckingham's cause, and a quality of disloyalty with which Richard was becoming increasingly familiar, Harry was captured by one of his own servants in attempting to escape back across the flooded Severn River to his stronghold at Brecon. Finally brought to bay Harry pled wildly to be allowed to speak with the King he had betrayed. Buckingham was brought to Lincoln. Remembering his own brother's disintegration in the face of death, and perhaps unconsciously afraid of the effect of Harry's silver tongued charm, Richard refused to grant him an audience. Condemned forthwith by the Council Harry Stafford went kicking and screaming to the block.

"I've got to tell him," were his last frantic words, "it wasn't my fault . . . . "

Who is ever at fault in this game of kingship, thought Richard bitterly surprised at his lack of emotion when Harry's death was officially reported to him. A cold lump settled in his chest crowding his heart. Otherwise he felt numb.

BOOK IV

THE KING

IX

AND THEN THERE WERE TWO

"Where is Richard?" Cecily, Duchess of York flung open the doors with her own hands and confronted her last son.

"Mother!" he advanced gladly to embrace her.

"What have you done?" Cecily demanded coldly.

"What do you mean?" Richard almost stammered in confusion at the sudden attack from such unexpected quarters.

"It wasn't his fault!" Richard with alarm noted the frightening wildness in his mother's eyes.

"Come, Mother," he soothed trying to lead her to a chair. "Speak no more riddles. Tell me whose fault what wasn't."

"I am not a child," Cecily shook him off, "and neither are you."

Richard was now thoroughly frightened.

"Let me call your women," he said with an attempt at calm. "You are unwell."

"Rather dismiss your men," she commanded in her habitual proud voice to which the House of York always harkened. Richard harkened now. With a gesture he dismissed his attendants. He waited. Proud and erect she faced him with all the grandeur of her regal bearing. Only her eyes were strange to him.

"You have executed the wrong man!"

Richard was stunned.

"If you mean Buckingham, he was a traitor and was condemned as such."

"That is not why he was executed."

"What are you driving at, Madam?"

Cecily pointed a long finger.

"You had him executed because he murdered your brother's

sons."

"He was executed because he rebelled against the Throne — executed by order of Council."

"Guided by you."

"And if so?"

"He was not responsible for their deaths although he accomplished them."

"How do you know?"

"Because I ordered the deed done."

Richard staggered as if he had been struck by a mace full in the stomach.

"You what?" he whispered hoarsely.

"I ordered the deaths of Edward and Richard Plantagenet because they were a menace to your throne. Buckingham was but an instrument."

"I don't believe you."

"It's true nevertheless. Now we are even."

"Even?"

"That strumpet killed my sons. Now she'll know what it's like to suffer as I have done."

Richard stared at his mother in incredulous horror.

"They were your grandsons!"

"They were *her* sons."

"And you had them murdered, two helpless children, in cold blood!"

"To save your throne."

"No, Madam," Richard's voice was heavy with loathing. "You cannot hide your foul deed behind even so high a motive. You murdered your own grandsons to revenge yourself against another woman. You are mad! The high flung love of England that you have so long professed is just a shield for your madness."

Bitterness boiled over in him.

"What is this House of York I have condemned my mortal soul to redeem? Rotten to the core. Edward's licentiousness, George's shallow jealousies, your mad vengefulness, and more terrible than all these, my own stupidity. Where are those high ideals," he asked her scathingly, "that were all for the good of England and the glory of God? They were not ideals but greed for the glory of York. Only scavengers destroy themselves.

"A king cannot afford to be a man, you preached at Edward. And what are you to whom York looks for my father's guiding principles? Nothing but a woman! A crazy, vengeful woman!"

192

The sagging figure that had been the proud Duchess of York crumpled in a sobbing heap at Richard's feet.

"To think that I was ever afraid of Dame Marguerite," his voice shook with cold fury, "when it was my own mother that I ought to have feared."

When Richard had ceased to speak the silence lay heavy upon them. At last he slowly but firmly moved toward the door of his chamber. Squaring his narrow shoulders he turned to look once more at his mother.

"Whatever it is that has brought me here, I am nevertheless King of England and King I shall be. Not for the Hastings, the Stanleys, the Northumberlands, nor the Buckinghams — not even for the Yorks. These care not a fig for England but only for themselves. For the good people of York, the Thomas Wrangwyshes, the Rob Percys, — yea, for men like Frank Lovell, who wanted Margaret but had to give her up to York's ambitions — for these I shall try to make my sacrifice worth while. I thought I was doing it for you and Edward and even George's sorry memory, to restore your glory. Yes, I shall strive for the good of the real England and for the love of Anne who is twice the woman you are!"

With cold courtesy, Richard held the door open for Cecily but made no effort to help her rise. As she passed him she would have spoken had he not waved her to silence.

"Although, Madam, you could not remember that these boys were your grandchildren, I shall endeavor with all that is within my power to remember that you, no matter what you have done, are yet my mother."

When she had left him, Richard leaned his back against the door and closed his eyes on the pageant of his wasted life and dreams.

"Anne!" he cried out in his heart for all they might have had. "What have I done and what have I done it for?"

"It's the King who needs you most," Scogan reported as he rode into the inner bailey at Middleham. "There is naught you can do here."

Wearily Anne made ready for yet another journey to the London she despised and the husband she loved. Scogan shook his head sadly as he watched that slight figure with a hectic spot on each cheek trot across the drawbridge and off to the South.

"Make him happy," were her last instructions about her son. "Nothing else matters."

"Would we had realized that years ago," she murmured to herself in fruitless regret for all they might have had.

But was it not she who had told Richard that there could be no turning back now? She squared her tired shoulders and did not look back to see Edward waving good-bye from the battlements.

As he had promised himself, Richard's Parliament, called in January of 1484, did more for the common man of England than any King had done since Magna Carta was wrenched by the public from the unwilling hands of King John. From his Parliament at Richard's instigation came the right to bail, protection for the little man against packed juries, and the abolition of the hated royal extortions wryly called benevolences.

If the barons noses were sorely disjointed by legislation forbidding hidden feoffments in land transactions, the populace was wild with joy at these concessions which eased their plight. Richard for a time enjoyed a certain peace that comes with restitution. He was so busy that though he kept Anne constantly as his side, he did not notice the paling cheeks by day nor the increasing thinness of her body as he held her in his arms at night. In the steady quietness of their mature love which was their only joy, they hoped for another child. As the months passed and they were still denied Anne felt a mounting dread that she could neither define nor shake off.

"Let's go home, Richard, for just a little," she begged. "Everything is in order."

Richard hesitated. Home! This he wanted more than anything.

"There is one thing that is not in order," he replied gravely. "Something I must resolve, Beloved, before I can think of home."

Anne sighed heavily.

"Now what?"

"Elizabeth must come out of sanctuary."

"Holy Mother of God! How will you accomplish it?"

Richard stopped his pacing and looked helplessly down at his wife.

"I thought perhaps you could advise me. You are a woman. What would you do?"

"Stick that silver dagger you're always fussing with in your gullet, if I thought what she thinks," Anne declared flatly.

"What does she think?"

"That you did away with her sons!"

"But she knows that Buckingham ... " his eyes fell. He turned his back to hide the expression on his face.

"He didn't do it, did he Richard?"

There was a long silence.

"Yes," finally, "he did the deed."

"Richard?"

"Yes?"

"Have you ever lied to me?"

He stopped suddenly in fear. Slowly he turned to face her.

"Anne!" his whisper rasped. "You don't believe *I* did it, do you?"

"Nay, Beloved," she reassured him quickly. "I know you too well. I have no doubt that if aroused you would commit a crime for England, but it would be bold not silly. This deed is worthy of a woman's mind. England gains naught by their deaths and you stand to lose all."

Richard tried to digest her canny reasoning.

"You are holding something back," her brown eyes accused him. "Is that not lying, in a sense?"

Again he turned from her to hide the inner conflict that must be reflected on his face.

"I have no right to burden you further."

"Uncertainty is the greatest burden you could put on me. Don't let something lie between us that will spoil the perfection of our confidence in each other. This is all we have left."

Richard knelt and laid his face in her lap.

"Who would have thought, my Pigeon, that my love could destroy you, too. Everything I have ever tried to love is gone save you . . . and our little Edward. And he . . . ."

"Shhh!" she touched a finger to his lips to still their anguished cry. "It is better left unsaid."

"So is what you would have me tell you."

"The knowledge of our son's frail health is the easier to bear because we share it. Is that not true, my love?"

"Of a surety, but that is a sorrow, not a horror."

"And is this secret you withhold so horrifying that a wife . . . ."

Suddenly the dam broke and Richard poured out the awful knowledge of his mother's perfidy. Anne at first recoiled in unbelief and then sat quietly during the painful recital of the secret that had torn at Richard's heart these past weeks.

"Why did you not tell me at once, Richard?" she asked gently stroking his dark hair.

"She is my mother," he said with quiet dignity, "my own flesh and blood."

"She did not feel such loyalty to her grandsons, who are also her flesh and blood. You must let it be known immediately."

"That I cannot!"

"Why not?"

"I cannot condemn my own to the block. If it should ever become public knowledge, the King could not condone such a thing even in his mother."

"Even if it means that King must bear the onus of her crime?"

"How so?"

"You are not unaware of the rumours that Bishop Morton has carried even into France that you are responsible."

"I am responsible," Richard cried. "Had I not unseated my brother's son he would be alive today."

"And England would be in the throes of a bloody civil war over his regency. Even the death of two children is better than the lives of thousands."

"Say not such a thing!" Richard thundered springing to his feet. "They were not just two children. They were Edward's sons, my nephews. Whether I handled the death instrument or not is immaterial. By assuming the throne, even to maintain peace in England," he quickly injected to head off her protest, "I signed their death warrants. This knowledge will dog me to the grave. I will not add the burden of my mother's dishonor and death to my already ragged conscience!"

"By your silence you will dishonor yourself for all time," Anne persisted.

"You will not betray my confidence," Richard blazed.

Anne's eyes stung with hurt.

"I shall never betray you, Richard," she said sadly, "although others will. You are too just for your own good. Edward was right. A king can only rule by might, justice will get him nowhere!"

"Don't say these things, Anne. If you take such beliefs away from me, my life will truly be a waste."

"Isn't it already?" she asked him bitterly.

"Not as long as I have you," he said. Sinking again to his knees he clasped her slight body to him as she sat. He turned his face against her breast. "But leave me the remnants of my ideals," he pled.

Richard was amazed anew at Elizabeth Woodeville's indestructible beauty. Haughtily, as if he were still the King's little brother and she yet the Queen, she received him seated in state in her chambers at Westminster sanctuary. At her side, stood her eldest daughter Elizabeth, Edward's counterpart in looks. Magnificently tall and beautiful, Elizabeth Plantagenet had the golden blondness of her father. The almond shape of the Plantagenet blue eyes and the cold disdain that flashed therefrom was purely Woodeville.

"Madam," Richard began ill at ease. "I have come to implore you to desert this ignominious role and assume your rightful place at court."

"What is my rightful place, my Lord?" The old jealous hatred glittered in her eyes.

Richard cleared his throat and felt a little foolish. Was he not after all the King? he asked himself.

"As Queen dowager," he almost snapped.

The delicately plucked eyebrows rose.

"If, as you have been at pains to point out to the world, my Lord, I was not Edward's lawful wife, how can I be termed Queen dowager?"

"We will forget all that," replied Richard gruffly feeling at a distinct disadvantage.

"You may forget it, my Lord," Elizabeth spoke icily. "I will not."

"As you wish." Richard was now thoroughly annoyed. "But do you choose to remember it in the bleakness of your chosen confinement here or in the sumptuousness of court life which," bitterly, "is your natural habitat."

Suddenly Elizabeth Woodeville changed her tack.

"What have you to offer?" she asked abruptly.

Richard was so taken aback he stammered like a child.

"What — what do you mean?"

"Make me an offer. What is it worth to you to have me come out and pretend that we are all one happy family?"

Slow anger was beginning to burn in the place of Richard's initial confusion. So this was the bereft and broken hearted mother bargaining glibly with the man she reputedly accused of the murder of her sons.

"To me personally, Madam," Richard replied stiffly controlling his anger with supreme effort, "it is worth nothing. Therefore I offer you nothing. To the Council it is apparently worth seven hundred marks a year if you will cease to make a ridiculous spectacle of the royal house of England by seeking sanctuary like a criminal."

"Need I remind you, my Lord, that I am not the criminal?"

Richard clenched his fists.

"Need I remind you, Madam, that the Lords of the Council are aware that you have agreed to affiance the lady Elizabeth here to

197

Henry Tudor?"

"That is my right as her mother and guardian."

"Not if your action is construed as an effort to strengthen Henry Tudor's pretense to the throne. Unless I assure them otherwise, Council will name that an act of treason."

"You cannot harm me here," Elizabeth Woodeville snapped.

"Do you like it here, Madam? Do your daughters all desire to become nuns?" Richard smiled grimly. "I can see by the petulant look on the Lady Elizabeth's face that she cares naught for the cloistered life. I'll wager her four younger sisters share her feelings in every respect, a very natural desire for pretty gowns, gay music, the promise of husbands who are not exiles."

Elizabeth Woodeville was silent. For a time she watched her daughter with all her father's beauty and sensuousness written boldly across her face. Sudden decision seemed to take her.

"Very well," she agreed abruptly. "We'll come to court."

Something in the almond shaped eyes warned Richard that behind her sudden capitulation lay more than just the desire for the gaity of court life, fine garments, and proper sons-in-law.

"On one condition." A cunning smile touched the corners of her wide mouth. Richard waited saying nothing.

"That you, my Lord, make a public declaration of your intentions and swear that you will do my daughters no harm, now nor in the future."

He was caught. Although she had made no mention of her sons, the question lay silent between them. Now she was warning him of and, by forcing such a public statement, would acquaint the world with her suspicions. If he refused, she would remain where she was, a living reproach to his reign and a source of lively conspiracy. If he agreed, he would in a sense acknowledge to the world, if not guilt, certainly complicity. Oh God! And man thought he shaped the face of the world. Woman could outwit him every time.

What a choice! He thought of Anne and his faith in women was in a measure restored. Suddenly he had to be with Anne — to hold her in his arms and reassure her. Reassure her of what? It was himself who needed this reassurance that only her presence could offer.

"Very well, Madam, as you will," he agreed in a fury to be gone. "But I would advise you to recall your conniving son Dorset from behind the skirts of Henry Tudor. From now on the King will be responsible for the present and future welfare of the daughters of Edward IV. I warn you, I will be trifled with no further."

"Yes, your Grace," Elizabeth Woodeville murmured meekly,

acknowledging him as King for the first time. Her eyes, already busy with their plannings, were not upon Richard but her daughter. How beautiful she was, and useful she would be. With an enigmatic smile Elizabeth Woodeville arose and went about the necessary preparations for her royal re-entry into the world.

The joy of release from the cares of kingship and the seething political atmosphere of London was short lived. Scogan awaited them at Nottingham, tears streaming down his face now seamed with premature age.

"Edward?" Anne whispered.

Scogan could only nod.

"Oh, Richard!" Anne crumpled into his arms. "This is too much. I cannot bear any more."

Holding Anne gently in his arms, Richard asked across her bent head.

"When?"

"Quietly in his sleep in the early morning of April the ninth."

Richard stiffened. Just as quietly something, some little hope, died within him. Putting Anne gently aside, he strode out alone into the star filled night. Down the abrupt rocky hill on which stood William the Conqueror's Castle and into the fine forest through which he and Edward had loved to hunt, Richard stumbled, heedless of the rough terrain. At last he reached the River Trent. For a time he sat with his arms hugging his knees up to his chest and watched the effortless winding of the waters north eastward toward a final resting in the sea.

Would there be for him no final resting, he wondered numbly trying to crowd his mind with inconsequential thoughts to hide his misery from himself. The numbness passed and like the clamor of a limb mangled in battle, the pain forced itself upon his consciousness. With it came a panic that had been hovering for months on the edges of his mind.

Was he — and his house — forever damned?

April the ninth. His own beloved son had died on the very anniversary of the death of his beloved brother for the death of whose sons he was himself at fault. How had he ever thought that as king he could answer England's need for justice, restore her glory, and his brother's? England didn't want justice. England didn't want freedom for the common man, England didn't want restraint on its avaricious barons — and most of all England didn't want him. England wanted the glamor that was Edward, England wanted to be ruled by might not justice. Once again, as in his childhood he felt the awful misery of being unwanted, of being different. Was he, after all a man ahead of his times as some whispered sagely, or just a throwback as Anne had said long, long ago . . . in the beginning.

A throwback? Throwback to what? He was as unloved of a God that had passed judgment upon him and damned his soul as he was unloved of a country that would pass judgment and damn his methods.

He either slept or lost consciousness for when he came to himself the forest dawn was alive with bird song. He lay and watched a doe nuzzle his foot impatiently and stride away in dignified scorn. Deplete, he arose and made his way slowly back to the castle. Unnoticed went the cramped stiffness of his shoulder. He had no feeling left.

The kindness and sympathy with which the good people of York welcomed their King and Queen touched Richard deeply. Hope, that eternal mustard seed in the heart of man, germinated anew. Here at home where people knew him, he was loved and wanted. If he could but make all England feel the same. He must! As he had gained the love and loyalty of his brother Edward by first giving his own without reservation, so Richard now offered both to England.

He found, however, that he could not stay at Middleham. He caught himself waiting and listening for Edward's childish voice and light footstep. It were as though his son had just stepped out of his chamber shortly to return to share some new found treasure or knowledge with his father.

"I cannot stay," he finally burst out. Tears clouded Anne's eyes as she strove to busy herself into forgetfulness.

"Poor Richard. You have no heir to give to England," she sobbed.

He caught her roughly to him.

" 'Tis not an heir I've lost. England abounds with would be heirs," he cried bitterly. " 'Tis a son we've lost. That is not so easily remedied."

"And 'twill never be with me!"

"What are you saying?" Richard tried to turn Anne's wet face up to his own. She would have freed herself, but he held her fast.

"What are you saying?" he demanded roughly making her eyes meet his.

"That a King should have a wife who can bear him strong sons. You have sacrificed everything for England. Can I do less?"

The look in his eyes was terrible. He almost shook her.

"Do you dare to insult our love thus? Yes, I have sacrificed everything for England. And will you desert me now that I have lost all but you?"

"Nay, Richard," she clung to him in desperation. "You are all I've ever had of love and kindness. I could not give thee up if England did not need thee more. You must have sons."

Richard lifted her in his arms and carried her lightly to his favorite chair. There he cradled her to him as he looked with longing eyes out of one of his great new windows across the lovely moors of Wensleydale where their son would ride no more. He kissed her hair softly.

"What makes you think," he asked her quietly, "that I could have those fine sons by any other wife."

She looked up at him through tear drenched lashes.

"Of course, you could."

He shook his head gently.

"Had it not occurred to you, my little Pigeon," he smiled, "and by the way you are much too little. We shall have to fatten you up. Had it not occurred to you," he cuddled her closer, "that you might have had fine sons by another husband?"

Anne almost hiccoughed her surprise at such possibility. Her pale checks flamed.

"Never fear, your Grace," he teased her gently, "I shall not let you try. My wife you are, and you are stuck with me." His smile faded as he caressed her head against his chest. "Our childlessness we shall have to bear together as we have many other great sorrows."

Her only answer was to nestle closer into his arms with a sigh of gratitude.

"I love thee, Pigeon."

"I love thee, Richard." Her voice was heavy with sleepiness.

In the dying light of a May twilight Richard held his wife gently as she slept for the first time since Scogan had brought the news of their son's death. Thus Scogan found them as the flame of sunset was caught in the glory of the stained glass that Meg had sent from Burgundy. Redly it stained their strained faces, young again in sleep. Richard was unaware when Scogan lifted Anne from his cramped arms and took her off to bed, shaking his own head at her weightlessness. He returned to tend his master. *Let him sleep while he may,* Scogan decided covering Richard's legs with a fur robe to ward off the chill of the northern night. *He has not seen the worst of it yet.*

On the morrow Richard was in a fury to be gone, to throw himself into pain killing work. The channel was alive with French shipping that continued piratical practices in spite of Richard's warning to Louis. He wondered wryly if Louis had made it to Heaven or was in Hell still conniving to unify France and divide England. He thought the last was most likely for word had reached him that Henry Tudor had escaped Francis of Brittainy's sharp eye into France where he was being stroked and petted by the harassed regency of Louis' daughter, Anne of Beaujeu. If Henry would help her against the jealous French barons she would help him to gain his heart's desire — the throne of England. Since both were equally helpless, Richard felt no fear in this quarter.

However, news of a much more serious character reached him at Scarborough where he was busily fitting out his fleet to scourge the channel pirates and knock out the Scots — who were on the rampage again — in one fell swoop.

When he had heard out Frank Lovell's scurrier his heart melted in pity toward his mother. After the first shock of revulsion at her confession, Richard steadfastly refused to believe that if his mother were in her right mind she could have instigated the murder of her own flesh and blood. Her mind apparently unsettled, she must have been duped by her trusted and confidential servant William Colyngbourne. Richard could readily imagine how the wily Colyngbourne, whom he had known in Edward's household, had whispered in Cecily's ear adding fuel to the slow flame of sorrow and resentment that had burned away her sanity.

For the good of the realm and the security of your House, Colyngbourne must have suggested in regard to her grandsons. Egged on by such insinuations and by bitter hatred of the woman who had doomed both her golden sons, Cecily had been driven to order the deed that marked the final curse upon them all.

Colyngbourne, Frank Lovel sent word, had been found guilty of seditious correspondence with the Tudor pretender across the channel. Frank sent on a copy.

Return unto England with all such power as you might get before the feast of Saint Luke in order that you may receive all the revenues of the realm due at the feast of Saint Michael before the said feast of Saint Luke. If you, my Lord, with your part takers will arrive at the haven of Poole in Dorsetshire, I and my associates will cause the people to rise in arms and to levy war against King Richard so that all things shall be at your commandments.

Thus had Colyngbourne written from the very bosom of Cecily's household shortly after Buckingham had left London and just before Anne had brought him news of his nephews disappearance. Grimly Richard noted the practicality of the proposal date for Henry Tudor's invasion in order that his anticipated reign might begin in financial solvency. In spite of such wise advice, Henry had apparently not thought the moment or the backers auspicious. And so his mother's infamy had been for naught.

A paroxysm of anger against this man left Richard weak and shaking. That Colyngbourne was a traitor to himself as King was a crime meriting the traditional death by disembowelling. Richard could think of no fitting punishment for one who had used the Duchess of York as the instrument of destruction of the House to which she had dedicated her whole life and prodigious energies, and of her own final damnation.

After a soul searching effort he finally composed a letter to Cecily at Berkhamsted Castle where she had hidden to shrive herself of her sin by a strict religious regimen. No word had passed between them since their last shocking interview when she had told him of her perfidy. Now he wondered how he, with so much on his own conscience, could have seen fit to judge her. All the old affection tempered now with pity for her — and .unconsciously for himself — was in the letter he now sent her in the hands of Sir Richard Ratcliffe whom he chose to replace Colyngbourne in her household.

Madam,

I recommend me to you as heartily as is to me possible. He chewed his quill. She must be made to know that he could forgive her if God could not. *I beseech you in my most humble and effectuous wise of your daily blessing to my singular comfort and defence in my need.*

Perhaps if she could be brought to feel his need for solace in his own loss, she could in a measure forget her own.

And, Madam (why could he not say Mother?) *I heartily beseech you that I may often hear from you to my comfort, also be good and gracious Lady to my Chamberlain, to be your officer in Wiltshire in such as Colyngbourne had. I trust he shall therein do you service.*

I pray God, he added his petition to the ones she must be sending up in her lonely and frantic daily devotions afar off to the South, *to send you the accomplishment of your desires.*

Written at Pontefract, the third day of June, with the hand of, again he hestitated, then in sudden decision, he dashed off,

Your most humble son

RICARDUS REX

Then he turned out a proclamation for Frank Lovell to have issued against Colyngbourne which met with an instant and insolent reply tacked to the door of Saint Paul's Cathedral.

The cat, the rat, and Lovell our dog
Ruleth all England under a Hog.

But Richard was at sea commanding the naval campaign against the Scots and did not know of this impudent attack against his cognizance of the White Boar that he had chosen as his personal emblem to honor his friends of York. He trounced his recalcitrant neighbors to the north so thoroughly that they cried out not only for mercy but peace and a marriage alliance to cement it. This he was pleased to grant by affiancing his sister Elizabeth's daughter Anne to the heir to the Scots throne. Returning triumphant and sun tanned to York, Richard set in motion another innovation that had long been close to his heart. He organized a Council of the North as a governing body to handle affairs while the King was in his far away capital of London. At the head of this body he placed John de la Pole, Earl of Lincoln, his sister Elizabeth's son and his own staunch friend and supporter. At the same time he appointed Lincoln Lieutenant of Ireland, thus nominating his nephew as his heir. So Richard mended his dynastic fences before he hurried south taking Anne with him to prepare for the traditional court celebration of Christmas.

Richard determined to hide the fears and frustrations that beset him from his subjects behind a glittering facade completely foreign to his nature but reminiscent of Edward's past glories.

"Richard." Anne looked so small as she stood with her back toward him gazing out on the beehive activities of a festive London. Richard touched the soft locks that hung childishly to her slight shoulders now squared so bravely.

"I have promised never to leave you."

His hand stopped its stroking. Unacknowledged fear clamped cold fingers on his heart.

"I can no longer keep my promise."

He turned her abruptly to face him.

"What are you saying?" he demanded gruffly.

She swallowed hard.

"The doctor says we have very little time left together."

"What doctor? I'll have him. . . ."

She placed a thin finger on his lips.

"Shh, Beloved. Your own physician. Don't take on so. I would not spoil your Christmas, but . . . but . . . ."

"But what?" he felt little pain and no shock. He had known it was coming but refused to face the knowledge. He had heard that mortally wounded warriors on the field suffered no pain. The impact of the death blow destroyed all feeling. Thus it was for him now.

"I can no longer share your bed."

"No one forbids the King," he shouted suddenly wild with grief.

"Save the Queen," Anne made a poor effort to smile.

"No!"

"I must, Beloved. The disease is virulent. It must not strike the King. England needs you, Richard."

"Neither England nor the world needs me," he burst out bitterly. He drew her close into his arms despite her protests. "And if you leave me, little Pigeon, I shall not be far behind, what matter if by your disease or by another means. I cannot live without thee, Anne, I will not!"

Again she strove to quiet him, but he poured out his bitterness until dry sobs shook him, and he laid his head upon her silken lap and gave up to his grief. After he was quiet for a time she spoke gentle words to encourage him.

"We have faced great trials bravely before now. Together we must face your subjects out there," she waved in the direction of the great hall decked in the gala hangings of the season. "You owe them a fine Christmas over which no pall must be hung."

"I owe no one anything, save you. This I know now that it is too late."

"Come, Richard," Anne straightened her gorgeous gown and covered her girlish coif with an elaborate and heavy hennin. "They must not know," she warned smiling bravely into his eyes as she placed her wasted hand upon his wrist.

But in spite of the Queen's gentle gallantry, the court did know. Taking the cue from their Sovereigns, however, they celebrated with a taut gaiety not seen at Westminster since Edward's youth. Elizabeth Woodeville's smile was unreadable as she presented her daughter Elizabeth of York in a graceful curtsey to the King and Queen. With a shock Richard noticed that his niece's dazzling beauty was clothed in a garment identical in fabric and workmanship to the Queen's. He would have sprung from his gilded chair had not a soft hand been laid in mild restraint on his cloth of gold clad arm.

"I am fatigued, my Lord," Anne's eyes smiled confidently into his. "Will you see me to my chambers?"

With pride in her splendid courage he returned her lovely smile.

"Indeed, I will, my Lady," he replied for all to hear. "I am overly tired myself."

The last sight that Richard had in the great hall as he led his wife away was of Elizabeth Woodeville chatting busily with Lord Stanley, Henry Tudor's step father.

Deftly, with the touch of a master, had Elizabeth Woodeville opened her campaign. As she had tricked him into a public declaration of his intentions not to harm her daughters thus putting him in an ambiguous position, so she made his present position even more untenable.

"You must deny it, Richard," Frank Lovell told him gravely in Anne's presence.

"I will not dignify such an obscene rumour with notice of any kind," Richard snapped.

"Why must he deny it, Frank?" Anne reasoned. "Richard's friends — and I, beloved," she reassured the deep hurt in his eyes, "know that Richard would never dream of such a thing."

"Richard has nothing to fear from his friends," Frank argued. "It is his enemies, of whom Elizabeth Woodeville is the most deadly, who will make capital of a man's alledged intention to marry his niece, and that," Frank's kind voice was troubled, "while he already has a wife."

"Alledged by his niece's mother," Richard snorted bitterly. "What a snake she is!"

"And what a monster she will make you out if you don't deny her allegations that you intend to force her to give you her daughter when. . . ." Frank floundered and colored.

"When I am gone," supplied Anne gently touching Richard's hand.

"I'm sorry, Anne," Frank mumbled miserably.

"Nay, Frank, try not to grieve. And promise me you'll help Richard. He'll need you when . . .when. . . ." It was Anne's turn to stumble at the dumb anguish in Richard's eyes.

"I promise, Anne," Frank reassured her.

When they could get their emotions under control, the three of them discussed their problem as matter of factly as they could. Frank continued to urge that distasteful as it was Richard must make a public denial that he had any intention of marrying his niece, Elizabeth of York.

"The people believe what the King says aloud," Francis Lovell assured Richard. "That will stop the unfounded whispering that the Woodeville woman is fanning into a flame of conjecture."

206

But Richard steadfastly refused to insult his wife by acknowledging even the extistence of such a rumour. Rarely did he leave her side although the news that Henry Tudor would attempt to invade England in the summer to press his rickety claim to the throne reached him at Westminster early in January. As Anne weakened they seldom appeared in public. When they did, her head was high under its heavy and detested hennin, her lips smiling, and the enormous brown eyes now deeply sunken were bright with feigned gaiety. Richard marvelled at her stamina and although his heart bled inside he matched his mood to her own.

Toward the middle of a bleak and blustery March Anne made to arise and make her elaborate toilette for a function honoring the Spanish ambassador. She fell back with a cry.

"Richard!"

Instantly he was at her side.

"Anne, beloved."

She caught wildly at his hands, her courage suddenly drained.

"I don't want to die," she whispered.

"Don't, little Pigeon!" In anguish he gathered her wasted body in his arms and carried her to a chair.

"Are you afraid?" he asked gently trying not to join in her weak sobbing.

"Not for me, Richard. For you, I am sore afraid." she whispered. "You'll need me." With an effort she raised her hand to stroke his cheek. "I didn't want to leave you, Beloved."

The whisper ended in a wisp of a sigh.

How long he sat with her wraithlike body clasped to him in despair, he did not know. The room was dark when Archbishop Rotherham made bold to enter although his knocks on the heavy door had gone unnoticed.

Richard looked up at the Archbishop with unseeing eyes.

"Your Grace?" Rotherham inquired gently.

Richard lowered Anne's head from his aching shoulder and looked down at the beloved face that was still and cold, but at last free of pain. He could hardly make it out in the gloom.

"Is it night?" he asked.

"Nay, your Grace, the sun but hides its face in a great eclipse."

"And well it should," signed Richard wearily carrying his slight burden to the great bed where together they had shared such joy. Alone in its vastness, she looked lost. But it is I who am lost without her he thought as he walked resolutely to the door of the antichamber which was thronged with the well wishers, evil wishers, the merely curious, and the real mourners.

"The Queen is dead," he said coldly striding through their midst in a frenzy to be away.

"What a pity!" said his well wishers understanding the misery that he hid under the brusque exterior, a personal sorrow he could share with none.

"No feeling at all," whispered his evil wishers. "How long before he'll marry the niece?"

"Bad omen," conjectured the curious hastening out to embellish the news by hanging the eclipse on its telling.

The mourners, of whom there were many, wept openly.

X

AND THEN THERE WAS BUT ONE

Quietly Elizabeth Woodeville sat amidst her recovered luxury and let it be known that the usurping King was trying to force himself on her daughter. Gently she dabbed her eyes with a silken kerchief at this disgraceful offense against morality and his own brother's daughter.

Richard shrugged indifferently and calmly made preparations for his departure from London. His advisors felt no such complacency.

"Public opinion is a facile thing," commented Frank Lovell mildly.

"Remember her vindictiveness toward Desmond," worried Catesby.

"She has no power," retorted Richard with some sarcasm. "Your skin is safe."

"She has the power of indomitable will and a direct line of communication with Henry Tudor. Such rumours your friends will discount as I have warned you before, Richard," persisted Lovell with the easy intimacy of close friendship. "In the hands of a bastard born plotter like the Tudor who has nowhere to go but up, they can do untold harm."

Richard stood as he and Anne had stood so often gazing out on the bustle of London town.

"You can not hurt her now," Frank put his hand on Richard's shoulder and communicated his sympathy with a gentle pressure of his fingers.

Wanly Richard smiled his gratitude at his childhood friend. At least he still had that. Francis Lovell as Lord Chamberlain, Rob Percy as Comptroller of his household, these men had begun with him their apprenticeship at Middleham where, with Anne and Isabel and George and even Harry Stafford, they had played at knighthood under the stern arm of Warwick and the benevolent eye of Edward. Only these two were left to remind him that life had once held joy and love. Yes, and high hope and loyal endeavor. The throne had taken a terrible toll. Poor silly Henry, too pious to carry the crown for Lancaster and from whom Richard's own father had lifted the weight to transfer it to York — not to his own brow, but to his son's. Warwick who like Buckingham could not control unweaning ambition to wield the power if not the sceptre. Margaret, Isabel and Anne — all brought and sold in the political market place. George, the pawn, whose desires outstripped his abilities. And last of all himself. How could he measure himself?

By seeking at all costs to prove — to England or to himself? — that loyalty and just desserts were enough to maintain a benign rule that favored the common man over the baron, justice over might, learning over ignorance. And they were telling him that the very public whose plight he had sought so diligently to lighten were facile. That they could be bought and sold as easily in the market place by false rumour as had his sister, his wife, and Edward's only love.

Catesby cleared his throat nervously.

Poor Catesby trying so hard to be honest and yet stay on the right side. How many others were in his shoes, caught in the sticky web of expediency?

"Very well," he agreed hopelessly at last. "I'll deny it. But I'll vouchsafe that will only give the intention at least credence. That's all the Tudor needs to discredit me, if you are right."

It was Elizabeth Woodeville who received the King rather than Richard who received his subject. Although her head bowed, her eyes held no hint of submission.

"So this is why you agreed to come to my court?" Richard eyed her coldly. "Not for comforts and luxuries, not for position, not even for the good of your daughters. But for revenge." He thought of his mother doing lonely penance in Wiltshire. "Revenge exacts a terrible price, Madam, which you shall pay."

"You cannot send me back to the Abbey," Elizabeth Woodeville said sharply. "Public opinion would not permit it."

"I shall not try to test public opinion over something so inconsequential as yourself, Madam," Richard replied dryly. "And vengeance I shall leave to God who claims it as His prerogative. Your daughter, however, I shall send to Lincoln at Sheriff Hutton She will at least not be yours to barter to Henry Tudor, no matter how attractive the trade."

Richard watched Elizabeth Woodeville's mounting anger with grim humour.

"You were once the Queen and as such, of an honorable estate. With this you were not content but must needs foist a greedy family on the realm to sap up strength to feed your own power. Now, I have offered you the next estate in honour, that of Queen Dowager with which you still are not content.

Elizabeth Woodeville was almost panting with rage. Fury mottled and obscured the seemingly indestructible beauty of her face. She looked as if she wanted to spring on him and scratch out his eyes.

"She probably does," Richard thought wryly while aloud he warned,

"I'll wager your position as Mother-in-law to the Tudor — if you ever achieve it — will not be to your liking."

Richard did not underestimate the danger. A defeated cause must always find a champion. Such a one had the House of Lancaster found in Henry Tudor. The Tudor's pretensions were tenuous to the point of non-existence, but dynasties had been founded and abolished on less. Richard wondered if Owen Tudor, wardrobe clerk, who had found favor and a bed with Henry V's widow were chuckling gleefully in his unmarked grave. Here rose his grandson — begat on royalty 'tis true, but without benefit of clergy — to vindicate his grandsire. Old Owen would be gratified to know that Henry had endowed him with no meaner ancestry than Cadwallader King of the Celts. And had not Henry's mother, now Lord Stanley's wife, sprung from the left hand blood of John of Gaunt, first Duke of Lancaster through his faithful mistress Katherine Swynford?

Richard looked his possibilities squarely in the face, found much wanting, and standing outside his own personality, watched himself set the course of his life by the lode star that had appeared on his horizon that bitter December night twenty-five years ago when his brother Edward had taken him shivering into his arms, his bed, his heart, and his destiny. Richard shivered slightly although the humid heat of May held the city early in its relentless grasp. Not the physical fear of invasion shook him now, but a raw terror that all his beliefs — the foundation stone of his existence — were up for a test that might find them wanting. Although his courage and resolve were undiminished, yet the emotional tragedies of his life that had followed one upon the heel of another had loosened his grasp on reality. Dimly he observed his own actions as one watches an eclipse through smoked glass.

No concern for London troubled him as he left his capital in the loyal and competent hands of Chancellor John Russell, guarded with dogged faithfulness by John Howard in Essex and Robert Brackenbury in the city itself. Reluctantly he parted with Frank Lovell because of his need to refit the fleet at Southhampton, but directed him to make haste to meet with the King's party shortly.

Taking only Rob Percy and Scogan with him, Richard turned west, forced by some inner compulsion that he did not understand into Wiltshire.

The King was kept waiting while the Duchess of York finished her devotions. When his mother finally appeared Richard was appalled. The regal bearing of the Duchess had become the gaunt rigidity of the nun. Her graceful hands, now boney, plucked feverishly at her beads. For a moment he thought she wouldn't know him.

"Richard, is that you?" Her voice held a querulous note as if she were anxious to be done with him and back to the strict regimen he had interrupted. The former brilliance of her beautiful eyes was now a vacant hardness.

"Mother!" Suddenly without willing it he knelt and kissed her hands.

"Aren't you yet the King?"

"Yes, Mother, why?"

"The King of England kneels to no one." Something of the grandeur of her former proud dignity returned to her voice.

"Of course, Madam," he arose and tried to walk as tall as she would have him.

"Why are you here?"

"To ask after your health, my Lady Mother, and — and to seek your blessing." He felt himself once more a child. He would have knelt again had she not prevented him. A boney hand touched his dark hair.

"I thought I would not see thee more, Richard."

His throat filled. He bowed his head.

"Thou has suffered much. Be not dismayed."

The dam of self control broke and at his mother's knee he poured out all the bitterness and despair that had beset him. The love that was bursting in his great heart but that his very nature had prohibited his knowing how to give, except to Anne, had now no where to go.

"Everything I touch is cursed," he cried out. "My brother, my son, my wife and . . . and. . . ."

He ceased his frenzied pacing and looked down at Cecily who had sunk disconsolately into a chair.

"Even your mother," she finished for him.

Cecily stiffened suddenly. The air of expectant waiting enfolded her again. She arose signaling for silence, looking beyond him.

"What is it?" Richard demanded, turning. There was nothing.

"Shh!" Cecily cautioned him impatiently. "Don't you hear?"

"Hear what?" Richard's spine began to tingle.

"The voices."

"I hear nothing."

"But you will, my Son, you will."

Richard stood helplessly by while his mother's rigid body passed him in the direction of her voices. Her lips moved soundlessly as she fingered her beads. He thought he had lost her again but at the door she turned back and for a moment she was Cecily, Duchess of York, her eyes full of the old fire.

"Tis not your fault, Richard. Tis but the fault of birth. If a man becomes King, he must cease to be a man. He cannot serve two masters — his manhood and the state. These two tyrants are irreconcilable."

She smiled and beckoned. This time she let him kneel for her blessing.

"You are so like your father," she murmured touching his bowed head. "Be not remorseful, my son. Look with pride on your accomplishments — a prospering nation, a people who love you and whom you have freed from baronial tyranny, justice in the courts — these things are no mean feats. You are a man ahead of your time."

Was this his answer? But what good is a man for whom the world is not ready?

"And the price I have paid!" he cried out hopelessly.

"Who knows better than I the cost of Kingship? Have I not paid with a husband, two sons . . .," she stopped. Her eyes suddenly dull again looked beyond him. ". . . and two grandsons," she whispered as she passed him by.

"Is it worth the cost?" he called after her.

"To whom?" Her words came back to him. "You or England?"

The answer to this question he sought in the inner conflict of his soul and purpose as he rode northward with Scogan and Rob Percy. His servant and his friend respected his troubled silence. Scogan tended his master's bodily comfort, Rob Percy stood by quietly awaiting his friend's need. When they reached Nottingham Frank Lovell was already there to discuss the defenses with his Sovereign.

"Not yet," Richard shook his head still under the spell of the irresolution his mother's questions had aroused.

"Dickon?" Rob Percy spoke tentatively. He had not used that name since his friend had become his King.

Richard smiled his quiet gratitude.

"Yes, Rob." Mayhaps he could yet be just a man.

"Let's go once more to Middleham."

Richard hesitated. Could he view once more with equanimity the scenes of his only joy?

"Let's try," Frank answered his question aloud.

The three friends galloped off together with Scogan shaking his head and trying to keep apace.

"A man can never return to his youth," he could have told them. "It will only make it hurt the worse."

And he was right.

Dickon Plantagenet, Frank Lovell, and Rob Percy were no longer there. Nor were Anne, Meg, and Isabel, George, Harry, or Edward. Nor could they even find their stern task master the Earl of Warwick. There were only a king, a viscount and a belted knight. In silent dismay they looked at one another across the overgrown tennis court. No happy voices of breathless contestants broke the eerie silence. Sorrowfully they turned to go.

Unable to face his lost joy at Middleham or his new found sorrow at Westminster, Richard took up his abode on his craggy rock at Nottingham. Besides, here at the heart of his kingdom, he could keep a watchful eye on any port where the hated Tudor might choose to land. Engrossing himself in the work of his realm, Richard became the blurred outline of a figure to his subjects. A darkness seemed to settle on him as well from within as from without. With the unflagging will that had driven him up to this point, he forced himself to waste no time in regretful contemplation of his fractured life but drove himself and his companions feverishly to the accomplishment of the impossible — a rule of justice rather than might.

Could it work? It must!

Quietly he looked to his defenses requesting rather than demanding allegiance of the barons whom he had rewarded liberally to his own impoverishment but who still felt that he had robbed them by his championship of the common man against their traditional predatory rights.

214

Lord Stanley was the first to test the foundation of his policy.

"Your Grace," he knelt obsequiously, "I beg leave to depart for my estates which are sadly in need of my presence."

Richard said nothing as he watched the play of expression on the narrow, mean face of his Constable and Steward.

"Your Grace will recall," Stanley's thin lips curved down his chin while the lines at either side of his prominent nose deepened perceptibly, "that I have been in constant attendance of your court ever since your Grace's accession."

Indeed he had, thought Richard wryly and for good cause. His wily Lordship had eternally stood with one foot in either camp ready to light with catlike agility on the winning side.

"You see fit to make such a request at the moment of expected invasion, my Lord."

"Just so, your Grace. Should an invasion occur, I should be in a better position to muster my men to our cause."

The ambiguity of *our* did not escape Richard. His eyelids hooded his cold eyes. Stanley returned his look blandly.

"And who will fill your invaluable place here?"

"My son Lord Strange would feel himself honoured, your Grace."

"Such a position," Richard told him pointedly, "Lord Strange might consider a dubious honor."

Lord Stanley lowered his eyes.

"My house desires nothing more than to serve England and England's king."

Richard laughed harshly.

"That statement could be a two edged sword, my Lord."

"Does your Grace doubt my loyalty?"

"Should I?"

"Your Grace has only to command and I shall stay."

"No, I shall let you go."

"Your Grace," Lovell urged, "is this wise?"

"No, Frank, it is not," he looked coldly at the still kneeling Stanley. "But a man, even a king must follow his destiny. You are free to choose your allegiance, my Lord Stanley. If you betray me, I shall in all probability not be here to punish you. But God will, never fear."

Stanley squirmed on his boney knees. Richard watched him for a moment in grim amusement before he raised him.

"You are free to go, my Lord . . . as soon as you have summoned your son."

July burned itself away in watchful waiting for Richard in his eyre. For him it was a pleasant time in a sense. He was surrounded only by those whom he loved and whose loyalty was beyond question. With Frank and Rob he spent satisfying days in hunting through the wild beauty of Sherwood Forest. Occasionally they laughed together boyishly as they swam naked in the Trent. Scogan sat waiting on the bank to towel their shining bodies vigorously and stuff their bellies with the succulent fish he had caught up stream while they frolicked in the icy water below. To Richard whose stomach had always protested the rich foods of the court, it was heaven. His spare frame had begun to fill out, his wounded spirit to find a certain ease when at the end of this first week in August a sweaty, dusty scurrier knelt at his feet and babbled the news that Henry Tudor, armed with French weapons and the sweepings of French jails had landed at Milford-Haven a week gone.

"I'm glad!" Richard declared although the growing serenity on his face was shattered. "Reality is less terrible than anticipation."

"But, your Grace," cried the terrified scurrier on whom Richard was trying to press a fresh fried fish, "Rhyp ap Thomas has joined him."

Richard laid his fish aside. So! The test had begun and he had lost the first round.

"Send for Norfolk . . . and the men of York."

He had almost said send for the Earl of Northumberland. But here again he realized that there was a choice to be made. Should Henry Percy, remembering his ancient jealousy, make the wrong choice, the men of York could always come without him.

And they did. But the delay caused as the men of York awaited word from their Commander made Thomas Wrangwysh grumble. Hastening his troops southward to the aid of their beloved Sovereign, Wrangwysh cursed Northumberland and promised himself and all his personal gods that he would avenge the Yorkists if aught befell their Richard while Henry Percy, in full array, sulked with standard furled.

The rising sun glinted on the simple gold circlet that crowned the helmet of a figure, slight even in full armour, upon a huge white charger.

"Remove it, Master Richard," pled Scogan astride Mohomet at his master's flank. "Both friend and foe can mark you out."

"And well they shall, Scogan." Richard felt free for the first time in his life. The thirty two years of his existence had driven him inexorably toward this moment. At last it was here and he could either prove himself or go down in the trying. He thought of his mother praying her life away for York. He could not pray, but he could fight. Pride filled his voice.

"I am King of England for all the world to know and if die I must, I shall die King of England."

"A priest, your Grace?"

Richard shook his head proudly and clasped his lance tightly.

"Nay. If our cause be just, God will reward us with victory. If not, it were blasphemy to plead His aid."

Trumpets blasted the Sunday dawn.

Under the banner of the White Boar Richard rode out closely surrounded by his friends, Viscount Lovell, his chamberlain, Sir Robert Percy, his comptroller, Sir Richard Ratcliffe and William Catesby, Sir Robert Brackenbury his Constable, his secretary John Kendall, and his body servant Scogan. Lord Stanley was there, and the Earl of Northumberland, but on the periphery where they could threaten or bolster Norfolk's flank. Where were the men of York? Richard's narrowed eyes peered to the North but could not see Wrangwysh and his furious, sweating men racing too late to his succor. What they did see distinctly were the three camps of his enemies. Lord Stanley's army and his brother William's stood motionless. Henry Tudor's army, taken by surprise in spite of tedious years of preparation, was endeavoring to move eastward in order to place the swamp between themselves and Richard who surveyed Bosworth Field from the summit of Ambien Hill. Henry Tudor was not to be seen. Disdainfully Richard turned his back on Northumberland who had accepted command of the flank with unreadable face.

There was a fierce exchange of arrows. The great mass of enemy troops began to ascend the hill. The royal army plunged down upon them. With a loud clash of steel the armies met. Fiercely they struggled back and forth and then drew apart panting. A shout arose. Norfolk was down! Richard's keen eyes suddenly perceived a red dragon banner. Henry Tudor. He also saw a scurrier speed from the Tudor in the direction of Lord Stanley. To inform Stanley that Richard's great general Norfolk was no more and he had best declare himself and come in on Tudor's side? Richard summoned Northumberland to advance in support of the royal army. Word quickly returned that the Earl declined to do so until Stanley should declare himself.

Sudden peace surged over Richard. So it was a personal combat after all, between Richard Plantagenet and Henry Tudor. He summoned his household knights and told them his plan. If he could but reach and destroy the Tudor before Stanley made up his mind, the day would be theirs. Would they ride with them? Only Catesby, trembling with fear, demurred.

"You must save yourself, your Grace," he urged nervously. "The way is still open to flight."

"You may take it then," said Richard coldly. "I cannot!"

Richard could not forbear to look into the faces of his faithful friends and touch his hand to theirs — Frank, Rob, Ratcliffe, Brackenbury, John Kendall, and last of all Scogan.

"You've no cause to go," he told his servant gently.

"I started with ye, Master Richard, there I'll end."

"Is this truly the end then?" Richard smiled at the seamed, devoted face.

"Mayhap," Scogan replied calmly handing Richard his battle axe before mounting his mule. "What e'er it be, I'm with ye."

Rising in his stirrups Richard called over his shoulder.

"We ride to seek Henry Tudor."

Each man nodded solemnly and lowered his visor. Down the slope White Scurrey carried his master, daintily picking his way as if unbidden he wished to delay the moment of decision. At the foot of the hill sudden exhilaration seem to seize both horse and rider. Through the slits in his visor, Richard saw the brilliant scarlet clad armies of the Stanleys slide by. Red dust rose in a shimmering curtain from under his galloping hooves and cut him off from the battle raging behind on Ambrien Hill, from all save the few who without question or thought of the future rode with him. He smiled joyfully. *Loyalty binds me!* It was true and he was vindicated.

Shouts and orders sounded as the red dragon flapped directly in front of him. His flailing battle axe cleared his way as easily and as cleanly as the scythe cuts the harvest. He had almost reached the red dragon when out of the corner of his eye he saw the red coats of Stanley closing in from behind.

"Treason!" he shouted as he saw Rob Percy fall.

"Richard."

A pair of wide brown eyes were smiling at him.

"Anne!" he answered joyfully.

He had not felt the blow.

Scogan cursing his deliberate beast finally found him there, his crushed head resting peacefully in the small of Rob Percy's back. Frank Lovell knelt at their side the blood from his nearly severed arm mingling with that of his two friends.

"Richard!" He was calling as he shook him gently.

"He cannot hear you, Master Frank. There's yet time for you to save yourself an you can."

As deftly as when he was but a child his servant hoisted Richard's mangled body across the back of his mule. Scogan's eyes were so blinded by the sweat which flowed in and the tears which flowed out, that he did not notice when the once proud head of his master, now dangling foolishly, struck the stone parapet of the bridge. An August noonday sun struck fire in the simple golden circlet as it bounced off and rolled to rest under a hawthorn bush.